DEATH
ON DELOS

DEATH
ON DELOS

Gary Corby

First published in the United States by
Soho Press, Inc.
853 Broadway
New York, NY 10003

Library of Congress Cataloging-in-Publication Data

Corby, Gary.
Death on Delos / Gary Corby.
Series: An Athenian mystery; 7

ISBN 978-1-61695-821-3
eISBN 978-1-61695-822-0

1. Private investigators—Greece—Athens—Fiction. 2. Nicolaos (Fictitious
character: Corby)—Fiction. 3. Diotima (Legendary
character)—Fiction. 4. Murder—Investigation—Fiction. 5. Sacred
space—Greece—Fiction. 6. Delos Island (Greece)—Fiction. 7. Greece—
History—Athenian supremacy, 479–431 B.C.—Fiction. I. Title
PR9619.4.C665 D43 2017 823'.92—dc23 2016054524

Map © Megan Corby

Interior design by Janine Agro, Soho Press, Inc.

Printed in the United States of America

10 9 8 7 6 5 4 3 2 1

For Catriona

*She was eight years old when I began these books.
Now she's a young lady about to take on the world,
and the world is in for a pleasant surprise.*

THE ACTORS

THE NAMES IN this book are genuine ones from the classical world. Some are still in use. To this day there are people named Nicolaos. It's also the origin of our Nicholas. Other names you might already know because they belong to famous people, such as Pericles.

But some names from thousands of years ago are unusual to our modern eyes. I hope you'll say each name however sounds happiest to you and have fun reading the story.

For those who'd like a little more guidance, I've suggested a way to say each name in the character list. I have included some deity names, a few place names, and a couple of nation names that might also be exotic. My suggestions do not match ancient pronunciation. They're how I think the names will sound best in an English sentence.

That's all you need to read the book!

Characters with an asterisk by their name were real historical people.

Diotima* DIO-TEEMA	A pregnant priestess of Artemis	"You can carry the next one."
Nicolaos NEE-CO-LAY-OS (Nicholas)	Diotima's husband	"We're on a mission from the gods."
Geros GE-ROSS	An old priest of Apollo	"You pollute the sanctuary by your very presence."
Anaxinos AN-AX-IN-OS	High Priest of the Delian Apollo	"This is a problem I find with many Athenians."
Pericles* PERRY-CLEEZ	A politician and General of Athens	"I fear you have some distance to go with your negotiation skills. Killing the other party is not the normal tactic."
Damon The modern DAMON	Head man of the village on Delos	"You're not like the other Athenians. They think too much."
Semnos SEM-NOS	Captain of *Paralos*	"Can I help it if I'm the most handsome man in Athens?"
Moira The modern MOIRA	An innkeeper	"One of the few things we got enough of on this island is goats."
Meren MER-EN (like Merryn)	A young villager and priestess of Artemis	"Apollo gets the glory on Delos, but we who serve the Goddess have the oldest temple."
Karnon KAR-NON	Accountant of the Delian Treasury	"A talent here, a talent there, and pretty soon you're talking real money."
Marika The modern MARIKA	Slave to Karnon	"You look like you might soon have a son of your own."

Philipos The modern PHILIP + OS	Assistant to Pericles	"I fell into a hole."
Axiagos, Enalkides and Orotheremes AX-E-AG-OS EN-ALK-EED-EEZ ORO-THE-REM- EEZ	Guards	"The pay's bad, but we get fed, and there's not much chance of dying, you know?"
Ekamandronemus EEK-AM-AN- DRON-E-MUSS	A slave with a long name	"Everyone calls me Ekamandronemus, sir."
Phaenarete* FAIN-A-RET-EE	Mother of Nico, a midwife	"Dear Gods, boy, did I teach you nothing about how to care for your wife?"
Sophroniscus* SOFF-RON-ISK-US	Father of Nico	Mentioned in conversation.
Euterpe YOU-TERP-EE	Mother of Diotima	Mentioned in conversation.
Pythax PIE-THAX	Father of Diotima	Mentioned in conversation.
Eileithyia* E-LETH-EYE-A	Goddess of childbirth and midwifery	"Hera, the mother of the gods, sent Eileithyia all the way from faraway Hyperborea to Delos, to assist with the birth of Apollo and Artemis. Everyone knows that."
Hyperborea* HYPER-BOR- RE-A	A mysterious land	"One of my assignments is to tend the graves of the Hyperborean Women."

Phoenicians* FO-NEESH-E-ANS	A sea-going people, a client state of the Persian Empire	The Phoenicians claimed to be the best sailors in the world, though everyone knew we Hellenes were better.
Kyzikos KIZ-I-KOSS	A province in the Persian Empire	"Kyzikos isn't just some Hellene city on the coast that the Persians happen to have conquered."
Breto & Melippos BRE-TOW & MEL-E-POSS	Sons of Marika	"You're only a child once, you know."

The Chorus

Assorted priests, priestesses, sailors, guards, villagers, and too many goats.

DEATH
ON DELOS

THE SACRED ISLE OF DELOS

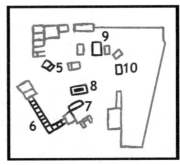

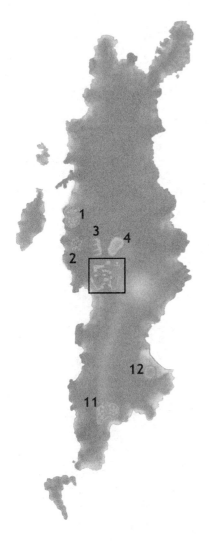

1. Abandoned Village
2. Abandoned Graveyard
3. Terrace of the Lions
4. Sacred Lake
5. Temple of Artemis
6. Stoa of the Naxians
7. Oikos of the Naxians
8. Temple of Apollo
9. Treasury Houses
10. Porinos Naos
11. New Village
12. Karnon's House

ARRIVAL

I T IS ILLEGAL to die on the sacred isle of Delos. It is also illegal to give birth there. I wasn't worried about death, but of childbirth we were in some danger, for my wife was heavily pregnant.

"Are you sure you're all right?" I asked Diotima anxiously.

"Yes, of course I am," she replied in exasperation. "You've asked the same thing a hundred times, Nico. You can stop now."

I would have to stop anyway, because the boat on which we traveled, *Paralos*, was about to touch land. I grabbed Diotima's arm, in case she fell over when the *trireme* came alongside the dock.

Delos was an island so small that you could walk around its coast in a day. Yet the long pier that protruded from her warm sands would have done credit to a major naval yard. In addition to being the birthplace of two gods, Delos was also the headquarters of the Delian League, the mutual defense alliance of the Hellenes, and it was here that the League's treasury was kept. It was perfectly normal for warships to visit, and for Delos to need port facilities that could host a major vessel, such as the one on which we stood.

Paralos was a trireme designed for war, yet kitted out with fittings of gold. Her scrubbed deck shone in the brilliant sun and there were colorful ribbons threaded into the ropes that the sailors used. Her crew, down to the lowest oarsman, could have attended a party without having to change clothes, so fine and gaudy were their outfits. Her captain was one of the most fashionable men in Athens. This was the first time I'd ever been on a warship and felt underdressed.

For *Paralos* was a very special navy boat. Her task was to carry sacred offerings wherever they needed to go, and to represent Athens on religious occasions wherever an Athenian might properly worship the gods. *Paralos* might belong to the fleet, but her orders originated with the temples.

It was on temple business that Diotima and I traveled. Every year the Athenians sent expensive offerings to Delos, in honor of the divine twins, Apollo and Artemis. This year, when the lots had been cast to determine which priestess should accompany the offerings, the job had fallen to Diotima, who had been a priestess of Artemis since she was sixteen.

"Stand by to dock," the steersman called from his position of power by the tiller.

"Oars in," the port and starboard officers called almost in unison.

The men pulled in oars.

The boat slid alongside so gently that it almost stopped itself.

It was like an elegant show that the crew had done many times before. I had been on serious warships, where each of these maneuvers would have been accompanied by much swearing and roughness. On *Paralos*, all was serenity. Except for me.

I glanced nervously over my shoulder at the ships lined up behind us. It was a large fleet. Fifty triremes. Fifty serious triremes from Athens, with Pericles at their head. A fleet that size could take on the navy of any other city and expect to win.

The priests and priestesses of Delos would be pleased to see Diotima and the gifts she brought.

They would be less thrilled when they heard what Pericles had to say.

THE TREASURE

A SMALL RECEPTION PARTY waited to greet us: two priests and two priestesses wearing *chitons* of bright material that reached to their feet and covered their arms. It wasn't the sort of garb anyone would willingly don on a hot summer day, despite which all four smiled at our arrival. Beside them stood a man who was dressed in faded robes of gray, and with a hood pulled over his head. He carried a long staff, which he did not lean upon, but held like a badge of office. He looked out of place beside the others.

At the head of this group was another man, dressed as colorfully as the priests but older, balding, and with an air of command about him. He smiled broadly as I helped Diotima onto dry land. His smile faltered as Diotima began to walk, or rather waddle, down the pier. The smile fell a little further with every step she took.

"My name is Anaxinos," he said, when we stopped before him. He spoke politely. "It is my honor to serve as High Priest of the Delian Apollo, and therefore Archon of the Sacred Isle." He paused, then asked, "Are you the priestess sent by Athens?"

"I am," Diotima said in a clear voice with a lift of her chin. "My name is Diotima."

Anaxinos glanced down at her maternal state.

"I hope you won't take this the wrong way, young lady,

but please tell me you won't be staying with us for long."
He said it kindly, but the message couldn't be clearer.

"I am somewhat aware of the problem," Diotima said
drily. "I've been assured that the dedication of the offerings
is a matter of days."

"That is true," the High Priest agreed.

"Then there is little chance of . . . er . . . an accident
while I am here, and in any case I was chosen by the Goddess."

Anaxinos raised an eyebrow at that. "Your High Priestess
in Athens agreed?"

"She did."

Diotima described how her name had been drawn from
the jar, in the traditional process of casting the lots to
select the priestess to accompany the gifts.

"They thought it must be some error, when the lot was
drawn with my name upon it," Diotima admitted. "They
threw my name back in. The High Priestess herself shook
the jar, very thoroughly, and drew again. When my name
emerged a second time, it was decided that such a message
from Artemis was impossible to ignore."

Diotima had told the truth, while neatly glossing over
just how controversial her appointment had been. This
assignment to accompany the offerings to Delos was a
prestigious one. When her name was read the first time
there had been gasps from the other priestesses. The
women could see the bump beneath Diotima's clothing
and knew what it meant, and they knew better than
anyone that it was strictly forbidden for life to begin or
end upon the sacred isle. The muttering had been so
intense that the result was checked, but there was no
doubt about it. For whatever reason, this year the Goddess had chosen Diotima to represent her.

"Your name came out twice?" Anaxinos said. "How very apposite for the divine twins, and as you say, impossible to ignore. Well, we shall make your stay with us as comfortable as possible." The High Priest turned to me. "You are the lady's husband?"

It was an easy guess, because it was inconceivable that a woman as respectable as Diotima should travel without her husband.

"I am Nicolaos, son of Sophroniscus," I said, by way of introduction.

"Just so," he said, polite but uninterested. "You are welcome."

The smiles of the priests and priestesses had not faltered during this conversation, but the gray man with the staff stared at Diotima with an odd expression. I guessed he did not like what he saw.

Behind us, the men had begun to unload the sacred offerings. They were particularly rich this year. Golden vessels, cast as household items too good for any house but that of the gods; the finest black figure pottery, which only Athens knows how to make; silver jewelry set in cases crafted by the most skillful artisans; a large portrait of Apollo and Artemis set upon solid board, by the famous painter Stephanos of Vitale; life-size statues of the divine twins, cast in bronze and painted for the utmost realism. For the priests and priestesses who dedicated their lives to honoring Apollo and Artemis, we had brought the finest food that Athens could provide. Amphora after amphora was stacked upon the pier, until I thought the decking must break under the weight: there was the best wine; and olives, for which Athens was famous, grown from the ancient vine that had been planted by Athena herself; fruits and vegetables in preservative; lambs on a tether, and enough of the always popular garos fish sauce to feed a small army.

The smile of Anaxinos returned when he saw these things.

Diotima spoke the formal words that she had been taught back in Athens. "I present to you, priests and priestesses of the Holy Isle, these small symbols of Athenian piety."

"You are doubly welcome for the gifts you bring," Anaxinos said.

"And especially for the food," muttered one of the priests in the background.

The other men and women, even the gray man, nodded in appreciation. It seemed that all was good in the eyes of the holy people.

"My colleagues will escort you to the sanctuary," Anaxinos said. "The sacred offerings will be installed in one of the treasury rooms, to await their dedication. Rest assured there is no more secure location in all of Hellas; the treasury of the Delian League is kept in the same place. The ceremony is scheduled for the day after tomorrow, to give you time to rest after the journey. We have a guest house prepared for you at the village."

"That is thoughtful," Diotima said.

"The village is at the other end of the island, I'm afraid. There's a rule against living within sight of the sanctuary. We didn't anticipate a pregnant lady. I'll order a donkey brought so you don't have to walk."

"Thank you."

I was impressed. The High Priest had everything in hand, and a ready solution for an unexpected problem. This man was a good manager.

He said, "The village is also where the stores are located. I'll ask your men to take the food and general goods straight there. One of the priests will show them the way."

"You are well organized," I commented.

"We do this every year," he said. "For you, this is perhaps a once-in-a-lifetime chance to see the most holy sanctuary in Hellas, the very birthplace of two gods. For us, this is our lifeline to civilization. The quality of what you bring defines our lives for the next year."

That certainly was a good explanation for the avaricious way the priests and priestesses had inspected the food as it was unloaded.

"Then I hope we have not disappointed you," I said.

"Athens has never disappointed us."

I hoped that wasn't about to change.

Anaxinos looked out to sea, shading his eyes against the glare of the sun, to where the fleet of triremes stood off from the shore. I could tell from the movement of his lips that he was counting.

"Tell me," he asked, "Are you two young people of importance back in Athens, to have such an escort?"

Diotima looked at me, and I looked at her. Neither of us wanted to deliver the news.

"Uh, not exactly," I said.

"Those ships are nothing to do with me or my sacred task," Diotima said flatly.

Anaxinos didn't seem to notice my wife's tone. "This is the first time in many years that I have seen so many warships off our island. Not even for meetings of the League do we see so much power assembled. Is Athens at war with someone? Where are they headed?"

The Athenian fleet chose that moment to land. There was only one pier, but that didn't matter; triremes are designed to be beached wherever the crew can find enough sand. The ships slid onto the beach as they are designed to do. Their crews jumped over the sides to secure the boats with long ropes. This continued all along the sandy coast.

"What in Hades do they think they're doing?" Anaxinos said. He sounded more incredulous than worried.

One boat didn't beach like the others. It glided up to the other side of the pier at which *Paralos* had docked. I happened to know the name of that trireme: *Harpy*. *Paralos* and *Harpy* faced those of us on land, side by side, with only the narrow wooden pier to separate them. Their battering ram prows pointed straight at us.

A man stepped off the new arrival. It was Pericles. He had carefully eschewed anything that smacked of the military. He wore no armor, but was dressed as formally as the High Priest, though the color of his clothing was more somber, the grays and reds of a man on a state mission. The chiton that Pericles wore covered him from ankles to wrists; across his shoulders he wore a *himation* of finest linen (his usual woolen one would have been far too hot in this weather); upon his head was a wide-brimmed hat that might have been for shade, but which I knew he wore to conceal his oddly elongated head. Pericles had always been sensitive about the shape of his head.

"Pericles?" Anaxinos said in astonishment.

Pericles took the High Priest's hands in his own, clasped them warmly and said, "Anaxinos, High Priest of Delos, I greet you. You are looking well."

Pericles's voice was pleasant, and rich in timbre. Pericles's voice was as famous as the man himself. There were those who said the secret of his success was his ability to enchant anyone who heard him speak.

It was apparent that these two already knew each other,

which on reflection was no surprise. Pericles and Anaxinos must have sat together at meetings of the League.

"I rejoice to see you, Pericles, as always," Anaxinos said, though his manner betrayed his confusion. "But what are you doing here?"

"A difficult situation has arisen, my friend," Pericles said. Then he delivered the news that had shaken all of Athens, when word had arrived from the south not ten days before. "I regret to tell you that the Persians have retaken Egypt."

"So we had heard, even here on isolated Delos," Anaxinos said. "Do you go to fight the enemy?"

"They are too strong," Pericles said. "So much so that we fear the opposite. The Persians could assemble a powerful fleet and attack the southern islands of the Delian League."

"Which includes Delos itself," Anaxinos said. He rubbed his chin in thought. "So you have come to protect the Holy Isle."

"In a manner of speaking," Pericles said smoothly. "In order to protect the members of the League we must have ships, and armaments for fighting men. We must have shield factories and shipyards."

"Yes, of course," said Anaxinos. "That is why we in the sanctuary maintain the treasury of the League, to pay for these things."

"Yet here on Delos, the treasury is exposed. Think upon it, Anaxinos," Pericles said. "The Persians could send a fleet to sack Delos and steal the treasury. The danger to your people is great, the danger to the funds even greater. So it is that we have come to remove the treasury of the Delian League," Pericles said. "We're taking it with us back to Athens."

The priests and priestesses who heard these words

exclaimed in horror. Anaxinos turned white, despite the sun. For a moment I thought he would faint. But he didn't. Instead he said, "You cannot!"

"I must insist," Pericles said.

"Have you discussed this with the other member states?" Anaxinos demanded.

"The need is urgent. The time required to confer is too great," Pericles said. "I'm sure you can see that. We must act."

The other priests and priestesses were glancing at each other in dismay. The priest in gray shook his staff.

"Then we must resist you," Anaxinos said.

"Resist?" Pericles said. He sounded surprised, and there was a shade of hurt in his voice. "My dear Anaxinos, this highly esteemed Sanctuary of Apollo has been an excellent custodian of the League funds, but a custodian only. The time has come for another to bear the burden."

Anaxinos looked uncertain.

"It is the safety of Delos that concerns us," Pericles said, pressing his advantage. "While the League treasury resides here, it is a temptation to any force strong enough to attack."

Anaxinos reluctantly nodded at these true words. He opened his mouth to speak.

But now the man in the gray robe stepped forward. He flung back his hood to reveal a short, grizzled beard, bright, angry eyes, and a stern, disapproving mouth. He beat his staff upon the ground until he had everyone's attention.

"I am Geros, the oldest priest, most versed in knowledge of the Gods, and the final authority on matters of temple doctrine, and I say that you cannot do this thing."

"Why is that, sir?" Pericles asked. I knew Pericles had a poor opinion of self-proclaimed experts, but he made an effort to keep his voice polite.

"Because it is heresy!" The old priest shook his staff in anger. "There is no greater crime than to remove treasure from a sanctuary. This all men know."

"And if the Persians attack you, as I fear?" Pericles asked.

"Then Divine Apollo shall protect us, as he always has," Geros said.

Personally I had more faith in Pericles's fifty triremes, but it would have been in bad taste to say so to the ancient priest.

Geros raised his staff and pointed it straight at Pericles. "Depart this place, before you do more harm."

"What harm?" Pericles demanded.

"When you come with such thoughts, you pollute the sanctuary by your very presence. I say to you, depart."

At these words several of the priests and priestesses shook their fists.

At that same moment, the sailors from *Paralos* walked past, carrying the sumptuous supply of food for the island.

"Shall we take with us the gifts and the food, too?" Pericles asked. "I remind you that for a century or more now, it is Athens that has supported Delos with our food and our gifts."

"So now you threaten to starve us?" Geros accused.

"I never said any such thing!" Now Pericles was losing his temper.

"Gentlemen!" said Anaxinos. He held up his hands to stop the argument. "Let there be peace here. We are all men of good will." He turned to the elder priest. "Geros, I am sure that Pericles has our welfare at heart."

Geros looked like he doubted that very much. He said nothing but, "Hmmpf."

Anaxinos then turned to Pericles. "Pericles, you must understand that what you propose is contrary to twenty-five years of custom, and that your actions are arbitrary and unexpected. But I have thought about it as you spoke, and there is a path forward. I shall announce a full meeting of the Delian League. Every member is to vote. If the member states agree, then you shall have the treasury."

That seemed fair. The priests and priestesses nodded.

"And how long will that take?" Pericles objected. "There are one hundred and forty-eight member states!"

"A matter of mere days if they travel with all speed—as you know perfectly well—and when the other cities learn what you're up to I'm sure they will make great haste to be here."

"Days to arrive, perhaps," Pericles said, "followed by months of endless wrangling. You know how these meetings go, Anaxinos. Men talk and talk, and in the end do nothing. What if the Persians attack in the meantime?"

"With your fifty triremes on station?" Anaxinos scoffed.

"I'm glad you mentioned that," Pericles said. He seemed to have regained his self-control. He sounded icy calm. "I point out that you are a village of priests. Whereas we are a fleet stronger than any other. I think that Delos must be sensible about this."

Everyone present gasped. That was an open threat, laid bare for all to hear. Athens had the power to take this money, so Athens would take it.

This encounter hadn't gone quite the way Pericles had promised me. Back in Athens, when he had told me of his plan, he had assured me that he would persuade the priests of Apollo.

"I will bring them to see reason. They are but priests, and I am the greatest orator in the world," Pericles had said with a complete lack of modesty but a good deal of truth.

Anaxinos, however, had a ready answer to Pericles's rhetoric. The High Priest, who had seemed such a nice man, punched Pericles in the face.

THE STANDOFF

"**A** RE THEY STILL rioting?" Diotima asked from the comfort of her bed. Her voice was tired, cold, and unforgiving.

It had been an easy pregnancy for the first ten months, the only problem being that Diotima had became increasingly and uncharacteristically irritable as the day of birth approached. Yet a wise man doesn't argue with a woman in her condition. Instead he ignores the irritation and looks after the mother-to-be.

I peered out from behind the curtains of the cottage we had been given to use. The cottage was a simple, one room affair with bed, chairs, and a table; but it had pretty appointments, such as the cushions on the chairs, and the curtains that covered the wooden shutters. The shutters and the door all squealed when you moved them—it seemed every hinge needed a touch of oil—but it was otherwise the perfect small home.

In the distance I could see fires burning and hear voices singing.

"It seems to be a standoff," I said.

As word of the Athenian invasion had spread, the priests and priestesses had come from all over the island to surround the treasury houses. Each treasury was a small building, all clustered together within the sacred precinct. At first there had been scuffles. I had decided my pregnant wife was not going to be caught up in a major fight—a fight which at that time seemed imminent—so, guided by one of the priestesses, I had escorted Diotima to the pretty house in the village where we were to live. There we waited throughout what was left of the afternoon to see what would happen next.

Meanwhile the people of Delos had sat themselves down in front of the treasury doors. As night fell they built bonfires. The people linked arms and sang songs of defiance and hymns to Apollo and Artemis.

The Athenian soldiers and sailors could do nothing but watch this display. The only alternative would have been to drag away holy people. Not even the most cynical Athenian was going to do that. The soldiers nevertheless tried to look useful by standing in a thin battle line, facing the singing priests. It was a complete waste of time because there was no enemy to fight.

This news and other updates we learned from the small stream of priestesses who returned to the village to collect food and water for the protestors. With the threat of open warfare over, Diotima and I wanted to return to the scene. But we couldn't stand with the people of Delos—we were Athenians, after all, and the locals would be wary of us—nor could we stand with the soldiers and sailors. Diotima and I were here to honor the Gods, like the people of Delos, not to deplete the treasury of Apollo. Thus we were neither one side nor the other. If we turned up to watch the excitement, then where we chose to stand would be a political statement.

"This is all your fault, Nico," Diotima said angrily.

"My fault?" I said, astonished. "What did I do?"

"What you didn't do, back in Athens, was dissuade Pericles when he told you of this horrible scheme," Diotima said.

"When was the last time I convinced Pericles to do any-thing?" I said to her.

No man likes to admit to his wife that he's any less than godlike, but there was no point trying to pretend that I was the equal of Pericles. I was still a young man, not even old enough to hold public office. He was the foremost man of Athens. On any question of importance the people always turned to Pericles for advice; no legislation could pass our assembly unless Pericles said he approved. In this case, it was Pericles who had proposed we safeguard the treasury. The people had instantly voted his plan into effect. Who was I to stop that?

"Besides," I said. "When you think about it, moving the treasury to Athens makes a lot of sense."

"Nico! How could you say such a thing?" Diotima said.

"Well, it's true," I said defensively. I couldn't understand why Diotima was so upset.

"It's a complete insult to the most sacred sanctuary in all of Hellas," she said. "Nobody can remove treasure from a temple without offending the gods. Think of the bad luck that Apollo and Artemis will send."

"Think of the even worse luck if the Persians raid and take the money. Pericles is right. Delos is far too exposed to leave anything precious here."

"Are you saying the sanctuary of the Divine Twins isn't precious?" my wife said frostily.

"You know what I mean," I said.

"I hope I don't," she replied. "I hope my husband has more piety than that!"

"In a war we can retake the island, if we lose it." I was becoming as angry as her. "But if we lose the fighting fund then we lose the war, and that's that! Anyway, it should hardly matter to you," I said. "Whether the treasury is in

Delos or Athens won't affect your life one bit, as long as they can spend the money on defense."

"Oh, Nico, of course it matters to me. Don't you understand? To dedicate the holy offerings on Delos is one of the highest honors any priest or priestess can have. I was chosen by the Goddess herself. But all that anyone will remember is that this is the year in which Athens stole the treasury, and now my special day is ruined."

Diotima broke into sobs.

It broke my heart to see her crying, but there was nothing I could think to do. I leaned over to give her a hug. "I'm sorry."

At that moment the protest singing at the sanctuary cut off as if directed by a choir master. The island went ominously silent.

"I wonder what's happening?" Diotima said.

I made a decision. "Let's go find out."

I helped my wife onto her feet.

PRIEST OF CHAOS

THE SANCTUARY WAS lit as bright as day by the bonfires and the many torches that men carried. We solved the problem of where to stand—with the Delians or with the Athenians—by splitting up. Diotima went to apologize to Anaxinos. This crisis was no fault of hers, but she felt the need to say something. I went in search of Pericles. I found him at the head of the Athenian force.

"Nicolaos," Pericles said as I walked up.

"Pericles," I replied. "What's happening?"

"As you see, we are making little progress."

Everyone was where we had left them: the Delians blocking the doors of the treasury, the Athenians looking for a way through that didn't involve hitting priests.

"This hasn't quite gone to plan," Pericles admitted.

Pericles sported a black eye. Anaxinos had landed Pericles a beauty. Whatever training they gave these priests, it seemed to include boxing. Pericles hadn't struck back when the priest of Apollo had knocked him down. To lay hands on one of the priests of the most sacred sanctuary in all of Hellas would have destroyed any hope of completing the Athenian mission.

For seven years now, I had been the man Pericles came to when he had a delicate problem that needed a solution, but I could be no help to him here. This problem wasn't delicate, and it wasn't so much a problem as a total crisis.

The longer the crisis dragged on, the worse Athens was going to look in the eyes of the other cities of Hellas.

"Where is your wife?" Pericles could not bring himself to say Diotima's name. Pericles and Diotima had never been on good terms; he had once tried to talk me out of marrying her. The world was a more peaceful place when the two of them were apart.

"She's apologizing to Anaxinos for what's happening," I said.

Pericles grunted. "It might not hurt to have a sympathetic Athenian on the other side. She can tell us what they're thinking."

I was pretty sure I could tell Pericles what Anaxinos was thinking, and without even bothering to ask the priest. In any case, it was not Anaxinos who led the resistance. It was the ancient priest Geros.

Geros stood before the assembled peoples of Delos as a military General might stand before his men at the start of battle. He faced the Athenians, and he preached.

". . . and so I say to you, Athenians, that this is not well done in the eyes of Apollo."

Geros was not a good speaker, but he was a passionate one. He raised his staff at every high note, which in the sing-song pattern of his speech seemed to be the close of every sentence. The staff rose and fell so frequently that men were watching the staff rather than the priest.

"You might say that the treasure you seek is not Apollo's to hold. In this I would agree! But you are to consider that this League of mutual defense among you and your allies is the Delian League—the *Delian* League." Geros carefully emphasized the word. "And we ask ourselves, why is it so?"

Geros raised his staff even higher. Then he thundered, "It is because your peoples sought the approval, the sanctity and the blessing of Lord Apollo, he whose greatest home is this sanctuary where we stand, on Delos! And the God in his wisdom listened! And what did he do? He sent the greatest good luck when the League met the enemy upon the waters at Salamis, and the sailors of Hellas—you people here before me—won the greatest victory in the history of man!"

Cheers erupted amongst the Athenians. It wasn't these men who had fought and destroyed the Persian fleet at Salamis; it had been their fathers, and my father too. But it all came to the same thing. Geros had made his point. If there was anything a Hellene believed in, it was luck. Good luck sent by the gods to reward righteous behavior, bad luck sent by the same gods to punish those who had offended.

Geros spoke more softly. "That is why your League is the Delian League. It is why the treasure must remain. For I remind you, men of Athens, that as Lord Apollo approved the investment of your treasury in this, his sanctuary, so he would be angered by its removal."

Geros didn't need to say the fateful words "bad luck." Every man who listened was already thinking it.

I didn't agree with a word he had said—Athenian sailors had won those victories against the odds, with not much luck to help them—yet even I was impressed by the old priest's passion and his belief in Apollo. The sailors of the Athenian Navy were convinced. I could see it in the way they stood, how they muttered amongst themselves and glanced at Pericles with worried looks. If Pericles at that instant had been handed the treasure to take with him, his own sailors would have refused to carry it.

Pericles knew it, too. "Will no one rid me of this trouble-some priest?" he said, as if to himself, but I heard him clearly, and so did the men standing closest. They looked askance at their leader. Among these was Philipos, a soldier to whom Pericles often assigned minor tasks.

"Surely you don't mean that," I said to Pericles. At the same time, Philipos asked, "Do you really mean that?"

"That was my frustration speaking," Pericles replied to us both. "When I first spoke to Anaxinos, he was about to agree with me."

"He did seem about to consent," I agreed.

"It fell apart when that old man opened his mouth."

In Geros, Pericles might have met his match. He gauged the reaction of the crowd. "I admit, I'm not sure how to proceed here."

"You could give up and go home?" I suggested hopefully. That at least would solve my marital issues.

"Don't be ridiculous," Pericles said shortly. "No matter what that foolish priest says, the logic of my position is unimpeachable."

"Geros isn't using logic. He's using emotion," I said.

"Yes, you're right, Nicolaos." Pericles looked thoughtful.

Anaxinos had been standing well to the side, watching events unfold. I was amazed he had not tried to take control. Perhaps he felt that it would be better to let things run their course. Now he walked over to where we stood. Diotima and a handful of priests were in his wake.

"Pericles, this situation is not good," Anaxinos said.

That was something we could all agree with.

"Have you reconsidered?" Pericles asked. "Can you order Geros to desist?"

"I am sorry, Pericles, but Geros is in the right," Anaxinos said. "This wouldn't have happened if you had agreed to my suggestion for a full meeting of the League. I want to repeat that offer."

"To ask a three-hundred-man committee to make a single decision?" Pericles said derisively. "No thank you."

"Then the standoff will continue," Anaxinos said unhappily. "I regret it."

Diotima shot me a frown, then shifted her eyes meaningfully toward Pericles. She seemed to expect me to talk him round. I shook my head very slightly.

"I have come to you for another reason," said the High Priest. He indicated Diotima. "This young priestess is scheduled to dedicate the holy offerings. Whatever the difficulties between us, the Gods cannot be neglected."

"I certainly agree," Pericles said at once.

"I am glad to hear it. Tomorrow we prepare. The ceremony will be the day after, precisely as Apollo rises."

"I understand," Pericles said. "My men will not impede the movement of any holy person." He glanced over at the protesters and smiled wryly. "Indeed, it seems to be the other way round."

"Quite so," Anaxinos said. He seemed embarrassed. "I bid you a good night, or as good as you can manage. Do your men have places to sleep? Have they been fed?"

Even in the midst of rebellion, Anaxinos was the perfect host.

"The men are accustomed to sleeping by their boats," Pericles said. "As to food, I'm not sure. We have a small number of supplies, but we didn't expect to be . . . er . . ." For once Pericles seemed lost for words.

"You thought to have the treasury loaded and be gone by tomorrow morning," Anaxinos finished for him. "Well, we'll see what we can do about dinner."

The High Priest turned away. The other priests followed, as did Diotima, who, before she departed, came to me as a wife should, squeezed my hand, leaned close, and murmured.

The other Athenians probably thought it was a wifely endearment. What she actually said in my ear was, "Talk to Pericles."

Indeed, that was my plan. Somehow we had to quell the tension, if only for my wife's sake so that her ceremony wasn't a disaster. I squeezed her hand back to show I understood.

I didn't get a chance to talk to Pericles. Instead, he talked to me. Once the Delians were gone he led me by the arm away from our fellow Athenians. Philipos watched us go with an odd expression. Was he curious? Or even jealous? If so he needn't have been. I'd never known a conversation with Pericles to be anything other than trouble.

"I misstepped in my approach to the priests," Pericles said to me quietly. "Though in hindsight it is hard to see what I could have done better."

"Perhaps if you hadn't bluntly threatened them with the force of the navy?" I suggested.

"I take your point," Pericles conceded. "The fact is, Nicolaos, despite appearances we are very close to agreement. Anaxinos sees that the Delian Treasury is really the property of the Delian League, but he cannot release the money because of doctrinal issues raised by the old priest Geros. Geros is the sticking point. Nicolaos, there's something I want you to do for me."

"Yes?"

"I want you to deal with the old priest."

"You want me to what?" To say I was horrified would have been an understatement.

A voice from behind me said, "Pericles, the villagers are driving sheep towards us."

Sheep?

"Not now, Philipos," Pericles said in irritation. "I don't think a flock of sheep are likely to savage our troops too badly, do you?"

"No, Pericles." Philipos sounded abashed, even sheepish.

"Then show some initiative, man!" Pericles barked. "Do what you think is best."

"Yes, Pericles."

When Philipos was gone I said, with some heat, "Pericles, I'm not going to kill an old man—"

"I didn't say kill him," Pericles interrupted quickly. "I said *deal with*."

"What does that mean?" I asked suspiciously.

"I want you to talk to him, to persuade him."

"Why me?" I said. Pericles had never praised my negotiation skills. Usually, he complained about them.

"You're the perfect person," Pericles said. "Geros knows you didn't arrive with the main force. Your wife is a priestess. She's to dedicate our offerings. Technically, you're here as a private individual. Geros will listen to you, Nico, where his ears will be closed to me."

"What am I to say?" I asked doubtfully.

"Tell the old priest that your sole interest is to avoid conflict," Pericles said confidently. "Emphasize the high regard in which Athens holds Delos. As gently as possible, ask what might persuade him to take a more relaxed view of relocating the treasury."

I'd been working for Pericles long enough to know what he meant by that. "I don't think Geros is open to bribes, Pericles."

"It's a question of finding out what he wants," Pericles said briskly. "Offer to take him on a holiday. Ply him with women and strong wine—he looks like he's never tried either—I don't care. Just get him to stop objecting."

"You're asking me to suborn a priest," I said.

"In a word, yes," Pericles agreed. "But I have every confidence in you, Nicolaos. You can do it."

THE DEAL

I WASN'T QUITE SURE how to go about bribing
someone—until now, no one had ever hired me to do
such a thing—but I was fairly sure it didn't involve making the offer in front of the target's friends, admirers, colleagues and acquaintances. Geros was surrounded by many
people who would fit that description. Somehow I would
have to get the priest alone.

In the meantime all I could do was watch and wait for
an opportunity. I found a good observation post away from
the crowd, upon the steps of the Oikos of the Naxians. The
Oikos was the sanctuary's administration center, built a
hundred years ago by the people of Naxos, who back then
had been the benefactors of Delos, just as the Athenians
were today. The Naxians in their time had made their
names immortal, and exceeded all of Hellas in piety, by
donating many fine buildings of outstanding merit. One
such gift was the Stoa of the Naxians, a beautiful covered
portico that adjoined the Oikos and ran to the east.

The Athenians had assembled on the well-trodden field
in front of the Stoa of the Naxians, which was the largest
open space within the precinct. The four treasury houses
lay on the other side of the field. That was where the
protestors had set up camp, to block access to the doors.
Between the protestors and the Athenians lay the small
but elegant Old Temple of Apollo, called by the priests

the Poros Temple because it had been built from poros limestone.

Anaxinos and a party of priests stood at the entrance of the partially-built New Temple, beside the Poros Temple. Diotima stood with this group. She saw me alone upon the steps of the Oikos and came to join me.

"Are you all right?" I asked her.

"I'm tired," she said.

She looked it, which was why I had asked the question. Her face seemed somewhat drawn, though perhaps that was an effect of the inconstant light from the bonfires. Diotima's black hair was invariably perfect—she favored carefully curled tresses that outlined her lovely neck—but tonight her hair hung limp and unkempt, and her face seemed thin.

I took her hand and helped her to sit down. "I'm not surprised," I said. "It's late at night, we woke at dawn, sailed from Athens to Delos, ever since have been caught up in a minor rebellion, and you're carrying an extra passenger. You should be dead on your feet."

"I saw you talking to Pericles," she said. "Could you persuade him to give up this scheme?"

"No, but he's worried," I said, avoiding a more complete answer to her question.

"He deserves to be," Diotima said in derision.

I debated whether to tell Diotima about the mission Pericles had given me, and decided against. This wasn't the time to worry my wife.

I had never before not shared my work with her, but this situation seemed special. Diotima might not be particularly understanding about Pericles's methods. The fact that Diotima and Pericles had never gotten along would incline her against his plan right away. Besides which, I had some dim presentiment that she might not approve.

Geros would either reject my offer out of hand, in which case Diotima need never know, or he would accept, in which case the Athenian forces would disappear with the treasury, and Diotima's special day of dedication would be free of conflict. Surely that would please her.

Thus the best course of action was to convince Geros to acquiesce in the matter of the treasury, without bothering my wife with the details of how that feat had been achieved.

"You should sleep," I told her.

"I will." She rubbed her eyes, and yawned. "I suppose you want to stay, to see what happens?"

"Yes. I'll escort you to the village first, though."

"I can make it on my own," Diotima said.

"I'll escort you anyway."

"I'm not a cripple, Nico!" She spoke angrily.

My father had warned me, when Diotima announced her pregnancy, that women with child could become a little bit irrational. "You just have to deal with it," my father had advised.

I hadn't believed him at the time, but I was starting to see that he was right. Of course my first duty was to look after my pregnant wife—in her current state she was hardly capable of doing it herself—but my perfectly reasonable efforts to protect her from all harm seemed to annoy her. It was inexplicable.

"What if you trip and fall in the dark?" I asked. "How would you get up?"

"What do you think I am?" she demanded. "A beached whale?"

"Well . . ."

"Thank you very much!"

"Can I help?" A voice emerged from the dark.

It was the young priestess who had shown us to our

house in the village earlier that day. Meren could not have been older than sixteen, yet already she wore the robes of a fully initiated priestess.

"I heard you mention the village," she said. "I'm headed that way myself. Would you like some company?"

"Thank you, Meren, that would be lovely," Diotima said. "Your invitation is beautifully phrased." My wife shot me a black look.

It seemed to me the young priestess knew the path to the village, as Diotima did not, and that Meren could run for help if anything happened to Diotima. I was content to watch the two of them disappear into the darkness, on their way to the other side of the island.

Meanwhile the standoff had turned into an impromptu party. The bonfires that lit the night were put to another use: villagers placed giant iron tripods over the flames and turned them into barbecues.

There really had been a flock of sheep approaching— Philipos had reported accurately. They proved to be older lambs, destined for the table. Despite the darkness, local shepherds had driven them from a nearby holding pen.

The barbecue proceeded at a great pace. It is the rule of our religion that no red meat can be eaten unless the animal's life has been given to the gods, but on holy Delos there was no shortage of either altars or priests to sanctify the meals.

The Athenians watched this with growling stomachs. After a while one of the more friendly priests asked the salivating Athenians if they would like a bite of the perfectly roasted lamb. No one turned to Pericles to ask permission. The Athenian army rushed forward—not to battle, but to dinner—and in the blink of an eye the Athenians and the Delians were standing around the giant bonfires, chatting and eating. The Athenians had given up hope of obtaining the treasure—at least, those not in charge had abandoned their mission—while the Delians fed their unwanted visitors with admirable good cheer.

Pericles threw up his arms in a theatrical display of despair. He marched off in a huff, in the direction of the beach and the pier. I supposed he would sleep tonight on *Harpy*. Anaxinos would surely have offered Pericles a bed, but I doubted Pericles would have accepted generosity in this state of impasse.

Pericles had left, but I saw Philipos had remained. He was as hungry as the rest of us. I wondered about him. Was he like me, someone for whom Pericles had found a use? Or was he one of those useless men who were desperate to be seen in Pericles's company? There were many such, these days.

When I first met him, Pericles had been an isolated figure. He had made himself the champion of democracy when it had seemed the democratic movement must fail at any moment. Friends for him had been scarce.

But now that the democracy was a huge success, now that Athens was in the ascendant, now that Pericles was universally acclaimed the greatest leader of our time, suddenly every social climber in the city wanted to call him friend. I would see these men in his courtyard whenever I visited his home. Pericles himself was never among them— he was always to be found working in his office upstairs.

I despised the social climbers. Why Pericles tolerated their presence I could not imagine.

Philipos, too, always seemed to be at Pericles's home. He hung about in the anteroom, beside the steps that led up to the office, like a loyal dog at his master's door. I had never spoken to him except for polite greetings. Whenever he was absent, it always proved to be because he was off on a task for Pericles, usually something involving the army, for Philipos was a veteran soldier, and Pericles's official position in Athens was *strategos*, one of the ten commanders of the armed forces.

Philipos had been a relative nobody until he began his work as assistant to Pericles. Like so many other men, Philipos had benefited from his association with our leader. I was embarrassed to admit to myself that the same could be said of me, though I liked to think that I maintained my independence.

The day's tension had desperately needed to be dispelled, and that was exactly what the ordinary folk of both sides did without thinking. The Athenians were inadvertently performing the job that Pericles needed: the priests were warming to the invaders. I wondered if that had been Pericles's plan. Or perhaps the plan of Anaxinos. Was either man that sneaky? I contemplated these deep thoughts as I watched the diners.

Geros was eating with his followers. They seemed to treat him with much respect. It seemed to me that Pericles was right. Geros was the key to the impasse. If he could be persuaded, all else would follow.

The sight of all that food was making me hungry. I was almost ready to abandon my vigil when a voice beside me made me jump.

"I think you're someone like me."

I turned to find a tall blond man with the broad shoulders of a laborer. He stood there, smiling at me in a companionable way. Whoever this new arrival was, I'd never heard him coming. Either I'd been concentrating on the scene more than I thought, or this man could move silently.

"What did you say?" I said.

"That you're like me."

He spoke in a friendly, casual voice, but I was startled at his words. Was he saying that he was an agent? Had he spotted me for one? If so, how?

"What do you mean?" I asked cautiously.

"I mean you like to stand to the side and watch things happen," said the tall blond man. "I've been watching you, while you watched everyone else. You're not like the other Athenians. They think too much."

"Is that bad?" I asked.

"People who think a lot get themselves into trouble," he explained. "But you don't! You stand apart and you work with your eyes all the time. Would you like some dinner?"

He held out a piece of flat bread, into which had been stuffed onions fried in olive oil, with slivers of succulent lamb. I dislike onions but love lamb. I took the food from his hand gratefully.

"What's your name?" I asked him.

"Damon. I'm one of the villagers."

"Not one of the priests?" I asked. "Don't they come from the village too?"

He shook his head. "Not really. All the priests and priestesses come from other cities. They moved here to serve the Gods." He paused. "Except for our girl Meren," he added. "She's the only local to become a priestess. We're all real proud of her. The rest of us aren't that smart." He laughed. "Someone has to do the real work around here. That's me and my fellows."

"I'm Nico," I said. I transferred the bread to my left hand and offered my right. We shook hands. "Thank you for the food. I wish I could offer you something in return."

"Don't worry about it." He shrugged. "Let's just talk."

"What about?" I asked.

"How come you're interested in Geros?"

I almost choked on my lamb. "He's an interesting man," I managed to say, after Damon had slapped me on the back and I'd recovered my breath. "Is he the one really in charge?"

"Instead of Anaxinos?" Damon shook his head. "Geros is like one of those irritating grandmothers who refuse to die." He nudged me with an elbow. "You know the type?"

"I'm not sure . . ."

"The type that hang around forever and demand everything in a querulous voice. They make life miserable for the lady of the house, and they think everything has to be arranged for their convenience. But no one says anything against the old biddy, because she's the master's mother, and you've got to respect the aged, right?"

Damon stopped speaking. He was obviously waiting for me to agree.

All my grandparents had died when I was young, but I'd been to the home of friends who had exactly that sort of lady. She was usually to be found sitting in the courtyard with her gouty feet up on the best dining couch, shouting orders at all and sundry.

"I know what you mean," I said to Damon. "What makes Geros so respected that people obey him?"

"He's been on the island since Zeus was a boy. He knows more about the traditions of Delos than all the other priests combined. If you need to know the right ritual for some obscure event, then Geros is your man."

"How come he isn't the High Priest?" I asked, in between mouthfuls of dinner.

Damon shrugged. "It was before my time, but I think he got passed over. Well, you can see why."

I could. Geros was divisive. Anaxinos was a consensus man. Any committee would take Anaxinos over Geros.

"But Geros seems to be uncontrollable," I said.

"You got that right," Damon said with feeling.

"Anaxinos can't like that too much," I said.

"He doesn't." Damon laughed. "He never says anything in public, but you can tell. When Geros throws one of his tantrums, Anaxinos stands to the side with that false smile on his face and he waits for Geros to calm down. Then Anaxinos carries on as if nothing had happened."

"Like what's happening now," I said.

"Yeah, but this is a bigger tantrum than usual. This time the old priest has got everyone stirred up, and Anaxinos is doing what he always does: standing to the side and waiting for it to pass. Don't know if it's gonna work this time, though. You gonna stay out here all night?"

"Maybe."

"Well, I gotta go. Been a long day." He wiped his greasy hands on his tunic, leaving streaks of olive oil and lamb fat smeared across the fabric. This told me that Damon wasn't married, because no wife would have forgiven him (as I had discovered the hard way).

As he turned to go, Damon said, "The funny thing about that sort of grandmother is, after they die, everyone's kind of relieved, but no one's brave enough to say it."

The strange villager wandered off into the night.

THE OFFER

THE MEN OF Delos and Athens sat about the sanctuary. They kept warm by the dying fires and drank wine from skins that they passed among them. The women for the most part trailed back to the village, in twos and threes, yawning a great deal and telling their men not to stay out too long, and not to wake them when they returned home drunk at dawn.

The High Priest Anaxinos looked about him. He was still surrounded by his small group of loyal acolytes. One of the middle-grade priests said something, to which Anaxinos nodded. As a group they began the walk down the Sacred Way, the wide path leading in and out of the sanctuary grounds. Their route took them past where I stood on the steps of the Oikos.

Anaxinos stopped and looked up at me in a rather curious way. "Where is your wife?"

"At home, sir, or rather, in the fine cottage you lent us."

"It's late, you should join her."

"Yes, sir."

Anaxinos began to walk on, then suddenly asked, "Is all well with you?" He was ever the perfect host.

"Very well, sir," I said. "Thank you for asking."

"Good night, then." He walked on, and his gaggle of priests followed. The moon, which was three-quarters full, had shone bright upon the protestors. Now clouds came to cover Selene, goddess of the moon. It made little difference to the drinkers—they had their fires—but the surrounding darkness gave the scene a sinister air.

It seemed that the old priest Geros had only been waiting for Anaxinos to depart, for he soon took leave of his own followers. But he didn't walk south toward the village. Geros turned due north, the opposite direction. What surprised me was that he walked away without any friends to accompany him.

I knew this was my chance. I couldn't imagine catching the old priest alone at any other time.

I watched Geros walk quickly into the darkness beyond the fires, and I was suddenly gripped by a fear that he might disappear into the night before I could catch up with him. I would be distraught if after such a long wait I missed my chance. I jumped down from the steps and hurried to follow.

I needed to skirt the barbeque pits—it would certainly look strange if I, an Athenian, was seen hurrying after the leader of the anti-Athenian protestors. Someone might even stop me. So I had to go around the fires, but should I circuit to the left or to the right?

I circled to the right. The ground beneath my feet was hard and easy to walk on, and luckily there were no loose stones, because in the dark I might easily have twisted an ankle. I had to wait a moment for my eyes to adjust, because the bright fires had blinded me.

As vision returned, I realized that Geros was nowhere to be seen. I cursed silently and hurried forward in the hope that I might catch a hint of his movement.

Without any warning my right foot slammed into stone. I was wearing sandals, but that wasn't enough to save my toes. I felt the toes crunch and the pain was immediate. I stifled my cry, but the surprise made me fall forward. My left knee hit the same rocks. I put out a hand to stop total collapse, and discovered that my assailant was a low stone wall, invisible at night unless you knew to look down. I cursed my luck.

The wall was too low to be useful for any practical purpose except to sit on it, which I did. I crossed my right foot over my aching left knee and rubbed the damaged toes. I would have to hope they weren't broken.

I guessed the wall must be the boundary marker for the sanctuary. Most sanctuaries have them, but this one was remarkably close by. The wall gave me an idea. Geros hadn't walked in my direction; if he had he would certainly have heard my accident. But he obviously knew where the wall was; he wouldn't have come this way intending to climb over it. Therefore I guessed that I would find a gate if I walked in the opposite direction. Now I knew which way I must go. When I passed the fires I had turned to the east. Now I headed west.

I had to hop to avoid putting pressure on my sore toes, then discovered that I also had to favor my left knee. It was a good thing it was dark, because my gait probably resembled one of those strange monkey creatures that the Egyptians keep for their amusement. I continued in this way with some caution, and was rewarded when I came to the corner of the sanctuary. I managed to avoid running into the adjoining wall. Here I found the gate I'd been looking for. It was the only way out unless Geros had climbed the wall in the dark, which seemed less than likely for a man of his dignity.

The pain in my foot and knee had subsided to a throb. I went through the exit to discover that I had walked into a graveyard.

It wasn't the sort of destination I'd been expecting. I knew it was a graveyard because of the funeral *stele*, stones erected to commemorate the dead. Some stood as tall as me, so that their silhouettes were discernible against the night sky. Two were close enough that I could run my hand over the inscriptions. The carved stone was gritty to my touch with sea salt, but even so I could read off the letters by feel. This made me stop and think.

Had Geros truly walked into a graveyard in the dead of night? If so, why? I could think of several explanations, but every one of them was macabre.

Still, the man was nowhere to be seen, and I was beginning to worry, for I was sure that I was approaching the coast. Delos was not so large that you could walk in a straight line in any direction for long without stepping into the sea.

I had to acknowledge that I had failed. Perhaps I would be able to catch Geros in the morning, when it was light and I could at least see the man I was attempting to bribe, though how I would corner him discreetly I couldn't imagine.

My attention was caught by a flicker of light in the distance. I realized it must be a torch. Whoever held the light seemed to be waving it about. It couldn't be Geros, who had left the bonfire without a torch. My immediate thought was that it might be sailors from one of the Athenian ships. But the navy had beached south of the dock, and we were north. Perhaps it was a sailor who had become lost.

No matter, it was someone with a light by which to see, and I was close to becoming lost myself. I decided to ask for directions back to the village. I made my way toward the light—with caution, for I had already learned one object lesson this night about the pitfalls of hurrying across unknown terrain.

So it was that I was staring at the ground, looking to see where I put my feet, when I ran straight into Geros. I almost knocked him over. He stumbled backwards.

"Look where you're going, you oaf!"

"What?" I said, then realized who I had hit. I felt I should explain. "I'm sorry, sir, I didn't see you in the dark. I was heading toward that light over there." I pointed, but the torchlight had gone. "That is, there was a light over there, but it's gone now."

"Are you a moth, to be attracted by lights?" he asked.

"No, sir. I wanted to ask directions."

"Got lost, did you?"

"Actually, sir, I was looking for you."

The clouds that had covered the moon chose that moment to depart, revealing holy Selene in all her glory. The old priest peered at me.

"You're the husband of that priestess the Athenians sent."

"Yes, sir."

"I don't know why you bothered coming to this island. You arrived with one small treasure, and then instantly tried to remove a far greater one. Hypocritical, don't you think?"

He had given me the opening I needed. I said, "That's what I'd like to speak to you about, sir."

"Yes?" He looked at me expectantly.

Now that I'd found Geros, I discovered that my voice had dried up. Pericles had told me what to say when I met the priest, how to make the transaction sound perfectly good and normal. But every word that Pericles had said had fled my mind. My tongue was paralyzed.

Geros glared at me. "Well, what is it? Speak up."

I stammered. "I . . . er . . . I mean, we . . . that is, Athens . . ."

Geros stamped his staff on the ground in annoyance.

"We'd like to pay you to withdraw your objection to Athens's taking the treasury of the Delian League," I blurted out, and winced at my bluntness.

Geros stared at me, in obvious complete surprise. I don't know what he'd been expecting me to say, but it wasn't this.

"You are offering me money to betray the Gods?" he said.

"Pericles also suggested wine and women, if money didn't suit," I said quickly. "I'll tell him you're not interested, shall I?"

Geros paused for a moment. Then he asked, "How much money?"

I was shocked. I think my jaw dropped. I had expected Geros to curse me and tell me to go away. I wouldn't have blamed the priest if he had struck me with his staff. Instead, he had opened negotiations.

"Umm, I confess I don't know," I said, because Pericles had never suggested a sum. "But I'm sure it would be a lot of money." That sounded lame, even to my ears. Desperate to put a more professional spin on my bribery, I decided to add, "Do you have any suggestions, sir?"

Geros rubbed his chin. "The Delian Treasury is the largest in all of Hellas," he said thoughtfully.

"Yes," I agreed. Everyone knew that.

"For such a treasure I think the offer should be not less than thirty talents," Geros said.

I tried not to gasp. You could buy a silver mine with thirty talents, and have change left over for a country estate.

"That is a lot of money," I told Geros. "It might be too much."

"You think I would help Athens for the price of a dinner?" Geros asked. He sounded offended.

"No, sir!" I said. "I merely hadn't thought about it."

"For a negotiator, you come strangely unprepared," Geros said. "Are you sure you represent Pericles?"

"I promise that I do. But the fact is, sir, I must consult my principal as to whether he would be willing to pay so much money."

"Then do so. I shall expect to see you later, with more details," Geros replied.

"How shall I approach you?" I asked.

"On the other side of this field are some abandoned houses. You will find me there after dawn. I assume Pericles can come to a decision very quickly. Until that time, this conversation never happened."

"Pericles will be swift in his reply, sir, but do you want time to reconsider this?" I asked.

"What do you mean?" Geros asked.

"I mean, are you sure?" Then I realized I was trying to talk the priest out of accepting my own offer. "That is, this is a very big step you're considering."

"Are you trying to back out of the deal?" Geros said suspiciously.

"No, sir!" I said quickly. Although, in fact, I had been trying to do exactly that.

Geros stamped his staff on the ground—it seemed to be his favorite way of starting and ending any conversation—then he marched off into the night. This time he walked towards the village.

I could hardly believe what I had heard. This man had spent the entire day preventing Athens from getting anywhere near that treasury. I had thought he was willing to defend it with his life. Now he was willing to sell it out?

The turnaround seemed so complete that I wondered if

this was some sort of elaborate trap. But if so, I couldn't see how. He could not have known about my offer in advance.

This left only the apparently indisputable discovery that the old priest was as greedy as every other man in Hellas. That thought somehow depressed me. I had wanted to think Geros was an honest man, even if he was a highly dogmatic pain in the ass.

THE ACCEPTANCE

"**I** ACCEPT," PERICLES SAID instantly, when I told him what had happened.

I had returned to where the boats were beached upon the sands. Pericles would normally have rated accommodation in the village, but the Delians did not have a spare cottage in which to house him. The official visitors' residence was already occupied by Diotima and me, and though I could easily be tossed out to make way for the foremost man of Athens, the same could not be said of a pregnant priestess, nor was Pericles so foolish as to even suggest such a thing. I took delight in knowing that my bed was better than his—not that I'd had a chance to use it.

In any case, Pericles had brought with him his General's tent. Pericles was renowned across Hellas as a statesman, but this was a misconception. All ten of our military Generals owned massive campaign tents, which served as headquarters when at war, and in which they slept. Thus Pericles had set up home on Delos in canvas quarters that were almost palatial.

I had to argue with the guard at the entrance to force him to wake our commander. The common men had no idea what mission I was on, and I was not about to enlighten them.

Pericles was usually the height of perfectly dressed fashion, but after the guard shook him awake, Pericles staggered to the tent's entrance, bleary-eyed and with his hair unkempt. I had never seen him look so completely like a normal man.

He took one look at me and said, "Come in."

The guard stood aside.

Pericles sat rather heavily upon a camp stool. He poured a cup of watered wine, offered it to me, poured another for himself, and said, "What news?"

I told him.

Pericles sat a little straighter by the time I finished.

"I confess, when I sent you on this mission, I had little hope of you succeeding. You must be more persuasive than I thought. You have done well, Nicolaos."

"Pericles, the amount he asks for is enormous," I warned him.

"But what we gain is even larger," Pericles said. "Though of course you are right, it would be cheaper if Geros wasn't an impediment. When must you reply to him?"

"At dawn, at a place on the island far north of here."

Pericles glanced out his tent. "Dawn approaches. You had best be on your way. Tell Geros yes."

TO SAY THAT I was exhausted would be an understatement. I'd barely had a chance to sit down since we'd arrived. Now here I was dragging my feet across the sands of Delos once more. I couldn't stop yawning. I tripped over stones that normally my feet would have missed. I closed my eyes on one flat stretch, merely to rest them, and it was a conscious effort to open them again. I consoled myself with the thought that when I met Geros, it would be a quick conversation. Then I could go home to the cottage in the village and sleep for the rest of the day. I need only tell Geros yes; the details could be sorted out later, though no doubt Geros would be anxious to hear how we intended to pay him.

Pericles already had that worked out. He told me that an account in Geros's name would be created at one of the new banks springing up in Athens. These banks were an innovation of the last decade: organizations which held money for their clients and invested their funds in various enterprises. No one had ever thought of such a thing before, but they had proved remarkably popular.

"But Geros is on Delos, where there's no bank," I said. "How could he use money that's in Athens?"

"He writes a letter to the bank, with instructions on what he wants done," Pericles said. "If he wants a thousand drachmae for spending money, then a courier will arrive on the next boat with his coins. If he wants to buy a farm, the bankers will pay Geros's money straight into the other man's bank."

"That will work?" I asked. It sounded too easy.

"Merchants do this all the time, Nico," Pericles assured me. "It's how one merchant pays another when they live in different cities."

"It is?"

"You don't think wealthy men send shipments of gold across the sea, do you? Dear Gods, no, every pirate in the Aegean would be waiting for them! The banks simply keep a tally. The point is, with the money in a bank in a city far from Delos, no one here will ever know Geros is a wealthy man. The whole transaction will be discreet."

The ease with which Pericles reeled off these arrangements suggested it wasn't the first time he had bribed an official from another city. That was both alarming and at the same time strangely reassuring. It meant my boss knew what he was doing.

"We will deposit the funds after we return to Athens," Pericles had finished. "Make sure Geros understands this."

I knew what that meant. Pericles intended to use part of the treasure that we removed from Delos to pay the man who let us take it. Thus the bribe would never appear in the official and well-audited accounting books of Athens. A treasure would depart Delos, and the same treasure, minus thirty talents, would arrive in Athens.

Delos looked different in the light of dawn, far less threatening, and less ominous. The place where I had run into Geros was indeed a graveyard. I had never doubted it, but was surprised to see that the graves were in a very poor state. What had not been visible in the dark were the funeral stele that had toppled over. No one had bothered to right them. Bits of stone had broken or chipped off some memorials. No one had repaired them, and the pieces lay where they had fallen. The ground was highly uneven with many potholes. It was no wonder I had had trouble crossing in the night—weeds grew up all around, tall enough to sway in the sea breeze.

I could hardly credit what I was seeing. On an island full of priests, no one had tended a graveyard? It beggared belief.

In the night, I had thought there were a couple of huts on the other side of the graveyard. In the light of day I saw that the huts amounted to a small village by the sea. The place looked like it had been sacked by raiders. There were perhaps twenty tiny cottages still standing, meaning that the roofs had not completely collapsed, nor the walls completely caved in. Obviously nobody lived there.

I could see why Geros had told me to meet him in that abandoned village. The remaining walls sheltered those inside from general view—necessary for any bribe transaction.

I picked my way around the fallen masonry to enter the misshapen village square. No one seemed to be around.

"Hello? Anyone here?" I called out.

There was no answer. I would have to wait for Geros to arrive.

I picked the most likely place to wait, the cottage in the best condition, with all four walls still standing. Like the others it was built of mud brick that had once been whitewashed. But years of storms had eroded the walls, and the whitewash had turned to a repellent brown color. The door and shutters had long since rotted.

I peered inside. The floor was littered with an astonishing amount of rubbish. Not only rubble, but hairpins, a few bronze rings tarnished to green, and a moldy leather sandal.

"Hello?"

No answer.

But there, lying on the ground with his cloak about him, lay Geros.

I guessed what had happened. Like me, Geros had been awake all night. He had lain down to rest while he waited for me and fallen asleep. If I'd lain down, I would have done the same.

Lucky bastard, I thought to myself. But there was bribery and corruption to be done, and I intended to do it so I could go home to get some sleep for myself.

I said, "Geros, wake up."

He didn't move. I wasn't surprised.

I touched his shoulder and, when that didn't work, shook him.

"Wake up!"

Geros was a solid sleeper. This called for extreme measures.

I bent over Geros, to roll him. As I did, my eye fell on the wall behind him. That corner of the room was very dark, even in the light of day. Now that my eyes had adjusted I saw what I should have seen before. There on the wall above Geros, written in letters of dark red blood, was a single word.

NEMESIS

Suddenly I had a horrible feeling. I heaved him over. Geros stared up at me with unseeing eyes.

There was a dagger plunged into his heart.

IT'S NOT MY FAULT

"**I FEAR YOU HAVE** some distance to go with your negotiation skills," Pericles said coldly. "Killing the other party is not the normal tactic."

"I didn't kill him!" I protested. Why didn't anyone believe me?

Perhaps it was because the body was still warm.

Geros was so recently dead that I had mistaken him for a sleeping man, even when I touched him. That meant the killer or killers could not be far away. I had prowled around the other deserted houses with the greatest possible care—I assumed Diotima would be upset if I got myself killed—before concluding that whoever had done in Geros had fled.

That left me in a quandary. Should I raise the alarm, or should I search for clues? I decided I must raise the alarm.

I ran, with a sore foot that made me hop from time to time, across the graveyard to the nearest civilization, which as it happened was the sanctuary of the temple complex. There I found the priestess Meren wandering about. I told her to bring Anaxinos, but first of all to wake my wife and tell her what had happened. Meren gasped at the news that Geros was dead, looked at me strangely, and backed away.

"Did you kill—" she began to say, but choked on the words.

"No, I didn't kill him!" I said. I was astonished that she

thought I might have. It was the first hint that I might have a problem.

She nodded, then took off down the Sacred Way like a frightened deer.

I needed to tell Pericles, and wanted to do so personally, but I didn't dare leave the body alone for so long, and I wanted to be there when everyone else arrived, if only to judge their reactions.

I couldn't be in two places at once. Or three, rather, because I also wanted to scout the surrounding area at once for clues and for any hidden killers. In addition, I needed to search the ground around the body before it was trampled by a hundred new arrivals. I had rarely felt so torn by conflicting priorities.

There was nothing for it but to send Pericles a message and hope that he didn't explode. I rushed to the Oikos of the Naxians, where I would be sure to find a stylus and something to write on. The doors creaked ominously when I pushed them open. I'd expected the Oikos's doors to be unbarred, but I hadn't expected to see anyone inside at such an early time.

Yet there, to my relief, I saw two slaves. Both looked up at the sound of the door. One was a middle-aged man, and the other quite young. The young one looked like he might once have been a soldier from some foreign land, captured in battle. A lot of men became slaves that way.

"You can't come in here!" another man objected. He was a clerkish looking fellow, seated behind an enormous desk, bent over piles of papyrus.

I ignored him.

The older of the slaves began to say, "Master—"

"Shut up and listen," I told him.

The slave closed his mouth. I turned to the younger man.

"I was going to write a message, but you'll do even better. I want you to go to Pericles . . . do you know who he is?"

The slave nodded.

"You'll find him at the dock in a great tent. Tell the guard out front that you have an urgent message, and don't take no for an answer."

The slave nodded. He was listening closely.

"Say to Pericles that his presence is urgently required at the abandoned village at the north end of the island. Tell him . . . tell him that if he doesn't go there at once, he'll regret it."

I deliberately withheld the news of the death. This seemed to me the best compromise. I would keep an eye out for Pericles and waylay him as he arrived, to ensure he heard my version of events first.

"Have you got that?" I asked the slave.

He nodded again.

"Then run."

The slave ran.

I returned to the scene of the crime.

This time I knew to stop at the outskirts of the buildings, to look for clues. I would have liked to have found footprints, but the ground was too hard and rocky even this short distance from the coast, and covered with gritty sand that blew easily in the constant sea breeze. Closer to the shore there was sand and there was virtually no tide, so footprints would hold their shape, but there were too many, and they went in every possible direction. Unfortunately I knew for a fact that people had been walking back and forth in the night. Among them was me. It looked like the multitude of prints that you would see at any beach. I could think of no way to make sense of them before the hordes arrived.

The first of these was on his way.

Pericles is a far more athletic man than most people give him credit for. He arrived first, though he was probably the last to receive the summons. I saw him bounding over the gritty sand and potholes of Delos like an angry rabbit. Running at his heels was Philipos, a shadow that couldn't quite keep up.

I jumped out in front of the buildings and waved to them.

Pericles stopped before me, panting. Philipos ground to a halt earlier, favoring one leg.

"This had better be important," Pericles gasped. "The slave you sent made it sound like a matter of life or death."

"It's funny you should say that," I said, searching desperately for a way to make what I had to say any less distressing. "Because Geros is dead."

Pericles stared at me. He sent Philipos to check, presumably in some vain hope that I was wrong. That was when he accused me of the killing.

"It's not my fault, Pericles," I said. "I had nothing to do with it."

I hoped that was true. I hoped Geros hadn't died because of my offer of a bribe. That put me in mind of a very important detail.

"Pericles, we're going to have to tell the priests about the bribery. I'm sure it'll come out."

"You want to be executed for corrupting a public official?" Pericles said acidly.

"Is that a crime?" I asked, surprised.

"Of course it's a crime, you idiot!"

"Then how come you told me to do it?"

"Shhh!" Pericles looked left and right, to see if anyone was listening. No one was. "That's a detail we don't need to explore," he said.

"It's a detail Anaxinos will almost certainly become aware of," I told him.

"Then if it happens I will have to speak with the High Priest, to put these things in their proper light," Pericles said. "I am disappointed with you, Nicolaos. Very disappointed."

I would have to live with Pericles's disappointment.

Philipos now returned. "The priest is dead all right. Well done, Nicolaos."

"It wasn't me!"

Philipos pointed toward the sanctuary and said, "Here come the Delians."

Anaxinos walked, as quickly as he could, along the path that diagonally crossed the graveyard. For an older man, he had made good time. In his wake were several of the priests who never seemed to leave his side. Behind him came my wife, with Meren to assist her. I wanted to go to Diotima, but knew that she wouldn't appreciate the attention. Nor could I have reached her without passing by Anaxinos, which would have been awkward.

Pericles said to me, very quietly, "Whatever you do, Nicolaos, don't tell Anaxinos about the bribe."

We waited, and they came to us. I took Diotima's arm and quietly asked, "Are you all right?"

"Is it true that Geros is dead?" she replied, completely ignoring my solicitous question.

"Yes, I'll tell you the full story later," I whispered.

"You'll tell us the full story now," Anaxinos said. I had not spoken quietly enough. The High Priest of Apollo had overheard my words. "Where is he?"

I led the party to the house. Anaxinos, Pericles, Diotima, and I went in. There was barely room enough for us all to fit. The other priests and Philipos watched from the doorway. We all looked down at the corpse.

"There is no doubt that he is dead?" Anaxinos asked.

"I'm sorry, sir, there's no doubt," I said. I knelt beside the corpse and touched the murder weapon and the bloody rents in his clothing. "As you can see, there are multiple stab wounds; the blade must have gone straight through his heart."

I pulled the knife out of Geros's chest. It was hard to extract. I had to twist a little, to relieve the suction. The noise as it came out was sickening.

I held up the blade for all to see. It dripped blood. "Does anyone recognize it?"

"It is a sacrificial knife," said one of the priests. "We use them during ceremonies when a lamb is to be sacrificed upon the altar."

Diotima carried a sacrificial knife in her pouch at all times, but hers was much shorter, and the blade curved. This one was double-edged, straight, and thin. What this blade and Diotima's had in common was that they were both sharp enough to split a hair. It was the perfect assassin's weapon.

"Are there many of these on the island?" I asked.

The priest who had identified the knife snorted. "Not above a hundred or so. We priests all carry one." To prove it he reached behind his back and produced his own.

"There are always one or two left at every altar," another priest added.

"Then no one would notice if one of these was missing?" I said.

The priests shook their heads. "Not after last night."

No, they wouldn't. There had been plenty of sacrifices last night. Apparently Geros had been one of them.

"Is there any sign of a struggle?" Pericles asked.

"The ground is so littered that it's impossible to tell,"

I said. "I looked carefully at the ground inside before you all arrived. There are plenty of signs that people have been here."

"That seems odd for an abandoned home," Anaxinos said. "Surely we need only search for anyone who had been here."

One of the priests coughed.

"Yes? Speak up," Anaxinos commanded.

"High Priest, these old houses have long been used by anyone who wants to meet . . . ah, shall we say . . . for private conversation."

"Oh, I see," Anaxinos said. He turned a little bit red. "I suppose I should have thought of that."

"What it means," said Diotima, "is that there'll be more clues in this room than we can cope with."

I nodded. "Diotima is right. We could spend ages chasing down every dropped hairpin and every mislaid ring in this place, and all we'd do is discover an embarrassing number of otherwise innocent trysts."

"Besides," my wife added. "Even if we found any real evidence, the killer could claim it was dropped during an innocent meeting."

This gloomy conclusion depressed everyone.

As we spoke, Geros's blood, which was still liquid, had run the length of the incredibly sharp iron of the blade, collected at the point, and fallen to the ground in a slow but steady trickle. What struck me was that this was the only blood on the dirt floor.

Anaxinos noted the same thing. "He might not have been killed here."

"Not necessarily, sir," I said. "If a blow is struck cleanly enough, then the blade can act like a plug."

"I see," Anaxinos said. "Well, you'd know, wouldn't you?" He sounded angry with me.

"What do you mean, sir?"

"I mean I want to know why you happened to be here to find him."

I'd been expecting that question, but I hadn't been looking forward to it. I had an answer prepared.

"I had offered to meet with Geros," I said. "I wanted to see if there was some way we might . . . ah . . . assuage his concerns regarding the treasure."

Anaxinos stared at me. "So he agreed to meet in an abandoned house on the far end of the island?"

"Actually, it was his idea."

"A likely story."

"This negotiation was done on my orders, Anaxinos," Pericles cut in smoothly. "The location was indeed the choice of Geros. I think he felt that a more . . . private setting would allow differences to be aired without undue emotion."

Pericles had adroitly changed the subject, just enough to divert Anaxinos from an unfortunate line of questioning.

"Hmmpf." Anaxinos clearly was not impressed with Pericles's words. "I wonder that I was not invited to this 'private' discussion."

There was not much Pericles or I could say to that.

"This is a disaster on so many levels, I barely know where to begin," Anaxinos said.

"Why don't we begin with the dead man," Pericles said. "There is justice to be meted out."

"It's worse than that," Anaxinos said angrily. "Don't you realize this entire island and everyone on it is now ritually polluted? Dear Gods."

Uh oh.

Anaxinos was right. It hadn't occurred to me, and I could tell from the look on Pericles's face that it hadn't occurred to him either.

Where Pericles and I lived, and anywhere else on earth, if there was a murder then only the murderer was cursed, and the family of the victim impure until the rituals had been observed.

But here on Holy Delos, where it was strictly forbidden for anyone to die or be born, this murder meant that every person on the island was tainted with the miasma of unholy death; every building, every grain of sand, every handful of dirt, every drop of water and mouthful of food, every weed in the ground. Even the shrines and the temples were out of action until the balance had been restored.

"What must we do?" Pericles asked quietly.

"First the murderer must be punished," Anaxinos said. "Then there must be a sanctification. On every part of the island, and in every temple, including the shrines in every home. This is going to take days, maybe months."

I didn't like the sound of that.

"Athens will help in any way that we can," Pericles said.

"Athens caused this disaster in the first place!" Anaxinos replied.

"Anaxinos, I swear to you that Athens had nothing to do with this," Pericles said, oddly echoing my own words to him.

"Then you are calling one of my people a murderer," Anaxinos replied.

Pericles looked very, very unhappy. "Forgive me, Anaxinos, that wasn't my intention," he said.

"But it is your clear implication, because there is no other possibility," Anaxinos said.

Anaxinos was right again. If an Athenian didn't kill the old priest, then a Delian must have. Neither answer was acceptable to our leaders.

Every time Pericles tried to calm down Anaxinos, the

High Priest found a new and even better reason to be upset. The fact that he was right in every one of them made me deeply uncomfortable.

"I can only repeat that this murder was none of our doing," Pericles said. "I am as horrified as you are, Anaxinos. I will appoint an investigator—the very best in Athens—and he will find the culprit. This I promise you. We will bring the killer to justice, no matter who he is, and he will be fully punished as the law demands."

"I thank you, Pericles, but we have already appointed our own investigator," Anaxinos said. "Yours will not be required."

"I insist," Pericles said. "Our man is the very best."

"Ours is better. I'm told she has extensive experience."

She?

The High Priest signaled to someone I knew.

"I present to you the investigator who will solve this crime. Her name is Diotima."

THE DETECTIVE

"**W**HY DIDN'T YOU tell me?"

I tried to avoid shouting. That required a major effort of my throat muscles, which caused my voice to clamp down and made my words come out as a strangled gargle.

"I didn't have a chance," Diotima said. "Anaxinos spoke to me as we hurried here. Meren woke me; she told me what had happened. I threw on my clothes and ran out the door . . ." She looked down at her bump. "Well, anyway, I tried to run. The High Priest was running out his own door at exactly the same time. We looked at each other—I think he was surprised to see me—but I didn't give him time to order me back inside. I headed up the Sacred Way before he could say a word. Anaxinos joined me, and we spoke on the way." Diotima grimaced. "Apparently someone has told him that you and I investigate crime as a profession. I can't say I'm too pleased he heard. I wanted to be here on Delos in my role as priestess."

"I know," I said.

"Anaxinos asked me to look into the killing for him. I have the High Priest's full authority to question anyone."

"You should have told him no," I said.

She arched a lovely eyebrow at my words. "Are you suggesting that I, a junior priestess, refuse a direct request from the High Priest of the Delian Apollo?" she asked.

When she put it that way, I had to say, "No. You gave him the only acceptable answer."

"Exactly."

"But Anaxinos still should have asked me. I am your husband after all, and I'm the one Pericles hires!"

Diotima smiled. "You're not feeling jealous, are you, Nico?"

"Of course not. Don't be ridiculous."

"I thought as much," she said. "You'll be pleased to learn I said the same thing to the High Priest, that he should ask you. He told me you're too close to Pericles."

"And you're not?" I said.

"Whoever told Anaxinos that we're investigators also told him that Pericles and I hate each other."

"Someone on this island is a major gossip," I said.

"I thought so too. It had to have been one of the Athenians, but you know, it could have been almost any of them. Your association with Pericles has become well known."

"That doesn't explain them knowing about the antipathy between you and Pericles."

She shrugged. "*Agora* gossip. Or maybe one of the slaves in his household mentioned it. Idlers will pick up anything."

I wasn't so sure.

"Anaxinos has been quite clever," Diotima said. "He needed an investigator. There's no one on the island with anything like the necessary experience to solve a murder. There's never been one here. I'm a priestess, but my husband is a close confidante of Pericles and I'm an Athenian. To any observer, I'm the most neutral choice. Yet the High Priest knows I'm against the removal of the treasure and that I'm sympathetic to their cause."

"Yes, I agree," I said, conceding. "The High Priest couldn't have chosen better."

Everyone else had departed. Anaxinos and his priests had returned to the village. Pericles and Philipos had gone back to the boats. Soon a party of priests would return with a board which they would use to carry Geros's remains to his home. There they would prepare the body for burial.

That meant we—or rather, Diotima—had very little time in which to conduct the initial investigation.

"There's one thing you need to know right away," I said. "Pericles asked if there'd been a struggle, and I said there were no signs."

"So?" she asked.

"So I lied. Look here."

Geros had worn a formal chiton, as befitted an old and revered priest. The chiton is two large squares of material, one front and one back, both cut to reach from wrist to wrist and ankle to neck, pinned down on both sides and over the shoulders, and tied at the waist with a belt. Such clothing creates enormous swathes of extra material that is left to hang. More importantly, the sleeves were vast.

I pulled back the sleeves, to show Diotima what I had discovered.

"Cut marks," she said at once. "Geros tried to defend himself."

"Plus he was stabbed multiple times."

"By the same person?" she asked.

"There's only one weapon left in him."

"I don't see that it helps us." She chewed at her lower lip. It was a habit she had when she was thinking hard.

"It certainly doesn't help us if every man, woman, and child on this island knows every detail of the murder scene," I said.

"That's true."

She bent over to inspect the writing on the wall.

"Nemesis. It means revenge, or the goddess of retribution," she said. "Retribution for what, I wonder?"

"Did Geros write that word, or did the killer?" I asked. "It makes a difference to the meaning."

"Yes." Diotima looked closer at Geros's red fingers, then at the wall. "Do the bloody marks match the width of his fingers? I can't tell. Nico, can you . . . ?"

She left the question open, but I knew what she wanted. My wife wanted me to hold the dead fingers against the writing, to see if they matched.

Diotima was not normally squeamish about such matters. But to touch the dead meant ritual pollution, and I knew she didn't want to expose the baby growing inside her to the slightest risk. Who knew what effect an unsanctified mother might have on her unborn child?

I took Geros's right hand. I had to hold his fingers in my own or else they flopped too much. I carefully placed them against one of the down strokes on the wall.

It was something of an effort to hold the dead man's fingers steady while Diotima peered at the fingertips, then the wall.

"The writing *might* be wider than his fingers," she said.

"Or he might have used two," I added.

She frowned at the wall. "No, two of his fingers are wider than the writing. It might be a smaller hand using two fingers."

"Or he might have held one finger sideways," I said. "There's enough blood for it."

I dropped the hand.

"Can anyone be stabbed through the heart and live long enough to write?" Diotima asked.

I shook my head. "But everyone knows strange things can happen on a battlefield. Men take horrendous wounds and live for days. Others seem almost untouched by a strike upon them but drop dead on the spot. It's possible that the dagger didn't do as much damage as it looks."

We sighed in unison.

"You said you thought the killer arranged the body," Diotima said.

"When I first saw him, I didn't even realize that Geros was dead."

"He might have fallen that way," she suggested.

"If he curled up as he died. Maybe."

"You didn't notice the blood on the wall?" my wife asked in a way that suggested I had been unobservant.

"Not at first. It was dark in the corner. When I came in close and my eyes adjusted, then I saw it."

At the moment we heard wailing from far off. The party from the village was about to arrive to collect the body. We heard the wailing from far off.

"Quick, search him," said Diotima.

I tore open Geros's clothing. Nobody would worry about the tears—this clothing was destined to be burned.

I ran my fingers around his back, and particularly underneath the leather belt about his waist. Men typically keep things tucked underneath their belt, but Geros didn't. Nor was there anything about his shoulders. I silently cursed. I moved my search to his legs. This was deeply unpleasant because Geros had let go when death came, as happens to everyone. It did, however, suggest that he had died standing, because the stickiness and the stains ran down his legs, not sideways across his buttocks.

It was when I reached his thighs that I felt the leather strap.

"There's something here."

The wailing of the mourners was almost upon us.

"Hurry, Nico."

"I think it's a pouch."

I pulled, but it was buckled on tight. To loosen I would have to roll him over, and I didn't have time. I snatched my knife, which I keep under my belt at all times, jabbed it beneath the strap and sawed away. The strap broke. I pulled it out—there was indeed a small pouch attached—and threw it to the opposite corner of the room just as the first of the mourners entered.

First came the men. They carried between them a large board, exactly the right size to transport a body. The leader of this group was Damon, the man I had met the night before, who had brought me dinner. Slightly to my surprise he offered me a nod as he entered.

After the men came the women. Just like they would have in Athens, and everywhere else in Hellas, the women were letting off an awful cacophony of screams and wails. This didn't necessarily mean that Geros had been well-liked or particularly mourned. It was the traditional way to show respect for the dead.

Men and women alike had shorn their hair in ragged lumps. The women had rent at their clothing, so that it was artfully torn in a fine display of despair while at the same time not relinquishing their modesty.

I stood in respect to the mourners and moved away from the body. I carefully stepped back to the opposite wall, so that one foot discreetly covered the pouch that I had liberated. No one would see it if I stayed where I was. Diotima likewise had quietly exited the room. It was exceedingly crowded, rank with the smell of the dead man, and this part of the exercise was nothing to do with her.

Damon said, "Hello, Nico. Fancy meeting you here."

I couldn't tell if Damon was simple, or too clever for his own good.

I said, "Hello, Damon. I'd wish you good morning, but
. . ." I shrugged.

"I know what you mean," he replied. He, too, shrugged.
Then his mood brightened. "Ah, well. Come on, lads, let's
get Geros on his way."

The men obeyed him without question. They lowered
the body board beside the corpse. I hadn't realized, the
night before, that Damon was a leader.

Damon positioned himself by the head. Two other men
went to the feet.

"Ready?" Damon said, putting his hands to Geros's
shoulders. "One, two, three, lift!"

They lifted, with more care than I had shown when I
searched the body, and placed Geros upon the board.

Damon wiped his hands on his tunic. "That wasn't too
hard, was it?" he said cheerfully.

The men agreed. I noticed for the first time that none
of them were priests. These must be regular villagers. I
wondered how many of them there were.

Damon said, "Are we ready to go, then? Let's be off."

He stood to the side while two men at each end raised
the makeshift bier.

The women had ceased their wails while this was going
on. I suppose they needed to catch their breath. Now they
resumed their cacophony as the men edged Geros through
the door and down the path. The women followed the
men. I was relieved to hear the noise receding. I went outside, where Diotima waited.

Diotima wrinkled her nose. "You smell awful."

"That's no surprise."

I held up my hands, which due to the search of Geros
were covered with blood, urine, and feces. I was about to
wipe them on my tunic when I caught a glance from my

wife, thought better of it, and said, "Excuse me, I'll be back in a moment."

Diotima picked up the pouch under my foot while I went to the beach.

Washing in seawater is the official cure for the ritual pollution of having touched a dead body, and if there was anything Delos had plenty of, it was seawater. It was also very good for washing off the unfortunate remains of the victim.

It occurred to me that I hadn't had a chance to bathe since we'd left Athens two days ago, so I walked into the water as I was, clothing still on. I was surprised at how far I could walk from shore before the water was deep enough to wash me.

I scrubbed my hands thoroughly. I watched as Geros's blood and other bodily fluids parted from my skin and mixed with the seawater, to flow away on a journey to what distant places only the gods would ever know. I removed my tunic when my hands were clean. I washed my tunic, then lastly my body. I emerged from the sea, naked, streaming water, but thoroughly clean. I squeezed my clothing, then dropped the tunic on the sand to dry.

That made me stop and stare. There was something on the sand that I hadn't expected to see. Something important.

I rushed naked back to the abandoned village—it was only a hundred paces—where Diotima was still hunting for clues.

"Come with me," I told her.

"What is it?"

I grabbed her by the hand. "You want to see this before it disappears."

I dragged her back to the beach.

"Look!" I pointed.

Diotima looked.

"It's your wet tunic," she said.

"Look *beside* the tunic," I said.

Etched into the sand was a long furrow, not very deep, but deep enough that it was unmistakable. It ran from the water's edge to a dozen paces above the waterline. To both sides of the furrow were drag marks.

Light dawned in Diotima's face. "Someone's dragged a boat up here," she said.

People had already walked across the drag marks. That was no surprise considering how many people had been here this morning. That, and the breeze, would soon make those marks disappear.

"Within the last day," I said. "Look how the marks have already worn."

"I'm not sure it helps, Nico," Diotima said. "There are plenty of innocent reasons to beach here."

She was obviously less enthused than I was.

"What sort of boat?" she asked.

"A dinghy, from the look of it," I said. "You can see where the keel starts and ends, and it can't have been too heavy, or the indent would be much greater."

Diotima nodded. "On an island with a fishing village, that's not a huge help."

"Maybe," I said. But I didn't want to give away any evidence. I measured the length, width and depth of the marks, using torn strips from my clothing to mark the distances.

Diotima still held the leather pouch we had removed from the body.

"What's in it?" I asked.

Diotima opened the flap, put her hand in, and said, "I feel coins."

She pulled out three and displayed them in her palm. Two of these were silver *tetradrachms*. That was a four-drachm piece, the largest unit of currency for which any normal person would ever find a use. Merchants who traded boatloads of goods talked in terms of tetradrachms. Shoppers in the agora bought and sold in *obols*, and any one of these tetras was worth twenty-four obols.

It didn't make sense. Surely there was nothing you could possibly buy on Delos that would cost a tetradrachm. I said as much to Diotima. "Do they even use money on Delos? There are some small villages where the old style of barter is good enough."

"I don't know," Diotima said. "We'll have to ask."

The final coin was something I'd never seen before. It was duller than silver, not as yellow as gold. A fish of some sort was stamped on one side, letters I didn't recognize on the obverse.

Diotima prodded it with a finger. "It looks like gold, but it isn't," she said. She looked up at me. "This coin is not Hellene."

"No."

"But we've seen similar coins before," she said.

"We have?"

"In Asia Minor. In Persian-controlled Asia Minor."

She was right. Years ago, before we were married, Diotima and I had found ourselves on a case in the city of Ephesus, where we had come across a jar of coins. Those coins had been different from these, but they did share a certain style.

I said, "Is there anyone on Delos who knows about coins?"

"We'll have to ask."

"There's something else you need to know."

Diotima raised an eyebrow. "Yes?"

"Last night, when I passed from the sanctuary into the graveyard, I came through the gate in the northwest corner. It didn't make a sound."

"So?" Diotima asked.

"So have you come across any other gate, door, wheel, or axle on this island that doesn't creak and squeal when it's used?" I asked.

It was true. The climate of Delos was so warm and so relentlessly dry that everything that could turn squealed, even if only a little bit.

"Let's go look," Diotima said.

I pulled my tunic back on. It was still damp, but it would dry quickly in the warm weather. What was more annoying was the sand down my back. I would just have to live with it.

We crossed the graveyard. I knelt at the gate to inspect the hinges.

"They're wet with oil," I said.

I ran my fingers across and smelled them. "Olive oil. It smells and feels like quality product. You could cook with this."

Men use cheap, coarse final pressing oil to grease machines.

Diotima wiped for herself and smelled her fingers. "Cooking oil, I'm sure. Probably from the kitchens. I take it you didn't oil the gate, Nico?"

"Of course not."

"I wonder who did?" Diotima added it to her list of things to check. The moment the High Priest had assigned her to the job, she had pulled out that old scrap of papyrus and begun scribbling notes. She frowned as she completed the line. "This is a long list."

I said, "What's your plan? I suppose you'll begin with interviews?"

"Yes. Of course, I'll have to interview you first," said my wife. "You're the prime suspect."

"Me?" I said, horrified. "I expected that sort of response from Anaxinos, but not from my own wife."

"Well, you were the one standing over the victim's body," she pointed out. "Face it, Nico, if you were in my position, you'd be insisting that you did it, and demanding that we learn more about your dubious past."

"I like to think you're already familiar with my dubious past," I said bitterly. "You contributed to a lot of it."

"Not the parts of it that happened last night after I went to bed," Diotima said. "Anaxinos asked a good question. How did you happen to be the one to find the body?"

I had known this was coming. "You had better sit down," I said. "It's a long story."

I told my wife everything that had transpired while she slept.

Diotima managed to hold in her anger until I petered out to an unhappy finish, at which point she exploded.

"Nico, how could you!" she said angrily. "That is probably the most despicable thing you have ever done."

"I can think of a few others—" I began.

"You suborned one of the most senior priests in all of Hellas!"

"I want to point out that I tried not to bribe him," I said, getting angry myself. "I even said I'd go back to Pericles and tell him no. But when I made the offer, Geros practically threw himself at me. It takes two to be corrupt, Diotima."

"I can't imagine Geros agreeing to that."

"Nor could have I," I said. "But it's true. Straight away

Geros asked how much Pericles was offering. He couldn't wait to take Athenian money. I was as shocked as you are."

"I notice that didn't stop you offering the bribe in the first place," she said, even more angry than me.

"What was I supposed to do? Tell Pericles I didn't feel like helping Athens?"

"That would have been a start! Not long ago, you shouted at me and said, *why didn't you tell me?*"

"That was about Anaxinos making you the official investigator," I said.

"Well, now I say the same back to you, my husband, about Pericles making you the agent for his corruption."

There was nothing I could say to that. When I'd calmed down a little, I said, "All right, I admit my mistake was not telling you right away what was going on. It was the first time since I met you that I've not shared a job with you, Diotima, and it didn't turn out so well. But when I shouted at you, you pointed out, perfectly correctly, that Anaxinos had left you little choice but to agree. Pericles did the same to me."

"You don't have to do everything that man tells you."

"With Pericles? He's the most persuasive man on earth. You know how he can make any course seem like the right one."

"That's true," Diotima admitted.

"In a way, Pericles was right," I said. "If Geros hadn't died, it would have all worked out. Athens would have taken the treasure, Anaxinos would be relieved that the conflict was resolved amicably, and Geros would have retired a rich man."

"It would still be the wrong thing," Diotima said.

"Well, yes," I admitted. "But have you noticed how statesmen tend to be results-oriented people? As long as everyone gets what they want, they let the philosophers worry about the ethics later."

"Even Geros, it seems," said Diotima unhappily. "How could he have resisted Athens by day, then done such a deal in the night?"

It was the first time she had admitted that Geros had been a willing party in the arrangement.

"I don't know. The irony is, it's the fact that Pericles and Geros had a done deal that makes it certain that I *didn't* kill Geros."

"You can hardly say that to Anaxinos," Diotima said.

"No, he might not see it in quite the same light. The proof of my innocence is something I don't dare mention."

"What a mess," said my wife.

"You mean my alibi?" I asked.

"I mean everything!" she said, disconsolate. "Not a single thing on this island has gone right."

"Speaking of things not going right, what happens now to your dedication ceremony?"

"Completely ruined," Diotima said, and I put an arm around her as she suppressed a sob. "You heard Anaxinos. The whole island is polluted. The best we can do for Delos is find this murderer."

"What do we do first then?" I asked.

"Anaxinos talked of going to Geros's house. We should join him."

"I'll meet you there. I have to report to Pericles first."

I FOUND PERICLES in his tent, on a camp stool, leaning over a trestle table. He had a large piece of papyrus in front of him, onto which he was scribbling words as quickly as he could. He continued to write even as I delivered a report on developments.

He grunted at my news, largely ignoring me. Then I especially mentioned the three coins that we had found on Geros, because two of them were tetradrachms from Athens. This led me to the question I wanted to ask, and for which I didn't want Diotima present when I asked it.

"Those are big value coins, Pericles. It worries me. I need an honest answer."

"To what?" he said.

"My attempt last night . . . was that the first time Athens has bribed Geros?"

That made Pericles look up at me. "Why would you think it isn't?" he asked.

"He agreed too quickly. Far too quickly for my liking, and because those are *Athenian* coins. They didn't come from any other city."

"I see."

Pericles put down his stylus. He looked up at me with an expression that was a combination of exasperation, indignation, and typical Periclean sincerity.

"I absolutely promise you, Nicolaos, that Athens has never before bribed any priest of Delos. Not in my time as a leader, anyway."

"I imagine you'd know," I said.

"I would," Pericles said without a blush. "If this annoying priest Geros was found with tetradrachms, they didn't come from our coffers."

I had no choice but to believe him.

Pericles picked up the stylus and continued his scribbles. I had been watching this with a determination not to ask the obvious question, but now curiosity beat me.

"What are you doing?"

"*Harpy* must return to Athens for supplies. We can't eat the locals out of everything they have. That's obvious after last night's dinner. I am sending my status report to the people of Athens with the captain of *Harpy*. The people expected us to collect the League treasury and return at once. It behooves me to tell them it will be days at the very least. I'll have *Harpy* courier the message, and any personal mail the men want to send."

"Oh." I wondered if my name figured prominently in that report, as the reason why the Athenians didn't yet have the treasure. I decided I wasn't going to ask.

"You said *Harpy* would carry messages?"

"If you have mail, but you'll have to be quick. *Harpy* sails as soon as I'm finished here."

I could be very quick. I snatched an old piece of papyrus from the pile on Pericles's table—I carefully didn't ask permission—grabbed one of the writing brushes beside the ink, and wrote a few words for my family. I told them that Diotima and I were well, and warned them that we might be here for a few extra days. In fact, the delay might be indefinite, due to some pressing business, since Diotima and I were on a mission from the Gods. In closing I asked my mother, who was a midwife, as diffidently and as cautiously as I could, so as not to cause any alarm, whether she might have any quick hints on how to deliver a baby.

I handed this to Pericles and continued on my way, to the house of Geros.

THE HOME OF Geros, the second highest priest of the Sanctuary of the Delian Apollo, was as modest as every other house on the island. It stood in the middle of the row of homes that lined the Sacred Way from the New Village to the temples. There was no garden—well, Geros hadn't struck me as the gardening sort of man—nor was the home painted in anything other than the dull gray that seemed to afflict all wood left out to the elements overlong.

I knocked on the door, and was admitted by a worried-looking man of late middle age. He rubbed his hands absently and said, "Ah, yes sir, I was told to expect you."

I stepped into the atrium, whence I could see straight in to the inner courtyard, which was a hive of activity.

The villagers who had come to collect Geros from the scene of his death were now in the courtyard of his house. They were clustered about a table that had been carried into the center space. With them were several priests who sang a hymn to Apollo while a handful of priestesses prepared the body for the afterworld. The women washed Geros, dressed him in fresh clothes, placed a coin under his tongue, with which to pay Charon the Ferryman to cross Acheron, the River of Woe, and used a clean white rag to bind his jaw, so that his mouth remained shut.

They did these things very properly, as anyone would expect of holy people, with the dead man's feet pointing toward the door, to prevent his *psyche* from escaping into the world.

The villagers saw that their part was done. They took their leave, passing by me as they left. Damon gave me a wink.

I wondered why Geros's family were not performing these duties. I asked the house slave who waited beside me.

"There is no family," he said.

"None at all?"

"There was a wife, but she died long ago."

"They had no children?" I asked.

"The lady died in childbirth, sir," the slave said.

"Oh."

Such words made me uneasy at the moment.

"Are you the only slave?" I asked.

"Yes, sir," he said politely. "I do all the work, including cooking. I expect you wish to join the High Priest and the visiting priestess?"

"Yes. The priestess you mention is my wife."

"Then allow me to congratulate you both on your growing family, sir."

The slave showed me upstairs to Geros's private room. There I found Diotima sitting sideways upon a dining couch. She had a small pile of papyrus and wax tablets beside her. Anaxinos was wandering about in a distracted way.

"They must be here somewhere," Anaxinos said.

"What must?" I asked. They both turned at my words. I had surprised them.

"Keys to the temple complex," Anaxinos said. "Geros and I both have copies. I must collect his set, in the interests of security."

Anaxinos opened closet doors and poked around.

I had heard of keys, but never before come across any.

"What do they look like, sir?" I asked.

"Thin bars of bronze, about the length of my forearm."

Diotima read the documents by her side, while I helped Anaxinos search, opening boxes and a couple of chests.

"Are these them, sir?" I asked.

Anaxinos peered over my shoulder to see inside the small wooden box I had found. It had been sitting on the floor behind where the door swung, which was why neither of us had seen it at once. Within was a handful of exactly what the High Priest had described. The bars looked like they had been bent in the middle.

"That's them. Thank you."

I handed the box up to the old priest, who thanked me a second time.

"I expect you wish to remain and read all of Geros's correspondence," he said. The High Priest's tone told us what he thought of that.

Diotima replied. "There is always the chance that somewhere in here is a hint to any enemies Geros may have had, sir."

"We already know his worst enemies: the Athenians camped on our shoreline."

"There may be others," Diotima said. "Who knows what we might find? We can only look."

"Just so." Anaxinos paused, then asked, "Tell me, do you not find this distasteful?"

"It is necessary, High Priest," Diotima said.

"It must be an Athenian way of thinking," he said darkly, and departed.

"What do you have?" I asked, when we were alone.

"I have an embittered, disappointed old man who was angry at life," Diotima said. "Did you know Geros had a wife who died in childbirth?" she asked.

"The slave told me."

"The records are here." Diotima waved a thin sheaf of papyrus. "Read this." She handed me the papyrus. It was brown with age, but the writing was perfectly legible. I leafed through, reading quickly.

"His wife was pregnant here on Delos," I said.

"Yes."

I flipped to the next page. "She went into labor early. They tried to rush her to Mykonos." Mykonos was the nearest major island, where she could safely give birth among good midwives.

"She didn't make it," Diotima finished for me. "She died in transit, trying to give birth on the boat. Read the last page."

The final page was a diatribe against Apollo and Artemis, and the rule of life and death that had forced Geros's wife to lose her life on a tiny boat.

I wanted to crumple the sad pages, but instead I placed them carefully on the desk. Our victim had written those words after the greatest tragedy of his life.

"He had lost his faith," I said. "That explains why Geros was so ready to accept a bribe. He no longer cared about the Gods."

Diotima nodded. "I think so. Though how anyone could lose belief in the divine twins is beyond me."

"Is there anything else?" I asked.

"I cleaned out the room." She gave me the papers to carry.

At that moment an enormous rumble filled the room. It was my stomach. I suddenly realized that I'd been awake all night and hadn't eaten since dinner.

"Have you eaten?" I asked Diotima.

"Do you mean, did I stop for breakfast while hurrying to a murder scene? No."

I helped my wife to stand up. "You need to keep up your strength if you're going to grow a baby *and* solve a murder."

APOLLO'S REST

WE ATE IN the village, for the simple reason that it was the only place to find food.

In every other town, village, and city in Hellas there is always a temple in close proximity to the agora. On Holy Delos, another temple would have been surplus to requirements; there were three major temples and the birthplace of two gods just up the road.

Instead, there was something much more important as far as I was concerned: a very good tavern.

No village as isolated as the one on Delos has any right to a tavern like Apollo's Rest. It was small, but clean—maybe the cleanest tavern I'd ever seen—even the straw on the floor smelled like it had been recently replaced.

The woman within was plump, buxom, and friendly.

"You'd be the visiting priestess and her man. I've been expecting you," she said.

I was surprised. "You have? How did you know we were coming?"

"Well, there isn't anywhere else to eat, is there?" she said, reasonably enough.

"Good point."

"My name's Moira. Take a seat."

We took the best seats in the house, which was easy because every bench in the place was empty but for one.

The captain of *Paralos* sat in a corner, alone, with a bowl of food and a mug of wine to keep him company.

He nodded to us and said, "*Kalimera*, my friends."

"Good morning," Diotima replied.

Moira noted the direction of our gaze. She said, "He's a fine-looking man, ain't he?"

"Indeed, he is," Diotima said.

I was instantly jealous.

Moira hefted her expansive bosom a notch higher and went to see if there was anything else she might do for the captain, being careful to lean well forward as she did.

Moira in our language meant fate. It wasn't the most common name for a woman.

"Have you noticed how the locals take divine names?" I said.

"What do you mean?" Diotima said.

"The village head man is Damon." In Greek that meant a genius, evil or otherwise.

"So?"

"Our hostess is Moira—fate. Someone wrote 'nemesis' above the corpse. Do you get the feeling this place is obsessed with the human condition?"

"This is Delos, you know. You're reading too much into it, Nico. Anyway, it's not that unusual. My own name means Honored by God."

"The perfect name for a priestess," I said. "It suits you."

Our hostess—who apparently was Fate personified—brought us watered wine, bread, and goat cheese.

"One of the few things we got enough of on this island is goats," said Moira. "They help keep down the weeds. Enjoy the cheese."

I asked how such a fine tavern came to be in such a place, meaning no disrespect.

"None taken," she said good-naturedly. "There ain't many people on Delos, but we get a lot of visitors, and you know what? They all like wine."

"They certainly do." I held out my cup for more. "Where is everyone?" I asked as she poured.

"In mourning," Moira said shortly.

"Oh."

Diotima and I were so used to untimely death that it hadn't occurred to us.

"This is the first death we've had in years," Moira said. "No one's quite sure what to do. Everyone's playing safe, to make sure they do the proper amount of mourning, you know?"

"I know what you mean," I said. In Hellas, the rituals for the dead were such a big thing that everyone worried what the neighbors would think if you didn't show enough outward grief. So everyone compensated by going completely overboard.

"There won't be anyone out doing business today anyway," Moira said. "Not with the temples shut down on account of the pollution."

"I notice you haven't shorn your hair," Diotima said. "Didn't you know Geros?"

"I knew him all too well," Moira said. "The fact is, I won't be shedding a tear."

"You didn't get on?" Diotima asked.

"Nobody liked Geros. He wasn't the sort of man you're supposed to like, you know?"

I knew.

"But you had to respect him," Moira concluded. She tucked the amphora of wine under a meaty arm and returned to her place behind the counter.

Diotima had her scrap of papyrus out. She stared at her notes and frowned.

"What are you thinking?" I asked.

"That I'm confused," she said. "Let me say the order of events leading up to the crime."

"Sure."

"The Athenians landed yesterday afternoon, with you and me arriving first on *Paralos*. We delivered the year's offerings, and Pericles delivered the news that he was removing the treasure. This came as a complete surprise to the Delians. Geros was present to hear these things."

"Does that help?"

"Only in that it means Geros wasn't prepared for our arrival. I thought he was astonishingly quick at organizing the resistance."

"If you think Geros had some advance warning, you can think again," I said. "The vote among the Athenians to remove the treasure came only the day before the fleet departed. Any boat that beat us here would have to have been very, very quick."

"I see your point," Diotima said. "Yet Geros didn't stop to think for a moment. His instant reaction was that the treasure must not be removed."

"He likes having treasure around. Who doesn't?" I said.

"Let's move on, then," Diotima said. "Geros organized the resistance, which was effective. So effective that Pericles decided to bribe Geros." My wife glared at me.

"We've already been over that." I winced at the thought of having that argument again.

"But the details are important. You wandered in the dark, stubbing your toes on the sanctuary wall."

"They still hurt," I complained.

"I'll rub some ointment on them later," Diotima said absently. "Meanwhile, Geros had passed through the gate. The gate which had been oiled."

"Who oiled it?" I asked.

"Someone who didn't want that gate to squeak," Diotima said. "I already have that question on my list."

"The only thing special about that gate is that it leads to the abandoned village. Why was the old village abandoned?"

"We'll have to ask." Diotima scribbled another note, ran out of space, and turned over the papyrus. "Then you, Nico, saw a light in the distance." Diotima paused. "Are you sure that light was in the old village?"

"Where else would it be?"

"How about on the boat whose track we saw in the sand?"

"I like that idea," I said. I thought about it. "It's possible. You can't tell distance in the dark. If it was on the boat, that would explain why Geros didn't see it."

"Are you sure Geros didn't?"

"When I pointed it out, he acted like he didn't believe me."

"Maybe," Diotima said. She wasn't convinced. "When you ran into Geros he was coming the other way."

"Yes."

"Why?"

"Obviously he'd finished whatever he'd gone to do out there," I said.

"Then he must have been quick about it. Did you lose much time following him?"

"No," I said at once. "The only delay was when I hit the wall, and of course he moved faster because he knew the terrain. Still, I can't believe he had much time for whatever he was about. I assume neither of us believe he was out for a casual stroll."

"In the pitch black through a graveyard?" Diotima scoffed. "Thanks anyway."

"Then Geros did whatever he did, and I caught him on the return journey. The rest, you know."

Diotima consulted her notes.

"The window in which Geros could have been killed is actually very small," she said. "He was alive when you left him. At least, I assume he was still alive, unless you did it."

"Very funny."

"All right then. When you left Geros, which way did he go?"

"Toward the village. I told you that."

"Yes, but think about the timing," Diotima said. "You agreed to meet again at dawn. Dawn wasn't all that far away, was it?"

I thought about it.

"Just far enough away to be annoying. Not enough time to rest."

"You found your way back to the navy boats. You talked with Pericles, and by the time you finished with him it was time to return."

"Correct."

"Then why did Geros walk back to the village, if he knew he'd only have to turn around almost at once?"

It was a good question.

"I don't know," I said. "Maybe he didn't go all the way to the village. What else is in that direction?"

"The temple complex, of course," Diotima said.

"I think you must be right."

"When you left the temples, there were still men about the fires."

"Yes."

"Were the fires still going, after you parted from Geros?" Diotima asked.

I cast my mind back. "I don't recall seeing the glow," I

said. "But then, I wasn't looking either. There may have still been people there. They might have seen Geros."

"We'll have to ask around." Diotima wrote another line on her list.

"I'm more interested in the writing on the wall," I said. "Surely that's our biggest clue. Why 'Nemesis,' I wonder? Why paint any message at all?"

"Under the circumstances, why not?" Diotima said. "The goddess Nemesis awards to every mortal the fate that their actions deserve. She is the bringer of divine retribution. Rather appropriate for Geros, don't you think? He was willing to sell out Apollo and Artemis."

It was a fair point.

"Also, Nemesis is the daughter of Nyx, the night," Diotima added. "And Geros was killed by an assassin in the night."

"You think there's someone out there who fancies themselves to be Nemesis?" I asked.

"Who thinks of themselves as the agent of Nemesis," Diotima said. "It makes sense, Nico."

I asked, "Is there a temple to Nemesis on the island, by any chance?"

Diotima shook her head. "No, but there is a history between Apollo, Artemis, and Nemesis." She paused. "It's not a very pretty story, I'm afraid."

"Nor are most murders," I said.

"The story goes that long ago, in Phrygia, Queen Niobe boasted that she was a better mother than divine Leto, beloved of Zeus, because Niobe had had seven sons and seven daughters, while Leto had had only two children. But those two were Apollo and Artemis."

"Hubris is not normally a good idea," I said.

"No," Diotima agreed. "The Gods were outraged by

Niobe's arrogance, Zeus in particular, since he was the father of the slighted children. Annoying Zeus is just . . . not a good idea."

"No."

"Zeus sent Nemesis to deal with Niobe," Diotima said.

"Nemesis killed Niobe?"

"Worse than that," Diotima said. "Nemesis brought Niobe's words to Leto. Leto in turn asked her children Apollo and Artemis to kill the children of Niobe, which they did with far-flying arrows. Apollo executed the boys, Artemis shot the girls, all but one. In despair, Niobe asked for her life to be ended. Nemesis turned her to stone, but a stone which wept forever."

"Nemesis is not one for compassion, then," I said.

"Not even slightly," Diotima agreed. "Nico, if there's someone on the island acting as Nemesis, then they will kill without mercy."

On that cheery note, Diotima finished her breakfast, put down her bowl, and said, "I'm hungry."

I wasn't surprised. She had been eating non-stop for the last couple of months.

Diotima ordered a second breakfast from Moira. Our hostess eyed Diotima's tummy and said, "Aye, I know just what you need," and brought the largest bowl of cheese and fruit that I had ever seen.

I noticed that the captain of *Paralos* had smiled to himself when this happened. I realized that he had been sitting there throughout our conversation, having finished his meal, slowly sipping a cup of watered wine. Diotima and I hadn't made that big of an effort to keep our voices down; I guessed that he had been listening in.

I rose and crossed the room to speak with him.

"Kalimera, Captain."

"Kalimera, Nicolaos."

He remembered my name, but I couldn't recall his.

"Semnos," he said, when he realized my difficulty. "My name is Semnos."

We had only been on his boat for a day, and that as passengers. I complimented Semnos on his memory for names and faces.

"It's a job skill," he said modestly. "*Paralos* is sent on missions to honor the gods at temples and sanctuaries all around the Aegean. Sometimes I go places I haven't been for three years or more."

"Yet you seem at home here," I commented. Semnos did indeed look entirely relaxed within the local inn.

"Oh, I do regular runs to Delos," the captain said. "It's one of the major sites. There are Apollo and Artemis here on Delos, Artemis at Ephesus in Ionia; in Rhodes I represent Athens in the worship of Helios; on Samos we go to adore Aphrodite."

"You're busy," I commented.

"That's just the half of it. Then there are the Dionysian rites, the mystery cults, and the *orgia*," Semnos said. "You need to be fit for those, I can tell you."

"What? All of the rites?" I said, startled. There must be a hundred temples across the civilized Hellene world, and every one of them has its own celebrations. I said as much to the captain.

"I'm sent to all the main ones," he said. "The Dionysiac rites in Arcadia, the fertility rites of the goddess Bendis in Thrace, the crazed erotic dances for Cybele in Samothrace . . . there are a lot of them." Semnos sighed.

"You get sent by the navy to attend orgies?" I said, incredulous. I wondered how a man got a job like that. The queue when the position became vacant must be mind-boggling. I suggested as much to the captain.

"There are certain personal requirements that limit the applicants," he said delicately.

I was struck again by just how very handsome was the captain of *Paralos*. Even I thought he was good looking.

"Women must throw themselves at you," I agreed.

"Men too. You should see what happens at parties."

I decided not to go there.

"For all those places where the religious celebrations can become a little . . . shall we say . . . exuberant, if it's a rite in which Athenian participation is required, then I and the crew of *Paralos* are the men for the job."

"The rest of the navy must be jealous of you," I said.

The captain's shoulders slumped a little at my words. "Whether or not they're jealous I don't know, but I can tell you what they say about us. They call us the pretty boys."

"Not without foundation," I commented.

"This I grant." Semnos made an elegant, sweeping gesture of his arm in acquiescence, so smooth it would not have looked out of place on stage. "But can we help it if we're forbidden to partake in any fleet action?"

"Is that a problem?" I asked.

"Is it a problem?" he repeated, incredulous at my question. "Surely you jest. Yes, it is. They call us the pretty boys, but they call us another word, too, an ugly one. The other sailors call us . . . cowards."

"That's tough," I said.

"Every fitting on our ship is made of gold," Semnos said dejectedly. "My standing orders are to never, ever risk *Paralos*."

"That does make sense," I consoled him.

"You have no idea what a disaster it is. Only last month, *Paralos*, *Harpy*, and another boat were in transit to Crete. We ran into pirates, not far from here in fact. Do you know what happened?"

"I feel sure I'm about to learn."

"I was forced—forced, mind you—to turn around and head the other way. Like a . . . I can barely say the word . . . like a coward." The captain might almost have wept. "*Harpy* and her escort carried on and destroyed the pirates. They were commended later."

"Sorry about that."

"And on the same day, the other sailors jeered my men."

"You were obeying orders," I pointed out.

"Does that make it any better?" Captain Semnos said.

If I was hearing this correctly, the good captain was depressed because he was required to attend orgies instead of risk his life on the seas.

"You could transfer to another ship?" I suggested.

"I tried," he said morosely.

"They turned you down?"

He nodded. "Can I help it if I'm the most handsome man in Athens? They said my particular talents were needed on *Paralos*."

I tried hard not to imagine the Captain's particular talents. "What will you do?" I asked.

Captain Semnos squared his shoulders. "I must carry on, and serve where my state needs me," he said stoically.

DIOTIMA FINISHED THE cheese, fruit, bread, and wine, then we left the tavern. I would have liked to stay longer, but Diotima and I wanted to discuss suspects, and we both knew that every word we said in Moira's presence would be repeated across the island before lunch.

So we sincerely thanked Moira for the breakfast, and departed for our cottage. I lay down on the bed at once. I was so tired that I almost fell asleep in a heartbeat.

In fact, I did. Diotima had to shake me.

"Nico, wake up!"

"What? What did you say?" I said groggily. "I wasn't asleep."

She laughed. "You've been asleep half the morning. Look out the window."

I did. Apollo was halfway up in the sky.

"You let me sleep!" I accused her.

"I certainly did. You're no good to me when you're so tired that you can't even walk in a straight line."

I had to admit that was true. I also had to admit the sleep I had gotten wasn't enough. My eyes felt like someone had thrown grit into them, and the rest of me felt like the dead in Hades.

Yet some sleep was better than none, and in my army days they'd made us march through the night and then exercise all day. That was only seven years ago. If I could do it back then, I could do it now.

"What have you been doing while I slumbered?" I asked.

"Acquiring the list of Geros's associates," Diotima said. "Also, getting some new papyrus." She handed me a fresh sheet. On it was written a list of names, none of which I recognized.

"Where did you get this?" I asked, waving the list.

"The Oikos up at the temple has office supplies. I stole some papyrus."

"I meant the names."

"Oh, I asked Meren, the young priestess," Diotima said breezily. "She wrote down for me the names of everyone who was in Geros's group last night. You know, the ones who surrounded him like acolytes."

"Anaxinos had a group around him too," I said.

"Yes, I noticed, I was one of them," said my wife. "Pericles had a group with him, too."

"Yes, I noticed, I was one of them," I said. "But they all left before Geros."

"So did Anaxinos and his people. There weren't many left behind in the sanctuary to kill Geros, and based on the mess I saw up there this morning, most of them were drunk."

"Then let's think about who is likely to have been Geros's nemesis," I said. "Who stands to gain from his death?"

"The Delians would say Pericles," Diotima said at once. "I've heard the talk in the village. Everyone is convinced Pericles ordered Geros removed." She paused, then said, "Nico, they all expect me to prove that Pericles did it."

I put an arm round Diotima to comfort her, because I knew what that pressure felt like.

"Welcome to investigation," I told her. "Everyone but the detective thinks they know the answer, and they expect *you* to deliver the goods for them."

Diotima leaned into me. "I suppose I'll get used to it," she said, and sighed.

I wished her luck with that, because I never had. What I'd learned was that the only way to get rid of the pressure was to find the killer, with enough proof to convince everyone. The only real way to help Diotima was to find that murderer.

I said, "The Delians think it was Pericles, but we know what the Delians don't. We know that Pericles had already removed Geros, with a lot of coins, and coins never killed anyone. Pericles actually had the least to gain from Geros's death. This murder causes him immense trouble."

"Yes, I see that," Diotima said. "It's the same argument that exonerates you."

"Right." I nodded confidently. "So it had to be a Delian who killed Geros," I concluded. I was immensely pleased with my impeccable logic.

Diotima thought about it. "But as you say, the Delians don't know that Geros had been bought."

"Right."

"So the Delians had no reason to kill Geros either," Diotima said.

"Right . . ." I began. Then I realized the implications. "Oh. I didn't think of that."

It was Diotima's turn to nod wisely. "The Delians had no reason to kill Geros, because they believed he was protecting the treasure. Pericles had no reason to kill Geros, because he knew Geros had been bought."

"Therefore nobody had a motive to kill Geros," I said. "That's . . . unfortunate."

"Very."

We sat on the bed, side by side, contemplating the fact that we had talked ourselves into a dead end.

"I suppose there's one piece of good news," Diotima said, not sounding particularly happy about it.

"What's that?" I asked.

"If we can find anyone with a motive to kill Geros, we'll probably have our man."

"Maybe," I said, and didn't believe it for a moment. Life is never that neat.

I contemplated life's sloppiness. That inspired another idea. "Diotima, on the facts as we have them, Geros isn't dead, because no one had a reason to kill him."

"There's a certain paradox in that statement—" she began.

"Therefore the facts as we have them aren't right," I interrupted her. "What we need are newer, better, fresher facts."

"You sound like an agora salesman," she said. "What do you suggest?"

"Let's start with something small. Something we can understand."

"Such as?"

I reached into her pouch, and brought out one of the pieces of hard evidence that we had. I opened my palm to show her. "It's only a little thing—it might not lead any-where—but let's check out these coins."

THE HIGH PRIEST

WE WENT IN search of Anaxinos. We found him at his home. Diotima and I were admitted at once.

Anaxinos sat in his courtyard, upon a dining couch. I thought it odd that a man of his standing should be doing nothing at the busiest time of day until I noticed that, like so many, his hair was shorn. Anaxinos was in official mourning.

"High Priest of the Delian Apollo, may we intrude upon you?" Diotima asked in that formal, sing-song voice that seems to be the specialty of priests and priestesses everywhere. I made a mental note to ask Diotima some time if they were all taught to speak like that.

"I have been expecting you, Priestess," Anaxinos replied with equal gravity. "A pregnant lady must not stand in my home, nor must any guest. Please be seated and relax, both of you."

We sat, but we didn't relax. I didn't dare lie back for fear that I might fall asleep again. Diotima lay back, and I could tell from her expression that she was relieved to have the weight off her feet. I would have to be careful to make sure she didn't over-exert herself on this job.

The chief priest and *archon* of Delos rated the best home on the island, though it was barely larger than what you'd expect for a successful merchant in Athens. Nor were the furnishings particularly plush. The dining couches were

functional rather than ornate. They showed signs of having
been stripped back and re-oiled. By Athenian standards
this was a middle-class dwelling, barely better than the one
in which my own family lived. The tables and furnishings
likewise showed every sign of having been there for longer
than I would have expected.

Anaxinos's grief did not extend to spurning high quality
wine. I noticed a *kylix* beside him—a wide, shallow,
stemmed cup used at parties—and within it a wine that,
from the aroma, could only be from Lampsacus. I flattered
myself that I knew something about wine. Lampsacus was
one of the best wine growing districts in the entire world.

"Have you ever tried to carry a bed on a ship?" Anaxinos
asked me.

"Sir?" I said, surprised at the question. "No, sir, I haven't."

"You would find it very difficult, I think," said Anaxinos.
"Likewise dining couches and tables. They tell me that
such heavy things must be tied down upon the top deck. It
makes the boat unstable, you see."

"Yes, sir," I said.

"In the short time you have been in my home, you have
already evaluated every piece of furniture in my courtyard.
I see it in your eyes. I thought I would save you the trouble
of working out why so much of it is old."

"Thank you, sir," I said as politely as I could through
gritted teeth. It was perfectly normal to look at a host's
home. Why should Anaxinos call me out for it?

Anaxinos picked up the kylix, and, without bothering so
much as to glance at it, he drained it empty. A slave boy
who stood at the entrance stepped forward. In his arms
was a small *krater*—a jar used to mix wine with water. From
this he refilled Anaxinos's cup. Anaxinos set the cup down
beside him.

"I find, young man, that you are like most Athenians," Anaxinos said.

"Thank you, sir," I said.

"It's not a compliment. You are intensely interested not in the value of things, but in how much they cost."

"Oh."

"There is a difference, you see."

"Yes, sir," I said in a noncommittal tone. I had no wish to anger him.

"This is a problem I find with many Athenians," Anaxinos said. He seemed almost to be musing to himself. "It is success which has done this. I suspect there used to be a time when your people were honorable."

There is a limit to my patience. "If you hate us so much, sir, why do you deal with us?"

"You think I have a choice? The Sacred Isle is more important than me, more important than Athens." He leaned forward, his eyes intent. "The Sacred Isle used to be the protectorate of Naxos."

"Yes, I know."

"Would that it still were," said the High Priest. "But Delos has always been the plaything of whichever city was the richest, the most powerful."

Diotima and I exchanged a glance. We were both thinking the same thing. The High Priest of the Delian Apollo was drunk. My wife looked concerned.

Anaxinos didn't even notice our glances. He was still talking, in an intense mood, leaning toward us. "They say this island had temples even in the days of King Theseus. That is how old we are. So I must tolerate Athens, because above all else Delos must go on."

He picked up his wine cup, considered it, and put it back down carefully beside him.

"Athens will rise," the priest said. "Athens will no doubt fall, one day. But Delos will remain. A thousand years from now people will still be coming here to worship . . . two thousand, three thousand . . . it does not matter . . . it must always be possible for people to come here, in proper worship of the Gods."

"Yes, sir. May I ask a question?"

"You may."

"Did you hate Geros as much as people say you did?"

Diotima stifled a gasp, but Anaxinos had earned my question. I don't mind when people insult me—an investigator gets used to that—but when they insult my city, I fight back.

"What people?" the High Priest demanded.

"Oh, people," I said vaguely. "If you think the antipathy between you and Geros has gone unnoticed, you're wrong. As far as I can tell, every man, woman, and child on this island knows you hated him."

"I didn't hate Geros. Well, not much."

"Then how did you feel about him?" I asked.

Anaxinos picked up the cup again and stared into it. He spoke to the wine rather than us when he said, "I've been a priest all my life. I came here as a young man, not much more than a teenager."

He stopped speaking after that. He hadn't answered my question, but I felt some words were required, so I asked, "Did your father approve?" Because not many fathers would be pleased to see their sons go to a temple and never return.

"I was an orphan," Anaxinos said shortly.

"Oh."

"My father was the blacksmith on the island of Kea. My mother died in childbirth—it was my birth—I was the fourth son. I suppose she'd simply worn herself out. Childbirth is so very dangerous."

I winced. I didn't want to be reminded of what Diotima would soon be going through. The idea that our child could kill her was simply unthinkable, but I had to face the possibility.

Even in drunkenness, Anaxinos saw that he'd made a mistake. He turned to Diotima. "Oh, I'm sorry. I didn't mean to imply . . . that is, I'm sure you will be fine, Priestess, when you—"

"That's all right, High Priest; just go on with your story," Diotima said.

"My apologies." Anaxinos performed a small bow from where he sat. "To continue, my father died six years later."

"That's tough."

"My brothers threw me out. They were all much older than me, you see; I was a late arrival for my parents, and there are few things quite so useless as a fourth brother in a smithy."

Anaxinos spoke without bitterness, in a matter-of-fact way, which I found remarkable.

"The day after my father was buried, I was out on the street," he finished.

"Where did you go?" Diotima asked.

"I wandered about for days. I can't remember how long. I begged for food. I offered to work, but who gives work to a six-year-old?"

"You're lucky you weren't taken as a slave," I said.

"Luck is a relative thing," Anaxinos said. "At least as a slave I would have been fed. But it was a hard year that year. The crops had failed. No one needed another mouth to feed. I went hungry."

Anaxinos stopped to drink more wine. I couldn't blame him. Then his natural instincts as a host cut in and he offered us wine from his own hand. I accepted, Diotima declined.

"This is a terrible story, High Priest," I said.

"It improves. I eventually found myself at the Temple of Apollo," Anaxinos said. "Apollo is worshipped on Kea. The temple is small, but beautiful. I'd never been there before, barely knew what it was. My father had not been one for temple worship."

Diotima and I made sympathetic noises.

"An old priest found me next morning, sheltering under the porch, shivering and hungry. He knew of me. Everyone knows everyone on these small islands."

"Of course."

"The priest fed me. He gave me cast-off clothes, ragged, but better than I had. I slept on fresh straw under a roof.

"That wonderful old man—Gemellos, his name was— Gemellos would have been within his rights to provision me and send me on my way. But he didn't." Anaxinos toyed with the cup in his hands. He seemed to have ceased drinking in his reminiscences.

"Gemellos kept me with him, because he was kind. Then he discovered something about me that I had always known but never thought of any importance. Gemellos decided one day to teach me my letters. He thought they would help me when I left the temple. But he was wasting his time, because I already knew them. I can't explain it, I doubt my father ever taught me, but somehow I was an excellent reader." Anaxinos paused, then added, "It's the most important skill for any priest, you know."

Diotima nodded at that.

"So I stayed at the Temple of Apollo, and before the year was out I knew every hymn. I read voraciously. By the time I was twelve I had almost memorized Homer.

"Gemellos had wanted me to succeed him at the temple on Kea. I would have, too. But on the day when I was fourteen, when I recited the *Iliad* by heart from start to finish, he insisted that I must go to Athens, to learn all I could. Perhaps he thought I would return, but the priests in Athens sent me to Delos when I turned sixteen, and I have been here ever since."

I was impressed. This man had come from nothing—from less than I had ever been—to become one of the highest priests in all the land.

Diotima said, "I have noticed, High Priest, that you are almost a perfect host to guests. I suppose the terrible experience of your childhood is often in your thoughts?"

Anaxinos gave Diotima a searching stare. "You are remarkably perceptive, young lady," he told her. "You are right. When I was a starving child I was turned away by the wealthy, time and time again. Those rich people would have happily stepped over my body rather than hand me a piece of bread. Then I was taken in by a poor priest who gave me everything he had. The lesson was one from the gods. I resolved never to be anything other than a perfect giver in all things."

"You have succeeded, sir," I said.

"I have spoken too much," he replied. "But perhaps with this insight you will understand my contempt for Athens. You think you need more money? Think again."

"I understand your feelings," I said. "It does not change the fact that we need to find a murderer."

"Yes. You asked me before how I felt about Geros. I will tell you. Geros was a good priest. He was a few years older than me. When I arrived, he had already been marked as the coming man, the next high priest. His scholarship of Apollo, of the Gods, and of Homer was simply superb. But when the old High Priest died, the Hellenes chose me to succeed."

"Because you're the consensus man," I said promptly.

"No, because my scholarship was even better," Anaxinos said. "I didn't exaggerate when I said I was a good reader. If I have some ability to get on with people, then that's a bonus."

"How did Geros take that?" I asked.

"Not well," Anaxinos admitted. "From that day on, Geros never missed an opportunity to display superior knowledge. I think that's what rankled: not that I had been promoted, but that I was judged the better scholar. It's a primary function of the high priest, you know."

"What did you do?" Diotima asked.

"What everyone has probably told you I do," Anaxinos said. "Wait for him to wind down, then carry on. I have nothing to prove, young lady. I'm the one with the high priest title." He sat up a little straighter. "Now, what is it that you actually came here for?"

"After all we've spoken about, you will be disappointed to learn we came here to ask you about money," I said.

"What about it?" he asked.

"Is there anyone on Delos who can tell us about coins?" I asked.

Anaxinos looked at me oddly. "That is a most silly question."

"You mean there isn't. I thought as much," I said.

"Don't be ridiculous. Who do you think keeps track of all the treasure that arrives?" Anaxinos said. "Of course there's an accountant here. You want to speak to Karnon."

"Karnon?"

"You'll like him. He's an Athenian, and he loves money."

ANAXINOS GAVE US directions. As we walked away, Diotima was visibly upset.

"That was awful," she said.

"It wasn't fun," I agreed. "I'm sorry you had to hear that."

"I had no idea that Anaxinos hated Athens so," Diotima said.

"He was drunk," I said. "That probably has something to do with it."

"There's a poem that says wine is the window into a man's soul," Diotima said. "Nico, which do you think is the true Anaxinos? The perfect host when he's sober, or the bitter man when he's drunk?"

"Who knows?" I said. Then I took a moment to consider. "No, I think I do know," I said after some thought. "They're both the true man. The sober Anaxinos is a fine gentleman. Maybe he's too fine a man." I shrugged.

"What do you mean?"

"He's almost the perfect manager," I said. "He's nice to people—"

"That's his job," Diotima pointed out.

"Yes, that's my point. No one's perfectly nice. At least not normal men. We all have rough edges, our prejudices and our personality defects."

"So?"

"So Anaxinos isn't allowed to display any of those human traits. He's in charge of the most holy sanctuary in the world. He's required to be relentlessly nice to thousands of visitors every year. That would have to grate on any normal man after a while. It would certainly grate on me."

"You think when he's drunk he lets out all the frustrations he can't voice in public?"

I nodded. "We caught him at a bad time. Do you think he knows about the bribery?"

"I hope not," Diotima said with feeling.

"So do I, because if he knew, I don't think he'd hesitate to knife Geros."

"That was my thought too. Not only is Apollo his entire life, but he hates greedy men."

We walked in silence for a while, then I asked a question that had been building up inside me. "Diotima?"

"Yes?"

"How can you face the possibility that soon you'll have to give birth?"

"Well, it's not like I have any choice, you know."

"But so many things can go wrong."

"When you men are about to go into battle, do you think about what can go wrong?"

"Most do."

"But you get into line and you fight anyway," she said.

"Yes, of course." I didn't add that most men were more scared of being called a coward than they were of death.

"Well then, it's the same for us women," Diotima said. "Anyway, Nico, I'm not going to die."

"Right. Of course not," I said confidently.

We walked along in silence for a while. Then Diotima said, "Nico?"

"Yes?"

"If I die, you'll look after the baby, won't you?"

I was shocked that she even asked. "Of course I will. You know that."

"I mean, you can't let yourself be killed," she said. "What we do, sometimes it's dangerous."

"I know what you mean."

"Well, if I die, and then you die on some job, then our baby would be an orphan, like what happened to Anaxinos. You can't let that happen to our baby. All right?"

Usually when both parents died, the children would go

to live with an aunt or uncle. It was a sacred family obligation. But in our family, Socrates was only a teenager, and both Diotima's parents and mine were old; they would not live long enough to raise another child. There was no one else.

"I'll try not to die," I said. "I'll get a safe job in Athens."

THE ACCOUNTANT OF DELOS

KARNON LIVED APART from Delos's other residents. The priests and priestesses and the locals all lived in the village at the southern end of the island. This they called the new village. The sanctuary and the old village were toward the north of Delos.

Karnon had built his home on the west side of the island, over a low hill away from the main village and thus out of sight of everyone else. I wondered why. It must have been inconvenient every time he wanted something from the village.

Fortunately we had been warned. Diotima rode the donkey she had been given to get around. I walked alongside.

Karnon's home was easy to see in the distance. Like every other house on Delos, it was surrounded by a depressingly large amount of the unproductive, light-colored grit that passed for soil in this place, out of which grew weeds. A small herd of goats ate the weeds and completely ignored us.

There were two boys playing outside. They were wrestling. They stood up respectfully as Diotima and I approached.

"Hello, sir," they said, almost in unison.

They were both so covered in dirt that they looked like matching white ghosts with powdered black hair. I thought they must be twins, but then I realized one was a few years older than the other, slightly taller, and more filled out, though both were thin.

"We're looking for a man named Karnon," I said. "Is he your father?"

The boys said, "No, sir. We'll tell him you're here, sir." Again they spoke almost in unison.

They ran inside.

A woman came out.

"I am Marika, housekeeper and slave to my master Karnon. How may I help you? I hope my boys weren't too rude."

"On the contrary, I have never seen two better behaved," I told her. "We hope to speak with your master."

"That is possible. I asked the boys to wake him. Please come inside."

Diotima slid off the donkey and I grabbed her on the way down. Marika exclaimed.

"You look like you might soon have a son of your own," she said.

Marika helped Diotima inside, holding her arms and giving my wife attentions that, had I done the same, would have annoyed her. But Diotima accepted the same assistance from the slave Marika. I decided it must be a woman thing.

Karnon's home was the most comfortable I had yet seen on Delos. In fact, had I not known better, I would have thought I was back in Athens. I noticed there was an *andron* at the front of the house, just inside the door. That would have been the normal room to receive strangers, but with a lady visitor it would not have been the done thing. Instead, Marika led us to couches in the courtyard.

The courtyard was neatly squared off. The furniture was newer and more comfortable than that which the High

Priest enjoyed. The walls had been painted not more than a few years ago. Everything was free of dust. I hadn't realized how dusty everything was on Delos—I had become used to the thin layer that coated almost every surface— until I saw Karnon's house, which was spotless. I wondered at the obvious wealth and the comfort of this man. If this was what being an accountant brought you, then I was in the wrong profession.

Marika brought us wine, and bread and cheese for my wife. We were both thirsty after the walk. It was as we sipped this that Karnon entered.

I stood to greet him, as a guest should, and got an immediate shock. I had seen Karnon before. He was the clerkish-looking man I had seen in the Oikos this morning at dawn when I had discovered Geros dead. He had been the one behind the large desk, full to overflowing with papyrus.

Karnon greeted me, then Diotima. "Excuse me for not being awake to greet you. It's my habit to work late and sleep late."

"I am sorry to have disturbed you," I said.

"It's of no matter," he said. "Have you been treated well in my home? Have you sufficient wine? Something to eat?"

I wondered if hospitality was the favorite pastime of the residents of Delos. Karnon's words were so like those of Anaxinos when we first arrived. Diotima hurried to assure our host that his slave Marika had been the epitome of fine service.

"That is good then." Karnon sat down before us. "You came to see me about something?"

At that moment, the two boys ran through the courtyard, followed closely by a cloud of white dust that settled upon everything within reach, including not only the fine furniture but their master Karnon.

Karnon grabbed the elder of the boys by his arm, and then he laughed. "Here now, lads!" he said. His voice was mild, where most masters would have been furious. "One mustn't run through the courtyard, not when we have guests."

The sight was vaguely ludicrous as the white dust of Delos settled slowly on Karnon's bald head. I was instantly struck by the sight of the master and the two slave boys together. I was sure Diotima had seen it too.

"I'm sorry, sir," said the elder boy.

Karnon let go his arm. "You two better sneak out before your mother catches you."

"Breto! Melippos!"

It was too late; the junior miscreants had been caught in the act. The boys' mother stood in the doorway to the kitchen. In her hands she carried food for us and wine for her master.

"Leave them be, Marika," said Karnon. "You're only a child once, you know." To the children he said, "Go now, lads."

The boys completely forgot the stricture not to run as they headed for the exit.

"You are too soft on those boys, Karnon," Marika said.

Diotima and I exchanged a startled glance. Had we just heard a slave scold her owner?

Marika placed the food on tables beside our couches. There were olives and bread. Then she passed through the same exit as her children, shouting something about buckets of water and dirty clothes.

Karnon watched us as we watched the comedy unfold. "I run a relaxed household," he said, by way of explanation.

There was definitely something strange about Karnon's household. I decided the only thing to do was pretend that that episode hadn't happened.

"We're here about the death of the priest Geros," I said, then paused, waiting for a reaction. When I didn't get one I added, "I assume you know he's dead?"

"I heard. Murdered, apparently. Bad business, that."

That was one way of putting it.

"We wanted to ask you about some coins," Diotima said. She fumbled in her pouch, extracting the three coins that we had found on Geros. I took these from Diotima's hand and gave them to Karnon.

Karnon squinted at the coins. I wondered if he had bad eyes. "Surely you recognize the first two," he said.

"Tetradrachms from Athens," Diotima said. "Do people on Delos really trade in such high currencies?"

"Hardly," Karnon said. He put these down in order to inspect the third. He held it up to the light and turned it in his fingers.

"Now this one is interesting," he said.

"We didn't recognize the metal," I told him.

"I'm not surprised," he said. "This is electrum. It's a mixture of gold and silver. There are some places where the mines produce it." Karnon stopped to drink his wine before he added, "Of course, those places are all in Asia Minor."

"What on earth would a coin from Asia Minor be doing on Delos?" I asked.

"It's an offering, obviously, donated by a supplicant," Karnon said. He held it up for us to see. "Notice the winged deer and the fish stamped on the front? The design is unique. This coin is from Kyzikos."

"I've never heard of the place."

"It's in Anatolia. Whoever left the coin almost certainly came from one of the Hellene cities on that side of the sea. They probably got it in trade."

Karnon leaned back in his couch, wine in hand, and said, "I notice you haven't told me where you found these. You also haven't really told me why you are asking these questions."

Diotima spoke for us both. "They were found near the body of Geros."

"Oh? Why do you care?"

"We have been asked by Anaxinos to look into the murder."

"You mentioned something to that effect before, but you're both Athenians." He raised an eyebrow.

"It's complicated," I told him.

"Hmm," he said, clearly unimpressed. "Well, if you think the motive was robbery, you can think again. These coins are very valuable. No thieving murderer would have left them behind."

"Any idea why Geros would have been carrying them?" I asked.

Karnon shook his head. "He certainly had no need for them on Delos."

"Or where he got them?" Diotima asked.

"As I said, it's the sort of thing a supplicant donates to a temple. Geros probably got them from one of the treasuries."

"Which treasury?" I asked. "How do you know what's in each?"

"I'll answer you in kind. It's complicated." He chuckled. "I tell you what, come see me when I'm at the Oikos, up at the temples, and I'll show you how we keep the accounts."

I could think of few things less exciting.

"Is it the normal practice for a priest to carry treasury property?" Diotima asked.

"Geros may have been given the coins by a visitor and not yet placed them in a treasure house," Karnon said.

"Is that normal?"

"No. Or he may have removed coins to pay for something on temple business."

"Geros could do that?"

"He was the second most senior priest on the island. Of course he could."

This was frustrating. Worse, I wasn't at all sure that the coins had anything to do with Geros's death. I could tell from the expression on Diotima's face that she too felt stymied.

"I'm afraid there's nothing unusual in this—not for Delos anyway." Karnon looked from one to the other of us. "I know what you two are doing."

I said, with slight bitterness, "You do? Then I wish you'd tell us, because we're not so sure."

"You're on a wild hunt."

"Not particularly."

"You don't understand," he said. "That's an expression we accountants use."

"What do you mean?" Diotima asked. I leaned forward, suddenly interested, because Karnon was speaking with assurance.

"Like when a businessman suspects his partner has been stealing from the partnership. Then an accountant looks at where the money was spent. We don't know exactly what we're looking for, but we'll know it when we see it."

"Sounds like detective work," I said.

"May I ask a question?" Diotima asked.

"You and your husband have already asked many questions," Karnon replied. "Why seek my permission to ask another?"

"Yes . . . umm . . ." Diotima was nonplussed. I knew she had meant a more personal question, the sort that some might not like to answer, but Karnon had not caught her meaning at all. The accountant apparently took everything literally. "I didn't see you at the protests," Diotima said finally.

"Because I was not there," Karnon replied.

"I would have thought the removal of the treasure would have a bigger effect on you than any other man on the entire island," Diotima said.

Karnon nodded. "I think that must be true."

"Yet you were the only one who didn't protest the removal?"

"Ah, I see your confusion," Karnon said. "Let me make several things clear. Firstly, I am an Athenian. Athenians are not exactly popular on Delos at the moment."

"We've noticed."

"Though I must say, I am generally an exception to that rule. I have lived on this island for a long time. The villagers often think of me as one of them. Secondly, though I am an Athenian, I am a servant of the Delian League. My service is to the League, not to Delos, nor to Athens, for that matter."

"I understand," I said.

Diotima asked, "As treasurer to the Delian League, did you have advance notice of the Athenian plan? Did you know that they were coming to take the treasure?"

"I didn't," Karnon said.

"So you were as surprised as everyone when Pericles turned up, demanding the treasure?" Diotima persisted.

"I was astonished," Karnon said. "Before you ask, I am not happy about it. The amount of preparation that must go into moving that much money is beyond your wildest nightmares."

"It is?" I said surprised. "Don't they just pick up the gold, carry it to the ships, and sail off to Athens?"

"*Good God, no!*" Karnon almost shouted. He half-leapt out of his seat. "You have to count it before it leaves, and you have to count it the moment it arrives. Otherwise how will you know it all got there?"

I saw his point instantly. We were both Athenians; we both knew our fellow citizens. We both knew what to expect if Athenians were left alone with bags of gold.

I said, "Someone could steal coins or gold bars in transit."

"Of course they would," the accountant said. "Unless they knew for certain that every box, every bag, every tiny scrap of gold had been listed, counted, and weighed before it left the treasure house. That's why it's such a big job to move the treasure. That's what I was doing when you burst into the Oikos so early this morning."

"Sorry about that."

"Or at least, I was starting the planning. We will have to break every box out of storage to audit the contents." Karnon grimaced. "I tell you, this is going to take forever."

Karnon spoke with the authority of a man who knew his business inside out. I wondered if Pericles had thought of these things. He probably hadn't.

"What does moving the treasure mean to you personally, Karnon?" Diotima asked.

I saw why Diotima had persisted with her questions. Removal of the treasure must surely threaten Karnon's job. It certainly forced a major change in his life.

There was sudden commotion from outside that made us all turn to the door. From the indignant squeals, the exasperated shouts of a woman's voice, the thump of buckets, and the splash of water, I deduced that two boys were having a bath. Then there was sudden silence, if you didn't count the spluttering. The slave woman Marika reappeared with an empty bucket in each hand and a smile of victory.

Karnon turned back to Diotima and said loudly, "The removal of the treasure would mean I go back to Athens. My job wouldn't change. As I have told you, my appointment derives from the League." He shrugged. "I would simply move this entire household and everyone in it to another city. One where we don't have to ration water, or wonder whether the food supply will last until the next shipment."

"So you would actually prefer the treasure to move?" I said.

"Either is fine with me."

I decided to take a risk on something that I had guessed. I said, "I assume, sir, if you relocated back to Athens, then you would free Marika and make her your wife, so that she and your sons would arrive as free citizens."

I thought that was an easy guess. When the boys had run past Karnon, I had seen they were the spitting image of their father. The only difference was that he was bald, while the youngsters had straight, black hair. Karnon would not be the first man to fall for a pretty slave woman.

"My wife?" Karnon managed to look innocent. "I'm afraid you are mistaken. My wife lives in Athens. Her name is Strateia."

"Oh, I see," I said politely, the situation suddenly becoming a little clearer. "I thought, with the easy familiarity between you and Marika—"

"My wife is the daughter of a wealthy man in Athens," Karnon explained. "When I received this posting to Delos, I knew it would create something of a problem. You see, my wife is used to the greatest comforts in life. She is extremely fond of social events and enjoys the company of the wives of other successful men. Myself, I am happiest with my numbers. The opportunity to be accountant to the Delian League was one I could not resist." He stopped to think about it, then added, "No, not even to please my wife could I refuse such a posting."

"Then she was not pleased with your appointment?" Diotima asked.

"She viewed it as a hardship post, I'm sorry to say," Karnon said. "It was she who suggested that she remain in Athens, to look after our children, and my estate of course."

"Of course. Very sensible," Diotima said, as if this were the most natural thing in the world.

Karnon nodded, then he added, somewhat defensively, "We do see each other from time to time, whenever I'm back in Athens on business."

"I'm sure."

"So those excellent young men are not yours," Diotima said it as a statement.

"They are excellent young men, aren't they?" Karnon said enthusiastically. "But I must deny paternity." He said this with a straight face. "Marika had them with one of the men in the village."

"I see," said Diotima in a flat voice.

Karnon said, "I don't know the father. I would never be so rude as to inquire."

"No, of course not," I said as deadpan as I could manage, to match Diotima's effort.

"I merely ensure they are cared for," Karnon insisted.

"You seem to do it well."

"Thank you."

Karnon stood. We rose too.

"Are we finished?" he asked, in a voice that suggested the answer was yes.

"Thank you for seeing us," I said.

Diotima rode and I walked back to the village. It was midday by now, and thoroughly hot. The heat seemed to rise off the ground, as if we were walking on a giant cooking plate that had been set to simmer. Because of it my feet were hotter than the rest of me.

The donkey clearly had no interest in going anywhere at this temperature. I solved that by whacking it in the rear with a stick from time to time.

As we plodded along I said, "What do you think?"

"I think we just wasted out time. Those coins don't mean a thing," Diotima said.

"Unfortunately, I think you're right," I said.

"But we did learn something. Karnon is the only person we've met whose life would be disrupted if the treasure moved. You didn't believe him, I assume, when he said the children aren't his?"

"They're his, all right. He obviously loves Marika. Did you see the way he looks at her?"

Diotima nodded. "He doesn't want to go home. He wants to stay here with the woman he loves and his sons by her."

"I'm sure that's true," I said. "But that's only a motive to stop the treasure moving."

"It's a motive to kill Geros, if Karnon knew Geros had done a deal with Pericles," Diotima said.

"That's a big stretch," I warned her. "You said this morning that there was only a tiny window of opportunity in which to kill Geros."

"Yes."

"That means there's only the same tiny window for someone to find out that Geros had turned against Delos for money. How could Karnon, who wasn't even at the protest, possibly learn that Geros had been bribed?"

"Oh. I didn't think of that." Diotima looked deflated. "That makes it much more difficult for my theory."

"Look on the bright side," I said. "It means the only people on Delos with a reason to kill Geros are the ones who had a chance to learn that he had been bribed. That should be simple. There can't be many."

"I see what you mean," Diotima said. "But we also have to consider the other side."

"What other side?"

"The people who wanted the treasure to move, and didn't know that Geros had been bribed. That, my husband, means the Athenians."

I groaned. "This is so confusing."

"I thought a moment ago you said this was simple?"

"That was before I realized there were so many combinations."

"Then let's list them," Diotima said.

"All right."

Diotima said, "There are two sorts of people on this island: people who want the Treasury of the Delian League to move to Athens and those who want it to stay on Delos."

"That covers every possibility," I said.

"Then there are another two sorts of people," Diotima went on. "The ones who knew Geros had been successfully bribed by you, Nico, and the ones who didn't."

"Yes, and the vast majority could not have known." I paused, then said, "Do you realize we're starting to sound like Socrates?"

Diotima shuddered. "That's a scary thought. But you're right, this is the way Socrates would think."

Socrates, my little brother, had a tendency to be depressingly logical. Though he wasn't so little any more. He had turned eighteen just as we left for Delos, and was now serving his compulsory two years in the army. I wondered which recruiting sergeant had been given the job of trying to make Socrates obey orders without question. Whoever he was, the poor man would probably be suicidal before the year was out.

Diotima was thinking aloud. "Possibly only you, Pericles, and Geros himself knew about the deal, but that remains to be seen."

"I agree."

"Now let's list which of those combinations might want Geros dead," Diotima continued. "First there are those who want the treasure to remain on Delos. Of those, if they don't know Geros has been bribed, then they definitely want him alive."

"Very much so," I agreed. "That must be the vast majority of the Delians."

"Yes," Diotima said. "But if you want the treasure to remain on Delos and you know Geros is corrupt, then you definitely want him dead."

"Those people would be furious with him," I said. "They would have a very strong motive."

"The only problem is, as far as we know, the number of people in that category is zero," Diotima said.

"Yes, that is somewhat annoying."

"Let's move on," Diotima said. "And by the way, when I say move on, I mean this donkey is incredibly uncomfortable."

"He probably feels the same way," I said. "You could try walking?"

"I doubt I'd make the distance, in this heat," she said. It was the first time I'd heard Diotima even suggest that carrying the baby was difficult. "But every time this animal takes a step, every part of me goes up and down, but at different speeds."

"That's all right then, babies like to be bounced."

"Very funny."

"Go on with your analysis. So far, I agree."

Diotima held onto the donkey's neck while it negotiated a particularly steep hill. "All right. Let's say you want the treasure to go to Athens, and say you know Geros has been bribed, then you want to keep him alive."

"Of course. That covers Pericles and me," I said.

"On the other hand, if you want the treasure to move, and you don't know a deal has been done, then killing Geros looks like a good idea."

"Yes."

"That must include most of the Athenians," Diotima said.

I could only nod to that.

Diotima said, "On the face of it, there are many more Athenians who might have wanted to kill Geros than any other group: the ones who didn't know there had been chicanery. What if one of them struck Geros on their own initiative?"

I laughed. "Every one of those men without exception is a soldier or a navy man. Do you know the first rule of all military?"

"No, what is it?"

"Never volunteer. It's inconceivable that one of them would have . . ."

But by then we had reached the first outlying houses of the village. We wouldn't be able to continue the conversation on a public road surrounded by inquisitive villagers. There were people in the streets, doing the sorts of things villagers always do. Women were cooking, cleaning, or carrying baskets to and from the small local agora. Further down the road, fishwives sat together and gossiped as they mended fishing nets. Men hauled loads on carts, did carpentry on houses or fixed their boats. One was fixing a broken axle. Through a large open window I could see Moira in the tavern, serving drinks.

It was the stuff of everyday life, but every one of these people stopped and stared at us as Diotima and I passed.

Diotima noticed the same thing. "It's like they've never seen a pregnant woman," she said.

"No, they've never seen two Athenian investigators on the job," I replied. "They're wondering what we're going to do, and what it means for them."

"I wonder if it truly means anything to them?" Diotima asked.

"They think it does."

But Diotima was right. It wasn't at all obvious why an ordinary villager in Delos cared about what she and I did.

"Do you know what we don't have any of?" I asked Diotima.

"Clues?" she suggested.

"I was thinking a bit more specifically. We don't have a single witness."

"Well, you made sure of that, didn't you?" said my wife. She was still annoyed about my part in the bribery.

I sighed. It was because I had set up a clandestine meeting that no one had seen anything. Or at least, as far as we knew. Geros had been killed in the dark, in an abandoned village, after an all-night party that had left anyone still awake too drunk to be a witness, and those not drunk at home asleep in their beds.

For the first time in my career, we were facing a failure so total that we didn't even know where to start.

THE VILLAGE PEOPLE

I NOTICED DAMON BY the village dock. He noticed me at the same time and waved.

"There's my friend of last night, the one I told you about," I said to Diotima. "I didn't introduce you when he came to collect the body. Let's go say hello."

"Hello, Nico," he said as we approached. "Have you solved the murder yet?"

"Not quite, but we have hopes," I told him, and then wondered why I made the pretense. Wasn't it obvious we had got nowhere?

"It's hot today, isn't it?" Damon said.

That was like saying water was wet.

"Damon, I'd like you to meet my wife."

He held up a jar. "I thought you might be thirsty. I have watered wine, and cups too."

We sat by the water's edge, in the shade of some trees, with our feet in the water and our behinds on mats that had been left lying there, because the sand was too hot for comfort.

The wine tasted better than the vintage would have suggested.

"Geros sure got himself killed, didn't he!" Damon said, as if this was some remarkable achievement on the priest's part.

"I suppose he did," I said, then asked, "I know his wife

and child are gone, but did he have any other family? Any brothers, perhaps, anyone who needs to be told?"

"Nah." Damon shook his head. "You know the priestly families all come from other places?"

"You said so yesterday."

"Well, most get family visitors from time to time, but Geros never had a single family member come here to see him."

"That's sad," Diotima said. "Was he lonely?"

Damon shrugged. "Who can say? Geros liked to talk, but not about personal things."

"What about the homes? Do the priest families stay together? Or do the villagers and priests mix?" Diotima asked.

"Mix mostly, I guess," Damon said.

"I feel foolish to have to ask you," Diotima confessed. "All my adult life I've been a priestess, yet I know nothing about Delos."

"Do you want a guided tour?" Damon asked.

"That would be lovely," Diotima said.

Damon stood. Diotima tried to stand, couldn't, and was helped up by me holding her right hand and Damon her left.

"Ups-a-daisy!" he said, as if she were a child. "Let's start here." He spread his arms to take in the idyllic scene of the well-maintained boats and the blue water. "This is the dock for the fishing boats," he said, which was obvious enough.

"Fish is your main food?" I asked.

"Oh yes," Damon said. "Nothing much grows on the land, but we do our best. Almost everyone has their vegetable patch."

"Isn't that difficult?"

"Very, but we're desperate for fresh vegetables. We catch rain in whatever buckets we can, and of course we men pee on the gardens. It's great fertilizer."

I made a mental note not to eat the vegetables at Apollo's Rest.

"Right there is our agora," he said, turning so we followed his gaze.

It was completely deserted but for a couple of people walking through.

"Not much going on today?" I asked, with a raised eyebrow. In Athens at the agora you couldn't have seen the ground for all the feet on it.

"The agora doesn't get much use," Damon admitted. "When people need to trade, they know who to go and see. But it wouldn't be a village without an agora, would it? Over on the other side is Apollo's Rest."

"We've met Moira," I said.

"Yeah, she's a nice woman," Damon said. "She likes to clean things."

"So we noticed," Diotima said. "What about the villagers and the priests?"

"We're at the far south end of the island," Damon said. "Fisher folk live close to their boats, of course. We villagers live along the coast, mostly; the priests and their families live along the north road to the sanctuary, mostly. They call it the Sacred Way, but we just call it the north road. But everyone gets mixed up, too, like I said before."

"Have the villagers always lived here?" Diotima asked.

"This is the new village." Damon shrugged. "They say a lot of people left the island when the old village was abandoned. I wouldn't know, I arrived after that myself. We get new arrivals trickling in. Maybe one or two every year, sometimes a family wants to settle. You know how it goes. Nobody minds, so long as they're good people and willing to work."

"What's the story about the old village?" I asked. "Why was it abandoned?"

"You'll have to ask Anaxinos about that, 'cause I don't understand it at all. Apparently it's cathartic."

That made no sense to me. I made a note to ask Anaxinos, when he was sober.

"Do the holy people and the villagers get along?" Diotima asked.

"Oh yes," Damon said without hesitation. "You have to, on an island this small. It's like living on a boat, you know."

"No fights?" I prodded.

"Only over women. You know how it goes," Damon said. "The daughter of some priest family likes the handsome son of a fisherman and the father doesn't approve. Or some ambitious villager wants to marry his daughter to an up-and-coming young priest, but some other man wants the girl."

"So there's intermarriage," Diotima said.

"Sure is, once we've cleaned up after the fights."

None of this sounded like something an old priest like Geros would become involved in.

"Do the priests help out around the village?" I asked.

"They do if they want to eat," Damon said. "The younger ones, at least. The older ones have got other things to do. Come along!"

We came along. There was the sound of hammering in the distance, metal on metal.

"That's the smithy," Damon said when I asked about it. "Old Mandro is our man. We make him work over that hill there, close to the water but away from the village."

Damon didn't have to explain why. Sensible villages kept

their furnace far away from anything that can burn, such as, for example, their homes.

"Does he have much work?" Diotima asked.

"Lots, the way everything around here rusts so quickly," Damon said. "Then there are all the visitors at peak season. There are always a few people who need stuff fixed, and the ship captains who need repairs before they move on. Frankly, Mandro is overworked."

Damon's talk of repairs reminded me of something else. "The villagers do all the maintenance?" I asked.

"Oh, yes."

"Does that include fixing squeaky gates?" I asked. "Because almost every gate on this island has a problem."

Damon's smile dropped a little. "Yeah, sorry about that. Every time Anaxinos is making up a list of things we need, to send to Athens, he asks me what I want. I always tell him oil, and he writes oil, and then Athens sends us highest-grade quality cooking oil. It never occurs to those Athenian idiots that we might need to grease a hinge . . . no offense intended."

"None taken."

"We tried using fish oil, but it just isn't the same."

"When I get back to Athens I'll make sure they send you some real oil."

"Thanks. I knew you were a good man, Nicolaos."

Coming off the main road were narrow lanes, whose sole purpose was to lead to other cottages set back from the thoroughfares. The houses were only spread out enough to allow for small market gardens between each. As we walked, everyone we came across waved and bid us good day. One woman mentioned a boil that had been troubling her. It seemed an odd thing to say, but Damon nodded and sympathized.

I realized after a while that Damon was being careful to be seen by all the villagers in our company. He was sending the villagers a message; he was telling them that Diotima and I were all right to talk to. Yet he hadn't explicitly said a single word. Damon had done all this by example. When a man passed by going the other way, Damon mentioned the woman with the tricky boils. The other fellow nodded.

"Thanks for letting me know. I'll see her this afternoon," and he walked on.

"That's our doctor," Damon explained. "We've got a good one, on account of all the visitors who come here."

What Damon had done, directing a doctor to see a sick woman, was what anyone would expect of a village headman, but if so then Damon was the most unassuming village chief I'd ever met.

"What's that over there?" Diotima asked. She pointed inland, at a large, unusually flat piece of land. In the middle of it were three forlorn-looking tents.

"That's where the visitors camp," Damon said.

"Visitors?" I asked blankly.

"You don't think we keep an inn for everyone who comes here, do you?" Damon said. "Delos gets hundreds of visitors every year, maybe thousands. I don't know, I can't count that high. So they got to sleep somewhere, right?"

"Right."

"Well, that's the camping ground," he said. "Not that anyone's there at the moment. At peak season that field is full of tents," Damon said.

"How come there aren't many visitors at the moment?" Diotima asked.

"It's harvest time," Damon said promptly. "In most places, people are working hard, bringing in the food."

"Not here?" I asked.

"Do you see anything to harvest?" Damon asked. He swept his arm across the barren landscape. The stony ground on Delos rose towards the central spine, where there was either a very low mountain or a very big hill, depending on how you looked at it.

"We call it Mount Kynthos," Damon said, when I asked.

"Is there a stream that runs off the mountain?" I asked.

"Not even a small one," Damon said unhappily. "When it rains, which isn't often, the water flows down that slope in every direction and straight into the sea."

"Then what do you do for fresh water?"

"We conserve water like you wouldn't believe. There's a small lake north of the temples which is our only supply—"

"The Sacred Lake?" Diotima interrupted. "The place where Apollo and Artemis were born?"

Damon nodded. "That's it."

Diotima was shocked. "Don't tell me you drink from a holy place!"

Damon laughed. "Since the alternative is to die of thirst, yeah, we drink holy water. I wonder if that makes us more blessed? We pull water from the Sacred Lake in small buckets. Because when that runs out, there's nothing else. Have you seen the lake yet? No? Come along then."

"Is there some way we can avoid that road again?" Diotima asked. By this time we had returned to the beach next to the village dock. "Even with the donkey it's hard going."

"Are you all right?" I immediately asked, and held her hand.

"Just tired," she said. "And a little bit sore in the legs."

"No wonder," I said. I pointed to a weathered rowboat

that was beached not far away. The boat was chained to a heavy rock so that in a storm it could not be lost to the sea. I was surprised no one had stolen the oars, which lay within. "We could take that," I suggested.

Damon looked where I pointed. "Oh no we can't. That's the emergency eject system."

I didn't understand what he meant. "The what?"

"You know it's forbidden to die here," he said.

"Yes, of course."

"Well, if someone's got a bad illness, then we can ship them off to Mykonos to be treated, and if they die, they can die there. But if someone starts dying unexpectedly—you know how old people will have those seizures—they clutch their chests and keel over real quick."

"I know what you mean," I said. "Every month or so that happens in the agora, back in Athens, always to an old person who has lived a full life."

"Right." He nodded. "Well if that happens on Delos, then we're in trouble. We carry whoever's dying down to that rowboat quick as we can, and we row them off the island."

"Does it work?"

"Usually. A couple of times we've had to be bit loose about the definition of dead. But we figure, as long as they're still warm, they might still be alive. Right?"

"Sure," I agreed amiably.

"You never know when that rowboat might be needed. It's ready to go at a moment's notice. It's also illegal to move it, except to eject someone off the island."

That left us no choice. Damon led us up the Sacred Way, with Diotima riding the donkey. I was beginning to understand why the Sacred Way was such a well-trodden path. Almost anything that anyone wanted to do on Delos involved traveling along it. There seemed to be a rule that no matter which end of Delos I was at, what I wanted to do required me to be at the other end. I had already lost count of how many times I had walked that route.

As we walked along it yet again, I was struck by just how constrained life was on this island. I wondered that the people who had lived here all their lives hadn't gone mad. It must be like living in a jail.

We reached the sanctuary. Here business was returning to something that approached normality. Priests and priestesses walked back and forth on whatever business they were upon. I noticed that the Athenians, who had filled the sanctuary the night before, were now entirely absent. It was almost as if nothing had happened, except that the charred remains of the bonfire pits left a reminder of the night's excitement.

Damon led us across the sanctuary grounds to the low wall on the other side, the one into which I had stumbled the night before. The wall was completely obvious in broad daylight. In the center was a gate that I had missed. Damon opened the gate, which squealed, and we walked through to another complex of small buildings.

"What are these for?" I asked.

Damon shrugged. "Not much, these days," he said. "You'd have to ask Anaxinos, or maybe Karnon; he runs the administration. You know Karnon?"

"Yes, we've met him."

"I think this used to be where they ran the island and made all the decisions, you know? But now all that's done at the Oikos."

We passed by the small old buildings to reach an open area. To our left, in a long line above our heads, was a row of lions.

"Oh, they're magnificent!" exclaimed Diotima.

Indeed they were. The lion statues sat upon their haunches, their heads raised, all of them facing east, with expressions of the greatest reverence.

"That's the Terrace of the Lions," Damon said. "They salute the Sacred Lake."

The Sacred Lake turned out to be more like the Sacred Pond.

"That's it?" I said, incredulous. The lake lay on the right side of our path. If I had come across it anywhere else, I would not have given the lake a second glance. I had seen watering dams on farms that looked more impressive.

"It isn't much," Damon admitted, and rubbed his chin. He sounded slightly embarrassed.

"Not much?" Diotima said. My wife slid off the donkey and stood beside me, completely entranced. "Not much?" she repeated. "My Goddess was born on that lake."

She stepped down to the water's edge. I hurried to follow her.

Diotima stopped when her toes were wet. "Where?" she asked the single word.

Damon pointed. "You see the barge?"

We could hardly miss it. The barge occupied the center of the small body of water. It was well-built and rose from the water as a solid platform.

"The priests say that's where they were born," Damon said.

Diotima began to sing. She sang a hymn, a paean, that spoke of the birth of divine Artemis and her brother, Apollo, and of the blessings that they had brought to the world.

Damon and I listened in silence.

When she finished, Diotima continued to stand there,

silently. After a while, Damon offered a polite cough. He had work to do, he said, and he had now shown us the entire island. There was nothing north of where we stood but empty land.

I thanked Damon for his courtesy. Then I offered him, as politely as I could, a reward for his guided tour. He looked at the coins in my hand, grinned, and shook his head. "What would I do with those?" he asked. Then he took his leave. He walked back the way we'd come, whistling a tune. It took me a moment to realize he was whistling the hymn that Diotima had sung. I listened to it fade into the distance.

Diotima had stood there throughout the exchange, admiring the lake. "I could look at this all day," she said simply.

"You might get tired," I said.

She solved that by sitting down. I sat beside her.

"It's difficult to take in," she said. "Artemis, my goddess, was born right here."

"Is it that special?" I asked. "We've stood on the spot where Athena stood when she gave the olive tree to Athens. You've worked in the same temple where the Amazons used to worship. We've been to Olympia, where countless demigods have walked the ground. None of those places made you as excited as you are now."

"Oh, Nico, that's different," Diotima said. "None of those were so important to my goddess. Can you imagine what it must have been like here? Back when . . ." She paused. "Well, whenever it was . . . on this spot there was a Titan giving birth to two Olympian Gods."

"It's not the sort of thing you see every day," I admitted.

"There you are then. This place is sacred beyond all imagining. I knew it was before we came, but now I *feel* it."

The breeze blew a little stronger. It pushed back her hair from her face as she gazed at the Sacred Lake.

"I totally understand why people dedicate their lives to this place," she said.

"I hope you're not thinking of moving here!" I said, alarmed.

"No, of course not," Diotima said. "It wouldn't be good for our baby."

"Speaking of which, we need to think about how long this is going to take," I said. "We need you back in Athens before anything . . . er . . . drastic happens."

"I couldn't agree more," Diotima said with feeling. "We do have leads, Nico. More than we had this morning."

This was true. "Anaxinos has to be on the suspect list, after that strange conversation this morning."

"I hate to admit it, but you're right," Diotima agreed. "As I pointed out before, Karnon the accountant might conceivably have wanted Geros out of the way."

"Yes."

"What about your friend Damon?" Diotima asked.

"What about a motive?" I replied.

"Personally, I think he's strange enough that he could have done something unpredictable."

"It's my turn to say, I hate to admit it, but you're right." I sighed. "Damon's on the list, then."

We trudged away from the lake, me supporting Diotima with my arm.

"This donkey needs a name," Diotima said, when we reached the patiently waiting beast.

"Blossom?" I suggested. It was the name of our donkey back in Athens.

"You can't have two donkeys with the same name," Diotima said. "Why don't we call this one Pericles?"

"While I appreciate the sentiment, the real Pericles might not," I pointed out. "What if you say something like

'Don't poo on my foot, Pericles' while the two-legged one is present?"

"That would be a problem," Diotima agreed.

"Apollo's Steed?" I suggested.

We both turned to look at the completely stationary, utterly unimpressed creature.

"Plod?" Diotima said.

"Done."

Diotima climbed up on Plod, with my assistance. We worked out a good system. Plod stood beside the raised Terrace of the Lions. Diotima walked up the steps, from which it was an easy step down to get on his back. We began the journey back to the cottage.

When we came to the low wall I had tripped over the night before, Diotima made a joke about it being my own personal Nemesis.

"I don't think the wall is the killer," I said.

"It did you a decent injury though," said my wife. "I notice you're still limping."

"It will get better," I promised. But her small joke put me in mind of something else. "You know, I noticed Philipos has developed a limp, too."

"That's because Athenian men are clumsy," Diotima explained.

Walking across the sanctuary, with flowers in her arms, was Meren, the young priestess who had escorted Diotima to the cottage on the night of the protest.

I pointed her out to Diotima and said, "I saw her at the sanctuary when I ran here to report Geros's death."

"Nico, the girl's a priestess," Diotima said. "Priestesses do tend to frequent temples, you know."

"At dawn?" I asked. "After a long night of protests? She mustn't have had much sleep."

"She came with me all the way back to the village, and I left early."

"That's true," I agreed. "But the point is she was here when Geros died. I wonder what she saw?"

"You mean, as in a killer running away?" Diotima thought about it.

"It doesn't have to be that good a clue. Even if she saw someone hanging around who isn't normally here, that would help us. Who knows? Let's find out."

THE PRIESTESS OF THE NORTH

MEREN HAD COME up the Sacred Way and was walking towards where I had last seen her, after Geros's death. I hailed her as she passed. She stopped and looked from one to the other of us quizzically. "Can I help you?"

I said, "Only a simple question. Meren, when Geros died, I saw you at the sanctuary."

"Yes, I remember. I watched you run past me like a scared rabbit," she said.

I decided to let that pass. "Did you happen to see anyone else running around?"

"No, only you."

"On that morning, before you saw me, did you notice anyone around the sanctuary who isn't normally there?" I asked.

"No. Why do you ask?" Then she answered her own question. "Oh, you wonder if I saw the murderer."

The young priestess was quick-witted.

"Yes, or maybe some other witness," I said.

Meren thought for a moment. "I saw the slaves who work in the Oikos of the Naxians. But they're usually here early. We always wave hello. I saw Karnon too, he passed me by on the way. He's the accountant of the League."

"Yes, we know."

"I commented that he was up early. He said he had to start planning for the treasury to move. He was yawning a lot."

That was consistent with what Karnon had told us.

"Anyone else?" I asked hopefully.

"No."

We had got nothing new.

"What were you doing at the sanctuary so early in the morning?" Diotima asked.

"Oh, I'm here early every morning," Meren replied. "One of my assignments is to tend the graves of the Hyperborean Women. Once the supplicants arrive it's too crowded to do anything. Of course, at the moment we have no visitors, but it's a habit."

"Tend the graves of whom?" I asked blankly.

"You do not know of the Hyperborean Women?" she said. "Come, I will show you."

Meren led us across the grounds to the tiny temple in the northwest corner of the sanctuary. This temple was close to the gate that led out onto the graveyard. Like most temples, it faced east.

"There are two deities worshipped here on Delos," Meren said darkly. "But you would never know it to listen to those priests of Apollo."

"You don't serve Apollo?" Diotima asked.

"By no means. I am like you, Diotima. I serve Artemis. This is her temple."

The contrast could not have been more stark. There were two temples to Apollo at our backs, in the middle of the grounds, one new, the other a century or so old, both large, and both wonderfully elegant. The Temple of Artemis, on the other hand, was small and looked like it had been there since Artemis herself was a babe.

"Apollo gets the glory on Delos," Meren said. "But we who serve the Goddess have the oldest temple."

I was prepared to believe it.

Diotima asked, "You are a priestess, Meren, but you also seem to be a villager."

Meren nodded. "I am both. The only one, in fact."

"Don't the other villagers want to be priests?" I asked.

"Well, first of all, you need the education, and not everyone's interested," Meren said delicately. "I grew up on the island and absorbed the lore and the rituals quite naturally."

I thought that must have been a lonely upbringing, especially if she was bookish. I'd seen children playing in the agora, but not many.

"There are other priestesses," Diotima said. "There were two who greeted us when Nico and I arrived."

"Yes, that's true." Meren shrugged. "They are the wives of some of the priests of Apollo. If a man is offered a position as priest, you see, then he moves to Delos and brings his family with him. If his wife is bored then she might volunteer to serve Artemis."

"Ah, I understand." Diotima nodded. "The priests are chosen men, but the priestesses are afterthoughts. I'll wager no one ever directly appoints a priestess, am I right?"

Meren sighed. "Yes, you're right. Except for me. When I asked the High Priest if I might be a priestess, he made me recite all the hymns, and then perform the rituals. I did them all perfectly, and he appointed me at once."

"You should apply for the Artemision at Ephesus," Diotima said. "It's the largest, most beautiful temple to the Goddess in the whole world. You would love it there."

"Oh no, I couldn't!" Meren said. She seemed genuinely shocked. "Then who would serve the Delian Artemis?"

We had just pointed out that there were other priestesses, but Meren obviously considered herself essential staff.

"How old is the temple, really?" I asked.

"Nobody knows," Meren said. "They say that Homer himself worshipped in this place."

That made me feel strange. I was standing where the greatest poet who had ever lived had once stood.

Meren beckoned. "Come inside."

We squeezed through the door, which was low and narrow, like the temples of old. The Temple of Artemis was a bit roomier than it looked from the outside. The door had been cunningly placed so that in the morning, the light shone within, but there was no window at the west end and now in the afternoon, it was quite dark. It took a moment for our eyes to adjust.

"Look left," Meren said.

Diotima and I both swiveled our heads. To the left of the entrance were two sarcophagi, side by side, both carved of local stone.

"Here lie the two women of Hyperborea," Meren said. "Their lives were of the greatest holiness."

"I've never heard of Hyperborea," Diotima admitted. "Yet I am a priestess."

"It is a strange tale," Meren said. "They say it happened more than a century ago, when two women arrived on Delos. With them came five great warriors for their escort. The women were . . . unusual. Their skin was fair, as fair as the moon. Their hair was fair too, as bright as the stars. It is said that they were very beautiful.

"At first no one knew what they wanted, because they spoke a language no one had ever heard before. When they had learned our words, the women explained that they had brought with them a gift for the Goddess Artemis.

They said that the people of their tribe had received a vision, that the goddess required this of them, and in their holiness they had sent two priestesses."

"What about the men?" I asked.

"The warriors who protected the women were fierce. They wore skins, like Heracles of old. The priests asked the women whence they had come. They said that their people lived beyond Boreas, the freezing cold wind that blows to the far north, that they had traveled for many months and faced many dangers to be with us."

"So the women from Hyperborea delivered their gift," Diotima said.

"Yes," said Meren sadly, "and then they died."

"What!"

"It was illness," Meren said. "They both fell sick and died. The whole island wept. The women were buried with highest honors, here inside the Temple of Artemis. They are the only people ever to be buried within a temple on Delos," Meren said. "As the youngest of the priestesses of Artemis, it is my job to tend their graves."

"Did the men remain?" I asked.

"The warriors in their sorrow returned home."

"The tale is sad, and strange," Diotima said.

"It gets stranger," Meren replied. "People thought that was the last that we would ever hear from the Hyperboreans. But the next year, another gift arrived, sheathed in wheat for protection. With it came a message, that the Hyperboreans would never again risk their finest women on such a dangerous journey, but that every year they would send the Sacred Gift that was due, passed on by whomever was kind enough to carry it."

Diotima clutched my arm. The pressure was quite strong. I knew she had heard something.

"Ever since then, the Gift has arrived?" Diotima asked.

"Every single year," Meren said. "Passed on by one traveler to another. No one has seen the Hyperboreans since that first visit."

"That is remarkable dedication. Where is this land of Hyperborea that you speak of?" I asked.

Meren scratched her head. "That's the strange thing," she said. "Nobody knows."

WE THANKED MEREN and went on our way.

"Why did you clutch my arm in there?" I asked.

"Because the epithet of Nemesis is She Who Gives What Is Due, and the retribution she brings is often called her gift."

"Hello!" a voice hailed us.

We both swiveled to see Karnon walking along behind us.

"I suppose you've come to see the treasury, like you said you would."

We had indeed said that we would. I'd forgotten about it. Karnon seemed enthusiastic about his job.

Although at the moment he looked embarrassed. He shuffled his feet, looked around to make sure no one was listening, then leaned close and said, "Also, there's something I'd like to say to you. In private."

"Then lead on," Diotima told him.

THE TREASURY

KARNON LED US across the sanctuary, to a temple building in the northeast. "This is the Porinos Naos," he said. "It's a temple to Apollo, but these days it serves another purpose. This is where we keep the treasury of the Delian League."

Porinos Naos meant limestone temple in our language, which was appropriate enough, since this temple to Apollo was made of limestone. The blocks that made the walls were very, very weathered. Some of the decorations etched into the facade were almost completely worn away. The columns were broken in places, but still doing their job. The paint had worn to almost nothing, so that bare stone was the only color.

"I'd hate for all our temples to end up looking like this," Diotima muttered under her breath, but the accountant heard her.

"The priests stopped worrying about upkeep when the building was taken over by the League and lost its sacred status," Karnon explained.

This nondescript temple contained more wealth than perhaps any other building in all of Hellas. I marveled at what an odd thing that was.

Karnon walked up the steps. At the top there were two guards in armor and carrying spears, with their helmets pushed back upon their heads.

I raised an eyebrow. "Only two?" I asked.

"Two are enough to keep away inquisitive tourists," Karnon explained. "A hundred would not be enough to repel a serious attack from outside."

I didn't like that answer at all. The more I saw of the security on Delos, the more I was convinced that Pericles was right. The treasury was not remotely safe here.

I said as much. "Then some city-state, say, Sparta, could land here, grab the money, and sail off with it," I said.

"You mean like Athens is doing right now?" Karnon said sarcastically.

"Here!" I said. "That's uncalled for."

"Is it?" Karnon said. "I may be an Athenian, but I'm not blind to how the rest of the world will see our actions." Karnon took the key, which he'd been carrying over his shoulder. "Have you seen one of these before?" he asked.

"We were there when Anaxinos recovered Geros's keys. But I've never seen one used. How does it work?" I asked, fascinated.

"Here, I'll show you," Karnon said. "See this slit in the door?"

Diotima and I nodded.

"This key goes in that hole, but you have to angle it just right."

He moved the key to the hole, but the unwieldy tool slipped from his fingers. It fell to the stone floor and rebounded with an enormous clang.

"Curse it," Karnon muttered. "I hate it when I drop my keys."

He picked it up and tried again, this time with two hands, holding the key at the long end so that the kink was down. He pushed it through, jiggling hard as he did.

"These things are always sticky," he explained.

When it was all the way in he turned it in place.

"What's happening?" I asked.

"As I turn the key, the big curve in the metal is turning to lift the bar on the other side. That's why only this key works," Karnon said. "The bend has to be in just the right place to meet the bar."

Personally I didn't think these new-fangled keys were likely to catch on, and said as much to Karnon. "A slave behind the door is a much better idea," I said. "The slave can identify you, that key can't identify anyone, and then the slave only needs to lift the bar. What could be simpler?"

"I somewhat agree with you," Karnon said. "That works in every home in Athens, but in this case we'd have to leave the slave standing in that enclosed temple for days on end with nothing to do. We don't open this treasury every day, you know."

"Oh, I see what you mean."

We heard a clunky bang on the other side.

"That's it," Karnon said. He put a hand on the door handle.

"Is there any other access in?" I asked.

"What do you think?" Karnon laughed. "No, of course not."

"Then what if you lose the key?"

"I've never lost the key," he said flatly. "But if I did, then at great expense and at the cost of my job we could dig a hole through the wall."

Several priests passed by in a group. Karnon ceased speaking until they had passed.

"You shouldn't confuse the key with any security, in any case," said the accountant. "I have no delusions that it would stop anyone for long. The real security are the guards, and the fact that no one, and I mean no one, could run off with that treasure anytime soon."

Diotima said, "Karnon, a moment ago you seemed upset about Athens taking the treasure. But at your home, you said moving the treasury didn't bother you."

"You asked me whether the removal would affect me personally," Karnon said. He looked from one of the guards to the other. They were, of course, listening to every word we spoke. Both stared straight ahead, expressionless, and made no movement.

"Let's go inside," the accountant said. He opened the door.

"This is the most private place on all of Delos," he continued, when the door was shut behind us. "It's the only place I know of where nobody can overhear us."

"You brought us here on purpose. What did you want to say?" Diotima asked.

"Of course at my home I spoke the words that I did. Marika was listening. I don't want to distress her. Above all else, I don't want her unhappy." Karnon let us think about that for a moment, then went on. "This move by Pericles affects her deeply. How do you think she feels?"

"Not good?" I suggested.

"What am I supposed to do if I'm forced to return to Athens?" Karnon put his hands to his head. If he'd had hair, I was sure he would have pulled it out. "You guessed the truth, didn't you?"

"The moment we saw you together," I told him. "The boys look too much like you to believe any other story."

"My wife will see it too. If Marika and the boys return with me, my wife will make their lives miserable."

"Marika is truly a slave?" I asked.

"Yes."

Karnon had a terrible problem. Household slaves are traditionally under the orders of the lady of the house. Karnon's wife could persecute Marika.

"Is your wife the vindictive sort?" I asked.

"Why do you think I volunteered to live on this miserable island?" Karnon said with feeling.

"You could free Marika," Diotima suggested. "If you were forced to go home, that is. Marika and the boys could live here, or some more pleasant place, and you could see them from time to time."

"And Marika should live on her own?" Karnon said.

That was a good question. Freed slaves often had trouble making a living. Freed female slaves with children had very few options indeed, and none of them were pleasant.

"Besides, Marika's the one I want to be with, and she wants to be with me. What would my boys think of me if I abandoned their mother?"

I was pleased to hear that the accountant wasn't prepared to abandon his slave woman. There were plenty of men who would. The child of a citizen and a slave is a slave, by law. Karnon could have sold Marika and his two boys, and no one could have objected.

But I knew, from the tone of his voice and the set of his shoulders, that if I had suggested such a thing then Karnon would have punched me in the face.

I didn't bother to ask why the accountant didn't divorce his wife to marry his lover. He had already mentioned that the wife's father was a wealthy merchant, and Karnon would not be the first man dependent on his wife's dowry. If he divorced her then by law the dowry remained with the lady.

"Did you know Geros was preparing to hand the treasure over to Athens?" I asked.

"Yes. Or rather, I suspected. Geros has always had an unhealthy interest in the treasuries."

"The Delian League's treasure?"

"All of them," said Karnon shortly. "We'd had words in the past."

"Oh?"

"I caught him trying to talk his way in here once. He argued that since he had access to all of the sacred treasuries, he must also have access to this one. He was wrong. The Delian League has its own rules."

"Who does have access?"

"Me. That's it. No one enters unless I am present."

"Is it that precious?" Diotima asked.

"You tell me. I'll show you," Karnon said.

It was dark within the temple. Karnon lit a torch, using the flint that he had brought with him. His actions were so automatic, moving in the dim light, that I knew he had done this hundreds of times before.

As light filled the room I saw the temple was full, stacked from wall to wall and floor to ceiling with box upon box of coins, more coins than I could count if I lived to be a hundred. Stacked to both sides of the boxes were bars of silver, all the way to the roof.

I stepped forward to inspect the treasure, kicking something on the ground.

I looked down. The doorstops in this place were blocks of solid gold.

"Dear Gods!"

"You see before you the treasury of the Delian League," Karnon said.

"Why haven't you run off with all this wealth?" I asked. "I certainly would."

"How would I lift it?" Karnon asked. I could hear the humor in his voice.

It was a good question. I could see now why Pericles had turned up with fifty triremes. It would need that many to carry this much metal without risking the boats sinking.

"Does Pericles know there's this much in here?" I asked.

"Oh, yes," Karnon said. "I showed him in here once, when he visited for a meeting of the leaders of the League."

"Then the other leaders know how much gold you hold too," Diotima said.

"Of course they know!" Karnon said. "They read my accountant reports. Or at least, I hope they do."

"So since you know exactly, how much money are we talking about here?" I asked.

"There are something like four thousand talents in this room."

He spoke calmly, but I staggered in shock. I'd had no idea the treasury was that large. One talent was six thousand drachmae..

It was mind-boggling.

"How in Hades do you store that many coins?" I asked. "It must make a mountain."

"No, there aren't that many coins in our treasury," he said, laughing at my question. "Most of it is in the gold and silver bars that you see."

"Where does it all come from? All those bars of solid metal, I mean."

"Either delivered by the wealthier states, or converted by us from silver coin sent by the poorer states."

"You turn silver coins into gold? Are you magicians?"

"It's a bit simpler than that," he explained patiently, even perhaps with a touch of enthusiasm. "Most of the contributing states are poor island nations of fishermen and farmers. All they can send us, in accordance with the tribute lists, is an amphora or two of coins."

"Such a measly sum?" I said in mock horror. I'd never

owned as much as an amphora of coins in my life, and I never hoped to.

"It's not much," he agreed, oblivious to my sarcasm. "But it would be inconvenient to store so many random coins. I take the contributions from several member states, merge them together, and use the sum to buy gold bars. The bars stack much more easily."

"I can imagine. So the treasury of Delos is mostly this gold?"

"Mostly," he agreed. "We keep enough coins for ready cash. Those are the coins you see in the center. They're much harder to stack."

"How much is that?"

"Oh, not more than a few hundred thousand drachmae," he said calmly.

I felt faint. This man spoke of enough money to buy a medium-sized town, but he called it spare change. Dear Gods, no wonder Pericles wanted this money safe in Athens.

"How in Hades did you accumulate so much money?" I asked.

"The yearly contribution from all the member states is four hundred and sixty talents."

The only people who talked of money in terms of talents were state treasurers and the mega-wealthy. "You don't just store all that, surely?"

"Most of it goes on operational expenditures, to run the combined navy. That's what the money's for, after all. But I also scrape and save what I can. I've managed to make some good investments in profitable cargos, joint ventures, olive oil presses, shield factories, that sort of thing. That's with the spare funds, you understand." He shrugged. "A talent here, a talent there, and pretty soon you're talking real money."

The men who ran these finances lived in a completely different world to the ordinary men in the towns and villages. Enough money passed through this man's hands every day to buy an entire village.

Diotima was more level-headed. "You said 'something like' four thousand. Don't you know exactly?"

"I know to the drachma according to the official books. But you need to understand, when we're talking of such sums, even a very tiny error in the accounting could amount to a few thousand drachmae, one way or the other."

One way or the other. I was willing to bet that one way was a lot more common than the other. I suggested that, as delicately as possible.

"Then you'd be wrong," he said shortly. "I'm an honest man." And then, because he was honest, he added, "Anyway, I'd never get away with it. My books are audited like you wouldn't believe."

We exited the room, and Karnon locked it behind us.

"Let's go to my office."

As we walked, he said, "I wanted to show you that, so you would appreciate the scale of the problem."

"I'm glad you did," said Diotima.

"You suggested, when we first met, that moving the treasury was a simple matter."

"I see now that it's not," I said.

"The Oikos is about a hundred years old," Karnon said as we walked up the steps to his office. "I'm not sure of the exact age, but the building's still in better condition than the older administration site. Those are the buildings you'll find north of the sanctuary wall, close by the Sacred Lake."

"Damon showed us."

"Damon's a strange man," said Karnon. "But a good one."

"Is he the village chief?" I asked. "No one's ever said so, but he acts like it."

Karnon laughed. "As far as I can tell, yes. Certainly no one else does the job, and everyone seems to listen to him."

"He was here when you arrived?"

"Of course he was."

Karnon clapped his hands. One of the office slaves brought watered wine, bread, cheese, and olives. Anywhere else it was basic fare, but on Delos it was a good meal.

We sat upon camp stools at the great table where I had first seen Karnon, which had only been this morning. It had been a long day.

I knew I was going to regret asking it, but the question had to be put. "You said you invest some of the money?"

"Yes. It makes no sense for it to lie there doing nothing. I am free to invest a large portion. That way I can add to the fund's wealth using the fund's money."

"What do you do with it?" Diotima asked.

"Mostly I buy silver mines," he said, and I was struck again by the unreality of this man's life. "Farm property is too hard to move when I want to sell it on. Better to stay liquid." Karnon was warming to his subject, and becoming more enthusiastic with everything he said. "In addition I can manipulate the markets. I have another assistant who buys up gold and silver on my orders."

"But isn't it gold and silver from your own mines that he's buying?" I said, confused.

"Yes, and I lend him the money to buy it."

"That makes no sense whatsoever."

"Yes it does," Karnon said happily. "After my factor has accumulated a big reserve, I order my mines to lower production, until the market has fewer gold and silver ingots for sale than people actually want. That drives up the price.

Then I order my factor to sell his reserve. It raises the profit for the League treasury, you see."

I was shocked. "Is that legal?"

Karnon looked at me oddly. "Why wouldn't it be?"

As Diotima and I left the Oikos, completely convinced that Karnon was a financial genius, Diotima had one final question. "What will you do now?"

"I'll proceed at once with getting the treasure ready to travel. A final accounting, if you will."

"What about those silver mines you mentioned?" I asked.

"They're the easiest to transfer to Athens!" Karnon chuckled at our incredulous expressions. "We don't have to move a mine, you know. Only the deeds of ownership. Effectively, the League investments go wherever the treasure goes, without doing a thing. It makes my own job easier too. I only have to count what's here. Nothing can go wrong with that."

THE GIFT OF THE HYPERBOREANS

WE NEEDED TO find out about this mysterious gift that Meren had told us of, sent by a strange people called the Hyperboreans. If the reference to Nemesis written in blood referred to a gift then we needed to know it. Unfortunately we didn't dare ask anyone on the island. The very person we were speaking with might be the one with something to hide.

"Who among the Athenians might know such a thing?" Diotima wondered.

"I think I know," I told her.

There was one, and only one, Athenian on the island who knew about both transport and holy offerings.

We found him seeing to minor work on his boat. He had sailors scrubbing decks and was in conversation with one of his officers. Something to do with how the brightly colored ribbons in the main lines had faded.

"Sir!" I said.

Captain Semnos of *Paralos* turned around. "Ahh, the investigators. How goes it?"

"We wanted to ask you, Captain—I know this is extremely unlikely but I wanted to ask anyway—do you happen to know anything about the Hyperborean Gift?"

I waited for his answer. When Semnos didn't reply, but merely looked at me quizzically, I said, "Sorry to trouble you; I know you've probably never even heard of it."

"There you would be wrong," the Captain said. "If I'm slow to answer, it's because your question surprised me. I have transported the Hyperborean Gift on three separate occasions."

"You have?" I said, astonished at my luck.

He must have heard the joy in my voice because Captain Semnos said, "This pleases you?"

"It certainly does, Captain. You might be of assistance on this case."

"I can't imagine how. But I shall tell you what I know."

"How did you come to carry the Gift?" Diotima asked.

"When Athens realized that the Gift was appearing once a year, and that its transport was so problematic, our archons made it known that wherever the Gift touched, the people there could call upon Athens and we would carry it the rest of the way."

"That is generous," I said.

"It's my job," Semnos replied. "I did not exaggerate when I said it is my duty to carry out all religious duties on behalf of Athens that involve foreign travel."

"Then Captain, you might be the only person in the world who knows the answer to my question," I said. "Where does the Hyperborean Gift come from?"

"I have no idea."

"But you just said you transported it!"

"Let me explain," he said. "On the first occasion when I was called upon to carry the Gift, I had to travel to Dionysopolis to collect it." Then he answered my unasked question. "That's an obscure city far to the north of here, very close to Thrace."

"Then Hyperborea is directly to the north," I said.

"On my second mission, I had to collect the Gift from Elis. They said the Gift had arrived by boat from the north and across the sea." He paused, then added, "I hope I don't have to tell you that Elis is in the far northwest of the Peloponnese. It's near Olympia."

"Yes, I know. That implies Hyperborea is close to Etruria, where the Etruscans live…" My voice trailed off as I realized the implication. "Wait, that's impossible. Hyperborea can't be close to Thrace *and* Etruria."

The Captain nodded. "You see the problem. My third trip to collect the Gift took me to Byzantion."

He didn't have to tell me where that was.

"That is bizarre," I said.

"It is," Captain Semnos agreed. "You're not the only person who wants to find Hyperborea. I've tried to solve the puzzle myself. At Dionysopolis they told me it had arrived overland with a courier, from the north."

"That's what I'd expect," I said.

"Me too," the Captain said. "At Byzantion they said the Gift had come by boat. Nobody knew which direction the boat had come. It might have been from the north, which at least would match the Dionysopolis experience. It could have been the Black Sea. But remember at Elis they said the Gift carrier had come from far to their northwest."

"Always from the north then? That's what everyone seems to say."

"Yes, but those routes are so far apart, it's impossible the Hyperborean Gift could be coming from the same place."

"It does seem unlikely."

"Can you tell us, what is the Gift?" Diotima asked.

"I don't know that either. It is encased in a sheaf of wheat, to deliberately hide the Gift from view."

"Why?"

"I've always supposed it's so no one will see it, and thus be tempted to steal whatever treasure lies within."

"You were never tempted to peek inside?" I asked.

"Never," Semnos said in a flat voice.

"Not even a little bit?" I wheedled.

"I take my responsibilities seriously."

"What happens to the Gift when you arrive on Delos?"

"I hand it over to the priest in charge of the Hyperborean Gift. He places it in a special treasury dedicated to Artemis."

"Good. Then I can ask that priest about the gift?"

"No, you can't. That priest was Geros."

THE CATHARSIS OF DELOS

IT WAS TOO dark to do any more. We were in the summer, so the days were long in any case, but Delos was an island where there were no mountains or forests to the east or the west to block the sun. Dawn was as early as could be, dusk as late.

We made our way back to the cottage. Diotima was weary, understandably since she was trying to solve a murder while carrying a baby. I was exhausted. The only sleep I'd had in two days had been the brief period in the morning.

We were so tired that we stumbled through the front door, only to find a note upon the table. It was from Anaxinos. He apologized for his behavior of the morning, and invited us to dinner.

Diotima and I looked at each other in despair.

"We'll have to go," she said.

"We'll leave early," I told her in a firm voice.

We stopped only long enough to refresh and wipe ourselves down. In the absence of a ready bath it was the best we could do.

We trudged the short distance to the home of the High Priest.

"I want to apologize for my behavior today," Anaxinos said the moment we walked in. The High Priest had opened the door himself.

"I am mortified," he finished. He held his head in his hands as he said this, and I guessed that in addition to being mortified, the High Priest was also seriously hung over.

"There is nothing to be concerned about," I said quickly. I thought it important to be the one to reassure Anaxinos. It would have been socially awkward for a mid-level priestess like my wife to have to forgive one of the highest priests in the land. "All it means, sir, is that you're a normal man. It happens to everyone from time to time. We drink a little too much and say things we don't mean."

"Or things we do mean but shouldn't say," Anaxinos said grimly. "I won't disown my words. I deplore that you had to hear them. But come, you must rest and eat."

The courtyard was where any man of refinement would entertain. Anaxinos had outdone himself. Slaves already stood waiting with sumptuous dishes. There was fresh lamb and fish upon platters, spiced vegetables and, joy of joys, eel in garos sauce, my favorite meal.

"I understood that you would both be very tired," Anaxinos said as we took our places upon the dining couches. "I instructed the cook to be ready at once."

"You are the perfect host, High Priest," I said in appreciation, and I meant it. I was already digging into the dish of eel as wine was served. I noted that Anaxinos refused wine for himself.

"How goes the investigation?" he asked. The household knew his favorite foods and had already served him. He ate small amounts with dainty fingers.

"We have a beginning, High Priest," Diotima said. My wife normally ate sparingly, but that was before she had begun the baby. Now she ate everything in sight. She skipped the eel but dug her right hand into the lamb with determination. When Anaxinos saw her enthusiasm he signaled to the slave to leave the entire dish with her. This alone would have earned the priest my gratitude.

"Sir, I must warn you that the investigation will take some time," Diotima said.

"How long?" Anaxinos asked.

"I don't know."

"Is there anything I can do to help?"

There was something I wanted to know. I said, "Sir, what happens at meetings of the Delian League? What is your role?"

"Mine?" Anaxinos said in surprise. "I chair the meetings. The job falls to me as High Priest of the Delian Apollo."

"Then you decide what is to be done?" I asked.

"Not even slightly. The commanders of every nation are present to make the warlike decisions. I have no military experience, young man. I dedicated my life to the Gods at an early age. I dare say even you have fought more wars than I have. No, my job isn't to make war. It's to keep the peace between the war makers."

His exasperated tone made me ask, "Tough job?"

"You have no idea." The High Priest wiped sweat from his brow. "I used to think it was hard work to keep squabbling priestesses from scratching each other's eyes out, but that was before I had to stop squabbling Generals from going for each other's throats."

"I thought they were allies?"

"They are allies. I don't like to think how they behave with their enemies." Anaxinos paused. "Though come to think of it, a soldier's job is to be very rude to complete strangers. Perhaps that explains it."

"Can you think of anyone who might have had a motive to kill Geros?" Diotima asked.

"Well of course, there's me," said the High Priest. To

our shocked expressions, he chuckled and said, "Why are you so surprised? Was it not you, young man, who suggested as much this morning?"

"Suspects don't normally volunteer, sir," I said.

"Nor am I," Anaxinos said calmly. "I am merely pointing out the obvious, and of course, I didn't kill him. Can we take that as an assumption, for the moment?"

"Yes, sir."

"The next obvious candidate would be Pericles," he said.

"Yes, we know, but there are arguments against that," Diotima said.

"I'm painfully aware," said the High Priest. "What Pericles has done is not good in the eyes of the Gods."

I felt a sudden lurch in my stomach. Had Anaxinos learned of the bribery attempt? If so, this conversation was about to become very awkward.

I said, rather tentatively, "Sir, when you say you're painfully aware—"

"Surely it is obvious," the High Priest broke in. "Pericles could have simply used his men to force his way into the treasury. I'm sure that's what he would have done, if the impasse had lasted more than a few days."

I was struck by how differently Pericles and Anaxinos had read the situation. Pericles, the leader of Athens, had felt powerless in the face of Delian moral authority. Anaxinos, the High Priest, felt powerless in the face of Athenian strength. I wondered what might have happened if these two men had been allowed to talk for long enough, without interference from Geros.

Anaxinos sighed. "I must be honest, too. Pericles has his faults, but he wouldn't commit an outright crime."

Anaxinos seemed to know a different Pericles than the one I worked with.

"What of the villagers, or the priests?" I asked. "Are there any among them who disliked Geros?"

Anaxinos was silent for a long while. He seemed visibly disturbed. "Geros was a difficult man to like. But I don't think many disrespected him. I cannot imagine anyone killing him."

"Someone did."

"There are plenty of Athenians present to answer that need."

Anaxinos had taken us back to where Diotima and I had found ourselves in logic: that if a local hadn't killed Geros, then an Athenian had; if an Athenian didn't do it, then it must have been a priest or a villager. Neither answer was palatable. I already knew this conversation would chase its own tail all night if we let it. Instead I asked, "Tell me, sir, how the ruined village came to be abandoned?"

"Your own people did it," Anaxinos said.

"We did?" I exclaimed, shocked. I could not recall Athens ever attacking Delos, and if we had surely our city must have been cursed for all eternity. I said as much to Anaxinos.

"You misunderstand," he said. "The village you see alongside the sanctuary was the original. Priests and priestesses lived there since time immemorial. But then almost ninety years ago, the Athenians received an oracle from the sanctuary at Delphi, where lives the Pythoness who interprets the words of Great Apollo."

"What were Apollo's words?" Diotima asked. "I have never heard this story."

"Apollo commanded the Athenians to perform a catharsis upon Delos; a ritual cleansing. By their own efforts and at their own cost, the Athenians were to cleanse all the dead from within sight of the sanctuary here at Delos."

"The Oracle at Delphi commanded a change to how things were done on Delos?" I asked.

"It's the same god, after all," Anaxinos said. "Both Delos and Delphi serve Apollo. You surely know that Apollo is displeased by death."

I nodded. Everybody knew that dead bodies were hateful to the sight of Apollo. That was why funerals in Athens were always held before the sun came up, or after it descended.

"Thus it was that your ancestors arrived here in many boats," Anaxinos said. "They dug up every body in the village cemetery—"

"That must have been fun," I commented.

"I doubt it," Anaxinos replied. "The corpses, no matter how old they were, were relocated to the new cemetery here at the south end, out of sight of the sanctuary."

"Is that when the village was moved too?" Diotima asked.

Anaxinos nodded. "It was also the moment that it became illegal to die or be born on Delos." Anaxinos sighed. "Fortunately we have the much larger island of Mykonos not far off. If an inhabitant feels one event or the other coming on, then we ferry them off the island."

"What about emergencies?" I asked.

"For those we have the emergency eject system. You have seen it, surely?"

I nodded. "Damon showed me."

"It lacks dignity, but it works."

"The old village was abandoned so long ago, but people still call your village the New Village," Diotima said.

"We do," Anaxinos said. "We've been living in it for eighty-five years now . . . four generations. Still, I think we'll be calling it the New Village for centuries to come.

The Old Village . . . the abandoned one by the sanctuary, some say that's been there since the days of King Minos."

"Is Delos that old?" Diotima asked.

"Nobody can say for sure. Where our Temple of Artemis stands has been a place of worship since the days of Homer's heroes." Anaxinos shrugged. "I cannot say, but I can believe. When do you think the gods were born?"

Diotima sat there for a moment, before she realized that the High Priest was waiting for her to answer. "You're asking *me*?" she said.

"I am."

"Er . . ."

"This is an issue of theology, young lady," Anaxinos said sternly. "If you're to progress in your profession and your love of the gods, then you must learn to think in these terms."

"Oh. I am sorry, High Priest, I've never thought about it."

"Consider it now," Anaxinos ordered. "I particularly want to hear how old you think Apollo and Artemis must be."

Diotima gave the question some thought.

But I was sure I already knew the answer. I said, "Surely the gods existed at the same time as the world."

Anaxinos shook his head glumly. "You repeat a common error."

"I do?"

"He's right, Nico," Diotima said. "Keep in mind, Uranus came first. Uranus created the world, married Gaia the Earth, and she gave birth to the Titans. Of those, Kronos the Lord of Time was created at the instant the universe came into being. He married Rhea, and they were the parents of Zeus."

"Oh, I see what you mean," I said. Now that Diotima

had said it, it was obvious. "The gods must be younger than the world."

"Right," Diotima said. "Zeus in turn married his sister Hera, but was also on . . . ah, shall we say . . . friendly terms with Leto, and, er . . . a dozen other women. It was Leto who bore Apollo and Artemis. Which means that by the time they were born there were already people walking the earth."

"Then they must be very young deities," I said.

"Yes, but Delos is very old." Diotima looked in confusion to Anaxinos.

"What is old to us can be very young to the gods," Anaxinos said. "But what you say is true. The God I serve, and the Goddess you serve, are among the youngest in creation."

"I never thought of it like that."

"It is possible that the sanctuary has been here since the time of their birth."

"The buildings aren't that old!" Diotima exclaimed.

"No, they're not," Anaxinos said calmly. "But the ones underneath the current temples might be. We know for sure that our temples have been rebuilt, time and again."

We made our excuses early. Anaxinos, being the perfect host that he was, immediately jumped to his feet. He insisted that one of his slaves escort us to our home, though it was so short a distance.

IT WAS LATE at night. Something was prodding me in the back.

It was my wife.

"Nico?"

"Hmmf."

"I can't sleep. The baby's moving."

"Again?"

I rolled over. At home Diotima would have slept in her own room in the women's quarters, while I, as a married man and the eldest son, had a room of my own in the other wing of the house. But my job took us all over the world, and when we traveled we invariably shared the same room and the same bed. In the dubious inns where we often found ourselves, sleeping together was safest and besides, we liked it.

Usually.

I put a hand on Diotima's tummy. I could feel the little baby moving about beneath her skin.

"Doesn't that hurt?" I asked.

"No."

I reached underneath the bed for the small stub of candle and flint that I had left there. I sat up and lit the candle. In the dark of the night, with the shutters drawn, it gave off enough light to see what was happening.

Diotima was lying on her side. She said it was the most comfortable position.

We both watched fascinated as Diotima's stomach pushed outwards in different places, time after time. You could almost see the out-dents of little hands.

Whoever was in there was trying very hard to get out.

"I think it's a boy," Diotima said.

"What makes you think that?" I asked.

"A girl would be better behaved," she groaned. "Uh, Nico, my bladder . . ."

"Again?" I repeated.

"If you don't like it, you can carry the next one."

We had left a bedpan by the door. I went to retrieve it. Diotima squatted over the pan and did whatever it is women do with bedpans. Then she eased herself back onto the bed.

I picked up the pan to empty it outside. I used to leave it till morning, but the smell was a problem in the heat.

I opened the door to see people moving silently across the agora, in the dark, in single file, without torches.

I shut the door as quietly as I could.

"There are people out there," I said softly. I put down the pan, reached for the candle and snuffed it out.

"It's past midnight," Diotima said. She peered at the window. It was shuttered, but we should have seen light through the gaps. "I don't see their torches."

"They aren't carrying any."

That got her full attention, as it had mine.

"How many?" she asked.

"I saw five," I told her.

"Coming our way?" she asked. That sort of thing was always a risk in our profession.

"No. Transverse, right to left across the agora. I think they might be heading for the inn." That idea had only just occurred to me.

"At this time of night?"

"Maybe they're thirsty."

Diotima held up a hand and I helped her off the bed. She reached for her chiton and pulled it over her head. She didn't bother with the belt or sandals. I had already done the same with my exomis. By silent agreement we both reached for the daggers that we kept by our pillows.

"If this turns ugly, you get away," I told her. "Make for the Athenian camp. They'll protect you."

She nodded.

The cottage had only one door. I opened it a crack to peer out. There was no one there that I could see. I opened the door further, just enough to slip out, then realized Diotima would need much more.

The creak of the hinge seemed to echo across the entire village, but apparently that was my imagination, because nobody came our way.

I edged out and stayed low by the door. When I saw no threat I waved a hand through the entrance, and Diotima appeared.

At that moment two doors opened on houses on the other side of the agora. The residents walked out, not in a hurry, but slowly, and quietly. Like the people before, they, too, carried no torch.

Diotima put a quiet hand on my left arm to get my attention. Then she nodded to our left.

Apollo's Rest was invisible from our cottage. There was no window in the wall that faced that way; but from outside we could see the flicker of light within, from the gaps in the shutters of the building, and from the cracks around the door.

The inn door opened briefly and the people disappeared inside.

More people came from down the road, from the direction of the fisher huts. They, too, slipped into Apollo's Rest.

"It's a town meeting," Diotima whispered in wonder. "Why bother going to such lengths if the whole town's there?"

"I don't think the priests are invited," I whispered back. "If they were, there'd be no need for all this secrecy."

"Unless whatever secret they're keeping, they're hiding from you and me," Diotima whispered back.

Apollo's Rest was on the opposite side of the open space to our cottage. We crossed quickly, to reduce the chances of being stumbled upon by a late arrival. We crept toward the inn, careful to keep our backs to the cottage, so that our silhouettes would not stand out. I looked for any guards they might have left outside, but I saw none.

There was a large window around the corner from the door. We went there, just in case someone came outside. The door was firmly shut and all the windows were shuttered, but by creeping up and peering between the wooden slats we were able to see inside.

Diotima and I crouched side by side, with our eyes as close as we could get them to the lowest of the gaps in the side window.

Within was a tableau of the villagers; it might almost have been a mural, the way they were arranged. They sat in a semicircle. Damon stood at one end of the arc, Moira at the other. It was like they were the mother and father of the village. Between them was virtually every villager that Damon had introduced to us. There was not a single priest or priestess to be seen, excepting Meren, who sat amongst them.

At the center of the semicircle was the bar, and at the bar was a man, one of the fishermen, with a beer in his left hand. His right hand he waved about as he held forth to the crowd. From the way he moved I guessed he'd already had at least one mug of wine.

"The killing has endangered us all," he said.

"That's hardly our fault," Moira said. "We must endure the inquiries. Then we can get on with our lives."

"Aye, and what if they find out?" the man with the wine said. "What will happen to us?"

He drank from his cup, drained it, and refilled.

"The priests don't suspect," Meren said, from where she sat. "If they did, I'm sure I'd know of it."

"How?" the man demanded. "Do the priests tell you all their secrets?"

"No, but you can tell," Meren said. "The way they talk, the way their eyes move when we're about. They don't know. If they did, they'd be watching us all more carefully."

"What of the investigators?" another asked. "The Athenian priestess and the other."

"They have no idea what is going on," Damon said. "I've seen to that."

"This detective-priestess is a great danger," the man with the wine insisted.

"I don't see why," Damon replied, with his usual reasonable and mild tone. "The priestess is inconvenient, to be sure, but no more than that."

They were talking about Diotima. I was mildly offended that I wasn't inconvenient too.

"Then we're in the clear," the second man said.

"For now," Damon agreed.

The man who had been speaking sat down, which he did by dropping onto a crowded bench and making room by force. Then he suddenly stood up again and lurched toward the door. Inasmuch as he had been drinking non-stop and was likely already onto his third wine, the reason was clear enough.

Moira took the floor. She held a wax tablet in one hand and a stylus in the other. She made a final note on the tablet before she began to speak.

"Let's move on to the finances," she said. "The gift fund is in good shape, but contributions are due."

There were groans all round.

"Oh, come now," she said, without heat, indeed she sounded good-natured. I got the impression this was the usual response. "You know we owe the Goddess for our good fortune."

"Not exactly good fortune at the moment," someone complained.

"Hey, are you warm?" Damon asked sternly.

"Sure," said the complainant. He sounded defensive.

"Then it's good fortune, isn't it?" Damon said.

A stream of urine suddenly splattered between me and Diotima. I started; so did she. We had both been so intent on what we were seeing that we hadn't noticed the drunk fisherman walk up from behind and raise his tunic. Now he was peeing on us.

"Hey!" he exclaimed. He couldn't have failed to see us.

A hand grabbed me around the neck. It was a rough hand, covered in callouses. From the way she struggled I knew Diotima was caught too.

"Let go!" That was Diotima.

He might have been drunk, but this fellow was very strong. I thought about fighting back, but then realized I couldn't fight the entire village. Through the cracks I could see every head inside had turned in our direction.

I felt myself raised up and was marched toward the door, out of which the villagers were streaming.

"Look what I found!" our captor bellowed.

"Shhh," Moira said. "Bring them inside."

Diotima and I were pushed within. We stood in the center of their circle. The villagers stared at us with blank expressions. It was more unnerving than if they'd been angry.

"All right, so you have us," I said. "Do what you will with me, but don't hurt Diotima."

They looked surprised.

"She's a priestess of Artemis," Moira said. "We can't hurt her."

Every head nodded in agreement.

I breathed a sigh of relief.

"Then you're going to let us go," I said.

"Oh, we can't do that," Damon said. He turned to his fellow villagers. "What do you think?"

There was thoughtful silence for a moment. Then someone said, "Maybe if we transport them somewhere far away?"

"What?" I said, alarmed.

"You'd tell."

"Tell what?" I said. "That the villagers meet at the tavern in the dead of night? It's weird, but it's not a crime."

"Nico, there's something they're hiding," Diotima said. She turned to Damon. "Tell me, what is it you don't want the priests to know?"

Damon threw his arms up in the air in a gesture of exasperation. "See? That's exactly the problem, you with all your questions. You know too much. I like the transport idea. Maybe if we put you on a boat to . . . oh, I don't know . . . maybe through the Pillars of Heracles? You'd never get back from there."

"This is ridiculous," I said. "If you haven't committed a crime then you have nothing to fear."

"You'd be wrong about that," Damon commented mildly.

"What then? Is this about the theft of the treasure?"

One of the men spat on the floor. "Who cares about that?" he said. "We certainly don't."

"He's right," Damon said. "The treasure is only money. We're worried about something much more holy."

"What then?"

"I get it," Diotima said. "Moira talked about a gift fund."

Damon nodded. "Diotima has it. You asked before what it is that we don't want the priests to know."

"Yes."

"Ask again," he said.

"All right," Diotima said. "What are you hiding that is so serious it must be desperately protected from our priests?"

Damon laughed in that simple way of his. "It's very simple, Nico and Diotima."

He swept his arm across the assembly.

"We are the Hyperboreans."

THE HYPERBOREAN PROBLEM

"IT BEGAN LONG ago, in the days of my great-great-grandfather," Damon said. "He was the chief of our people. Our priestess, who was called Karin, came to him one day and announced that she had received a vision sent by our Goddess. The Goddess spoke to Karin and told her that in the land of the Hellenes she was worshipped with the name Artemis. She commanded Karin to carry gifts of worship to her faraway temple."

"The tale of the Hyperborean women," Diotima said. "Meren told us."

"Meren told you true," Damon said. "Except for one little detail. Karin and her friend didn't die of illness. They liked it here so much that they decided to stay. They adopted Hellene names and settled on Delos."

"Were your people angry?" Diotima asked.

"The people were upset at first, but when the guards explained what it was like here, how warm and lovely, the people understood. Over time, others departed to see this fabled land of Delos. They didn't return either, but sent back word that they had settled in the village, pretending to be Hellenes, and learned how to fish.

"In all that time, we continued the tradition of sending the Gift to Delos, and hid letters to our distant relatives in amongst the Gifts."

"How very remarkable," Diotima said.

"When my father inherited the chieftainship, he decided to move the entire tribe."

"Didn't the people on Delos notice?" I asked.

"We arrived in ones and twos, or a family at a time. People move between the islands all the time, you know? We adopted Hellene names, the Hellene way of life. Well, after we were all here we knew, we must keep giving the Gift, in thanks to our Goddess who had shown us the way here."

"Then you're the Chief of the Hyperboreans?" I said to Damon.

"I am."

"You've never been tempted to go back home?" I asked.

"You're joking, aren't you? We could stay in our native land, where in winter we need a pickaxe to break the water out of the buckets, or we could move here."

"I see your point," I said.

"Of course, we have to worry about sunburn, which wasn't much of an issue back home," he allowed. "But that's a price we'll willingly pay to avoid having our balls freeze off."

"A very reasonable attitude."

"The problem is, if the priests find out, they'll throw us off the island."

"I don't see why," I said.

"We're not even Hellene," Meren pointed out. "Strictly speaking, I don't belong here."

"Oh." I hadn't thought of that. "That *is* a problem," I said, because everyone knew Hellene temples could only be served by Hellenes.

"Meren is our priestess," Damon said. "It made sense to get her to join the Hellene temple, since it's the temple of our Goddess too."

"Very clever," Diotima said.

"Besides," Meren said, "it means I can tend to Great Aunt Karin."

I began to say, "Who?"

"You mean the priestess who brought the First Gift?" Diotima asked.

Moira nodded. "One of them is Meren's distant relative. We say great aunt, but it's more probably great-great-great aunt."

"Ladies and gentlemen," I said. "You don't need to transport us anywhere."

"I suppose you're going to promise not to tell anyone," Moira said skeptically.

"No, I'm going to promise to tell Anaxinos, eventually."

"We'll have you on the first ship out," Damon said.

"No, listen to me first." I sweated a little, despite the time of night. "Pericles wants the treasure of the Delian League—"

"We've already said we don't care about that—"

"And he doesn't care that you're the Hyperboreans," I interrupted. "Trust me, Pericles is not exactly the most religious of men."

"So?"

"So anything that gets him what he wants is fine with him. If I tell Pericles that you were instrumental to solving this case, and if I tell him that you are necessary to the stability of Delos, then Pericles will force Anaxinos to accept you."

"Hmm," Damon and Moira both said at the same time. Damon added, "Anaxinos won't like you for that."

"Anaxinos already hates Athens, and I don't think he's too keen on me anyway."

"I will add to that," Diotima said. "I think if you went

to the High Priest and told him your story, you might find him a little more flexible than you expect."

"I doubt it," Moira said.

"You might not know that Anaxinos has a history of being destitute and homeless," Diotima said. "I think he would listen to you with favor." She hesitated, then added, "Also, without Geros here, it will be easier for him to show ecumenical leniency."

"That's the truth," Meren said.

Damon's and Moira's eyes met. Something passed between them. Then Damon took a reaction from the Hyperboreans. Here and there I saw slight nods.

"All right, you stay for now," Damon said. "As to talking to anyone else, you don't say a word until I say you can."

"Fair enough."

"And remember this, Nico. I like you, but we'll all be watching you."

"Got it."

THE OVER-ENTHUSIASTIC
ASSISTANT

DIOTIMA SLEPT IN. I let her. She was so exhausted by everything that had happened the day before, I was worried she might fall ill if she kept up the pace.

So I tiptoed out of the cottage and made my way to Apollo's Rest.

"Kalimera, Moira."

She looked at me suspiciously. "Kalimera," she replied.

I put coins on the bar, more than were needed.

"Breakfast for me, please, and could you keep an eye on the cottage? When Diotima's awake, could you bring her your best breakfast, please? She's eating a lot at the moment."

"Aye," Moira said. "I know how that works."

She began to ladle out a lentil stew and yesterday's bread for me to eat.

I put more coins on the bar.

"You already paid," she said.

"That's for your gift fund," I told her. "That's how it works, isn't it? That's what you were talking about last night. You Hyper . . . er . . ." I looked around to make sure no priest was listening, but we were alone. "That is, you nice people keep a common fund, from which each year you buy your gift for Artemis."

"That's it," Moira acknowledged. "Everyone contributes. You caught me last night telling people that the contributions are due. We've got a few skinflints who need to be reminded once or twice, or three times . . ."

She put the bowl in front of me, and I immediately began scooping it in. I was starving. I said, between mouthfuls, "I suppose that means you're quite good at accounting."

"Not like that Karnon along the way, if that's what you're thinking," Moira said. "The man's like a demigod of coins."

"I know what you mean."

I finished the bowl, thought about buying a second, and decided I could steal food from the Athenian camp instead, because that was where I was headed. I had had an idea the other day that, until now, I hadn't had a chance to check. It was something for which I couldn't bring my wife. This was the perfect moment.

I left Apollo's Rest, and saw the village doctor crossing the agora. He was a tall man with a loping stride, difficult to miss. I hailed him. He stopped and waited for me to catch up.

"I don't do free consultations," he warned me immediately.

"I'm not ill," I told him. "Doctor, I wanted to ask you about Geros's body."

He looked at me oddly. "You're interested in dead bodies?" he asked.

"Well . . . yes."

"That is probably the most bizarre thing I've heard this year."

"Is it possible for someone who has been stabbed in the heart to write a word in blood before they die?" I asked. We needed to know if perhaps Geros had written that final word Nemesis as a message to us.

"It's absolutely impossible," the doctor said. "Of course,

some wounds that look like they went through the heart can miss by a fraction. In that case, your victim might live long enough for a final message."

That was good to know. But had the knife cut Geros's heart?

"Could you look at Geros and recognize if his wound was instantly fatal?" I asked.

The doctor snorted derision. "I doubt it. Do you know how many dead bodies I've seen since I moved to Delos?"

"No?"

"Not one," he declared. "Not a single one. Because it's illegal to die here." He patted his brow with a clean rag. "You have no idea how stressful that is."

"Why?" I asked, puzzled.

"Anywhere else in the world, and I mean *anywhere*, it's no big deal if a doctor accidentally kills a patient, right?" The doctor spoke imploringly, as if he needed my understanding. I felt I should nod, so I did. "I mean, it happens all the time, and no one ever complains."

"Er . . . perhaps the dead man?"

"They don't tend to say much, and the families understand that nothing is ever certain in medicine."

"I understand."

"*You* might understand, but the priests who run this island certainly don't. Whenever there's a risk of some seriously ill person dying, I have the priests shouting at me, demanding that no one is to die on Delos." The sweat ran freely. He patted his brow again. "I say priests, but Geros was the main offender. Perhaps now I'll have some peace and quiet while I deal with the sick."

"I suppose that means you're not very good with child-births either," I said.

"I'm probably a little bit rusty," he allowed. "The last

time I delivered a baby was . . ." He counted on his fingers. "Thirty years ago?" He answered my question with the sort of rising inflection that made me think it might have been forty years rather than thirty.

"Thank you, Doctor."

"See me if you need anything amputated. I might be weak on babies, but I'm damned good with an axe. Good day to you."

He strode off.

This, and his wild talk about accidentally killing patients, didn't instill any confidence in me that the doctor could help Diotima if the baby started to come while we were here.

That was bad news. We had completely overstayed our welcome. Diotima was yet to perform the ceremony she'd been sent to do. The investigation had seen to that. We couldn't leave until the murderer was caught.

I did some counting on my own fingers, and calculated that the baby was due soon.

I FOUND PHILIPOS exactly where I expected to find him: loitering close by Pericles's tent. He was sitting on a camp stool, with a knife in his right hand and a piece of driftwood in his left. He was carving the wood.

Even on the Holy Isle, Philipos managed to have an air of the military about him. Perhaps it was his closely shorn hair. Men who wore helmets often tended to cut their hair short, to fit easily beneath the metal and leather. His neck was thick, the sign of a man who often carried weight on his back, his body was stocky, and the skin of his face had the broken veins of a man who had spent years marching under a hot sun. Now he was doing what military men spent most of their time doing: he was waiting.

Philipos wasn't alone in his idleness. All up and down the narrow beach, Athenian sailors lay on the sand, in the shade of the boats they sailed, getting some sleep, or idly talking.

Ever since the debacle of the first night, the Athenians had kept away from the locals. After the death of Geros, Pericles had made this official, giving the men strict orders to avoid contact.

"Anything that makes matters worse has to be avoided," Pericles had told the men. "Don't let a fight start."

So the Athenians had been lying around, bored.

I said to Philipos, "You must be as bored as the common men. Have you had a look around the island?"

He shook his head. "I've stayed right here. You never know when Pericles might need me," he explained.

"Sure," I said, not believing that for a moment. "So you haven't been in to see the village?"

"No."

"Nor the temples?"

"Not except for the night of the protest." He looked at me oddly. "Why do you care? Aren't you supposed to be solving this murder? I suppose you know that you're holding up Pericles with all the time you're taking."

"*I'm* holding up Pericles?" I said, astonished.

"Of course you are," Philipos said. "Every moment you waste on this dead priest is time we could have spent moving the treasure. People are getting antsy, Nicolaos, and it's your fault. You need to get a move on."

"Those men don't look particularly antsy to me." I pointed at the long row of dozing sailors. "The men are getting paid a drachma a day to lie in the sun and sleep," I pointed out. "Do you see anyone complaining?"

"Did you know that some of the men formed a party and started walking toward the village in search of women?"

"Urrk," I managed to splutter. That would have been a disaster.

Philipos nodded. "I got word of it and alerted Pericles. He reached them before the men were halfway there. He turned them back." He paused. "That's why I'm alone here," he said. "The men know it was me who reported them."

Now that he mentioned it, there was a considerable gap between Philipos and the other Athenians.

Nobody likes a snitch, but this was Philipos all over. He had done the right thing in the wrong way. Instead of using his natural authority, he had gone to Pericles. If he had confronted those men himself he might have won their respect.

"The men might not want to talk to you, but I do," I said. "Let's go for a walk."

"Where to?" he asked suspiciously. "The last time you went for a walk with someone, they ended up dead."

"You don't think I did it, do you?" I said, incredulous.

"What am I supposed to think?" Philipos looked left and right in a most calculating way. Then he hissed, "I know what your real mission was. You don't have to lie to me, Nicolaos."

I had no idea what he was talking about. "Do you want to explain that?"

"You know I can't. Not here!" he said. "What if they find out?"

"Who?" I asked.

"Them! Everyone!" He waved his arms about wildly.

I wondered if Philipos had always been insane, and I just hadn't noticed. Even so, what I needed to say required privacy.

"Why don't we go for that walk?" I said.

"And what if I don't come back?" Philipos demanded.

"Then everyone will know I did it." I pointed down the beach, where the entire row of bored sailors had turned their heads our way. "Half the Navy is watching us."

That was in fact the reason why I wanted to get Philipos away. What I had to say wasn't for anyone else's ears.

"Very well," he said reluctantly.

Philipos picked himself up off the stool, with evident effort. There was only one way to go from where we were that didn't involve walking through crowds, and that was north, towards the scene of the crime. The coast on this stretch of Delos had sand, but it was a surprisingly narrow strip. The feet didn't sink in; it was easy to walk upon.

We walked in silence for some time. Philipos wasn't feeling talkative, it seemed. He was favoring his left foot. This was what I'd seen before, and it was the reason I needed to see him. He hadn't been limping when we arrived on Delos.

"How did you hurt yourself?" I asked.

"Twisted my ankle on that path to the village," Philipos said. "It's not as easy as it looks, in the dark."

I could sympathize, but there was a problem. "Didn't you tell me that you hadn't visited the village?"

Philipos negotiated an unstable stone upon the sand before he replied, "I didn't go all the way there."

"That seems strange."

"I turned around after I hurt my ankle," he said.

"Now there's a funny thing, Philipos," I said. "Because I've lost count of the number of times I've walked up and down that Sacred Way, and I can tell you it's the flattest track on this whole island."

Philipos shrugged. "I'm clumsy."

"You? An army man who regularly walks night marches?" I scoffed.

"I don't know what you expect me to say," Philipos said, becoming angry. "It's the truth."

"It's a lie," I said confidently. "But I know a place where it's easy to hurt yourself in the dark—the same place where I banged my foot into the wall—the area north of the sanctuary."

"I didn't walk into your accursed wall," Philipos said. "My foot slipped. It could happen to anyone."

"You're right, it could happen to anyone, and the place it's most likely to happen is the old graveyard. I noticed it myself. The graveyard is uneven, there are fallen stele all over the place. Some of those funeral monuments have broken up and there are round stones to snap an ankle. The place is just perfect for hurting yourself in the dark."

"So?"

"So that's where you hurt yourself," I said. "The only question is, when were you in the graveyard, Philipos?"

He said nothing.

"It must have been before Geros was killed," I wheedled. "When I summoned Pericles to the body, you came with him, and you were hobbling badly then. The ankle looks a bit better now, less swollen. I'll bet you'd only recently hurt it, when I saw you after I discovered the body."

By this time we had walked so far that we were in sight of the abandoned village. Philipos suddenly stopped. He looked down, kicked the sandy grit with his good right foot, and said, "All right, I admit it. I was there. I followed you that night. I saw you wait around on the steps of the Oikos. I saw you follow that old priest. When you followed him, I followed you."

"I didn't see you."

"It's like you said. I've spent more time in the army

than you. I've had more practice at tracking people in the night."

"Why did you follow me?"

"I wasn't, really. The man I wanted to follow was the priest. But after I saw you move, I could hardly let myself get in front, could I? You would have seen me. I had to trust that you knew what you were doing, that you wouldn't lose him." Philipos had fallen instinctively into his army role. He spoke to me like an officer to a difficult soldier. "Then you ran into that wall. It ruined my plan," he said accusingly.

"Sorry about that."

"It's a wonder your scream didn't bring everyone running," he said.

"I didn't scream."

"Yes you did." He smirked. "I realized before you did that the priest had turned left. I jumped the wall and followed until I reached that graveyard. But like you, I'd lost him. I hid behind one of the funeral stele, waiting to see if I could pick him up. Then I saw a light." Philipos pointed at the village. "It was coming from there."

That must be the same light that I had seen. It occurred to me that Diotima and I hadn't paid enough attention to that light. Who had made it? It seemed that not only had Geros been walking about in the dead of night, as had I and Philipos, but there had been a *fourth* person in what was supposed to be an abandoned part of the island.

"Very well then, Philipos," I said, "Now tell me what in Hades you thought you were doing, following me in the night."

"I told you," he said. "I wasn't following you, I was following Geros."

"Yes, but why?"

"To kill him, of course."

I put my head in my hands. "You're admitting to the murder?"

Philipos hung his head low. "No, I failed."

"In the names of all the gods, what on earth were you thinking?" I had to prevent myself from shouting.

"Pericles said it himself," Philipos said defensively. "Who will rid me of this priest?"

"He didn't mean it!"

"How was I to know that?"

I sighed.

"Besides," Philipos added, "I knew perfectly well you'd been sent to kill the old priest."

"I did no such thing!"

"There's no point lying, Nicolaos," said Philipos. "I heard Pericles give you the order. I approached when the two of you were talking together, remember?"

I had to think back to recall. Yes, Philipos had come up to warn Pericles about the approaching lambs.

"I remember. Go on."

Philipos drew in a breath. "As I walked up, I overheard Pericles tell you to deal with Geros. Deal with! Those were his exact words. There's no point trying to deny it," he finished in a conspiratorial whisper. "It's all right, Nicolaos, I won't tell anyone."

So that was the problem. A coincidence of two phrases from Pericles, both innocent. Well, mostly innocent, if you didn't count corruption and bribery. Philipos had heard the words out of context. He'd heard an order to kill.

"I figured it may as well be me who did it instead of you." Philipos shrugged.

"You enjoy killing people?" I asked.

"No. Even on a battlefield I never liked it much." He sounded unhappy to admit it.

"I'm not surprised," I said gently. "I've known real assassins, Philipos, men who enjoy it, and let me tell you, you're no assassin."

"Well, I've discovered that," he said. "But there's no need to rub it in."

"There's nothing to rub," I said. "Assassination is not fun. It's not even exciting. Mostly it's just scary."

"How would you know?"

"I know, trust me."

Philipos shot me a look. I stared back, daring him to ask the next question.

"There's the problem," he mumbled. "You know that, and I don't."

"I don't understand you, Philipos. You thought I was going to eliminate Geros, you thought the job was going to get done anyway, and yet you took an enormous risk to do something that wasn't your problem?" I paused, to let that sink in, then asked the burning question. "Why?"

Philipos looked away. "Pericles is a genius," he said.

"That's debatable," I told him, "But either way it doesn't answer the question."

"Yes it does," he replied with some heat. "As a man, I'm nothing special."

He paused, waiting for me to argue with his modest self-opinion.

I didn't.

Philipos glared at me and went on. "Pericles is guiding Athens. Have you not seen how much greater our city has become since he became our leader?"

I nodded.

"Then there is Aeschylus, who writes plays; and that Sophocles fellow too," said Philipos. His voice had quickened and his words held belief. "They are great writers.

Then there are all those philosophers with their thoughts, and the sculptors and the artists and Callias the diplomat. I am nothing special, but I am surrounded by all these great men who are changing the world. Men like you."

"Me!"

"You. Who does Pericles send on all the most important missions? I hang around his house, and he sends me on errands. He could ask me to do something important—I would do it!—but when something important comes up, something that needs a man of action, he turns to me and says, 'Send for Nicolaos.' Why not me? I'm not a statesman or a philosopher or an artist or anything like that, but I could do the job you do. Why doesn't Pericles ask me to be the agent?"

"You want *my* job?" I said, astounded.

"See?" he said bitterly. "You think I can't do it."

"No, I think you're insane," I said with considerable feeling. "Is that why you went to murder Geros? To prove you could do what I do?"

"Yes," Philipos said in a near whisper.

"I'll make a deal with you," I said. "From now on you can do all the dirty work that Pericles dumps on me."

"What?" he said, surprised. "I'm to be Pericles's agent?"

"Yes. You're welcome to it." The moment I said it, I felt a weight lift from my shoulders.

"Do you really mean that?" he asked suspiciously.

"I really mean it," I told him.

The fact was that I had already been thinking about quitting. I had been badly shaken when Diotima asked me to look after the baby if she died in childbed. I wouldn't admit it, not even to her, because it would imply less than perfect confidence, but I was terrified that she wasn't going to make it. If I couldn't admit it to my wife, I could at least admit it to myself.

A man with children to raise has no business risking his life day after day. I had reached the happy position that I didn't need Pericles's money to make my way. The rewards from previous jobs had seen to that. It was time to get out.

Philipos smiled when he realized that I meant it. I felt it only fair to wipe that smile off his face at once.

"The job's yours. But I'm warning you, Philipos, you won't like it."

"What does it involve?" he asked.

"Mostly it involves getting beaten, stabbed, kicked, punched, and spat on, and when you get the job done a thank you from Pericles and a protracted fight to make him pay you for services rendered."

"You're trying to talk me out of it," he said accusingly.

"You'll learn, soon enough," I promised him, thinking it was going to be fun watching Philipos discover reality. "In the meantime, you can tell me what went wrong with your murder plan."

"I fell into a hole," he said, shamefaced.

I had to suppress a laugh, but Philipos saw my expression.

"Well, you can't laugh. You kicked a wall," he said. "I saw you. It's not like I did anything worse."

"True enough," I said, and now I grinned. "So neither of us has a future as a dark assassin. What was this hole you fell in?"

"An open grave, in the graveyard. I went straight in and twisted my ankle when I landed. It hurt a lot. I could feel the ankle swelling." He gestured at the wrapping around his leg. "Well, you see it now. I decided if I couldn't make a fast getaway then I would have to abandon the attempt."

"Very wise."

"I climbed out, only to see you trailing after the priest."

"You saw me again?"

"I said so, didn't I? Geros was on his way to the village. I saw him go amongst the buildings. I abandoned my attempt. Then I saw you. I hit the dirt and lay still. You almost walked on me, you know. You're not very observant in the dark."

I decided not to rise to that. "What then?"

"I made my way back to camp, staying along the water's edge to avoid being spotted."

"Did you see Geros leave?"

"How could I? I was heading back to the fleet while you were still hunting him down to kill him."

"All right, then what did you do?" I asked.

"Went back to the camp, where you saw me."

Philipos's story made perfect sense. The only problem was, with only the smallest change in the details, he could have waited for me to leave, killed Geros on his way through the graveyard, left the body lying where I found it, and then returned to camp before I got there. Which would make it look like I killed the priest, which was what half the other priests thought anyway. Philipos could have twisted his ankle at almost any place on this island and at almost any time.

"Does this mean I'm your assistant now?" Philipos asked as we trudged back to the Athenians.

I thought about it. I still didn't trust Philipos. If there was any Athenian who could have killed Geros, it was certainly him. But his air of general incompetence suggested otherwise, and if he was acting, then he was doing a fine job of fooling me. Besides which, if I took him on, and he tried to ruin the investigation, then that would be a sure sign that he was the killer. All in all, I thought this might be a good test. I would find him a job that was important, but easily checked.

"Apprentice," I said firmly. "You're an apprentice. You have to start from the ground up, you know."

"Oh yes, of course. What do I do first?"

I tried to think of something that would keep him out of the way.

"There are boat marks in the sand, next to the Old Village. Go check them, will you? They might be eroded. Here are the measurements of the indents in the sand, from when we first saw them." I handed Philipos the shreds of tunic that I had used to record the lengths.

He frowned. "This seems very simple," he said.

"Now here's the fun part. When you've done that, find out which boat on this island made the marks."

"That seems impossible," he said.

"Nonsense," I said briskly. "Any decent apprentice could do it."

I thought to myself that would keep him busy for a while.

"NICO, WHAT IS it?" Diotima asked, when I walked in the cottage door. "You let me sleep in! What happened?"

"Add Philipos to your list of suspects," I said. "And by the way, he is now my apprentice."

"You're babbling." Diotima put a concerned hand to my forehead. "You don't feel feverish. Have you been drinking?"

She smelled my breath.

"Hear me out."

I told her everything that had happened. It was a surprisingly long tale. When I finished, Diotima fixated on the point most important to her.

"You're handing your agent work to Philipos?" she said. She was clearly dubious about that idea.

"We don't need it anymore," I told her.

"How will we pay for things?" she asked.

"Do you know how much money we've saved?" I asked her.

"I have no idea," she said.

Diotima had never paid attention to the family finances. My wife was a priestess first, a philosopher second, and an author third. None of those jobs involved large sums of money.

"We have the farm that Pericles gave me," I said.

"It's minute," she pointed out.

"It makes a small living," I allowed. "Father was pleased enough with the farm that he let me remain an investigator, rather than require me to join him as a sculptor."

"A good thing, too," my wife said. "You'd make a rotten sculptor."

While my father lived, he was the head of the family. As a sculptor he made enough to get by, but it wasn't much. My mother was a midwife, and that supplemented the family income. In recent years I had become the major earner, as a good son should. What pleased me enormously was that I'd managed to do this with the work I wanted, as an agent and an investigator.

"Then there's the money promised by the Egyptian public service," I said.

"I'll believe in that when I see it," Diotima said.

On our previous assignment I had been promised a very large reward from the head of the public service in the land of Egypt. That money hadn't arrived; Diotima was right to be skeptical, but I thought it worth mentioning, before I made the most important argument.

"I am now earning more money from commissions for private citizens than I am from Pericles," I said. "Do you realize that the work we do for the state—under commission for Pericles—pays us the least, but is the most dangerous?"

This was the essential point I needed to make Diotima understand. Since I had begun work for Pericles my name had become known. Other men, private citizens of Athens, had from time to time come to me with problems that had nothing to do with the state or the good of Athens. At first those jobs had been a small trickle, trivial issues like missing sons (usually run off with an inappropriate girl), neighbor disputes (it was astonishing how often men quietly moved boundary stones and tried to get away with it), and agricultural arguments ("He stole my best goat"). These were barely noticeable as a source of coins, but over the years the trickle had become a steady stream. The little jobs had led to more lucrative ones ("My business partner is stealing from me"; "Someone stole my boat"). I was now earning more from my private practice than from work for the state. What was most important, those private commissions were always family squabbles, or business matters—much less likely to get me killed than my work for Pericles, which was invariably fatal for someone. I was aware that I was starting to push my luck.

"I see," Diotima chewed her lower lip, a sure sign that she was thinking hard. "You're right, Nico, but can Philipos do the work?"

"Do we care?" I countered.

"What will Pericles say?"

That was a good question.

"Pericles can't force me to take his commissions," I said confidently.

"Hmm." Diotima had her own views on that. "Should I point out that you've made a major suspect your apprentice?"

"What better way to maintain tabs on a suspect than to keep him close to us?" I said.

"I can think of several better ways," Diotima said. "Also, he must be the oldest apprentice in the history of Athens. Do you think he did it?"

I paused before saying, "He's given us enough evidence to prosecute him, if we wanted, and I doubt he could defend himself in a trial. As far as we know, nobody saw Geros alive after Philipos's adventure in the graveyard, and what's more, he exactly fits your motive scheme of an Athenian who didn't know that the fix was in."

"Then it's very possible he is the murderer," Diotima said.

"Yes, it's possible," I agreed. "We'll have to be very, very careful around him." I glanced at the position of the sun. "We need to go." Time was flying away on us.

"What do you make of Philipos's story of the open grave?" Diotima asked, as she rode and I walked along the Sacred Way for the umpteenth time.

"It's bizarre," I said. "It doesn't make sense."

"Yes," Diotima agreed. "Why mention such a thing if he's the killer? He could have invented a loose stone to trip on. Everyone would believe that."

"Why mention it if he isn't guilty?" I replied. "You're the detective, my dear. You'll have to decide."

There was a knock at the door. I opened it to see a man I recognized. It was the slave whom I had commandeered on the morning that Geros had been murdered, the one I sent to take the news of the disaster to Anaxinos.

"I have a message from Karnon," he said.

"Yes?" I waited for him to tell it to me. Instead, he handed over an *ostrakon*, a broken piece of pottery into which a message had been scratched. It said, "Come at once. Disaster."

The slave led us to the Oikos of the Naxians. Inside,

Karnon was pacing ferociously back and forth. He alternately swung his arms behind his back, then clenched them in front again in angst.

What could have caused such agitation? I could think of only one answer.

"Who's dead?" I asked.

"No one," he replied. He stopped pacing, but could barely stand still. "It's worse than murder."

"What could be worse than that?" Diotima asked.

Karnon stared at us in abject horror. "We've been robbed."

THE GREAT TEMPLE ROBBERY

"**A**FTER WE SPOKE, I thought I should continue my accounting of the treasure," Karnon said. "I wanted to be absolutely sure that I had my sums right before anyone moved a drachma."

Karnon had led us to the Porinos Naos, the temple in which the fighting funds were stored.

"And?" Diotima prompted.

"And the loose change boxes all came up correct. But with the enclosed boxes, they are numbered and weighed. That's the fastest way to get a quick estimate, you know."

"I understand."

"The boxes came up with the right weights, but . . ." Karnon gulped, and nodded at his slave, the one who had summoned us. "But Hermes here noticed that one of them had a loose top. That's not so surprising, because these things are extremely heavy. Do you recall that I said the loose change is in coins, but the long term storage is all precious metal?"

"Yes."

"Those cases break open quite easily. They're small, to cope with the weight, but only made of pinewood. It wouldn't be the first time someone dropped a case and it splintered to pieces. The slaves hauled out the broken case and called me over to witness. Whenever a case is to be opened, I must be present. It's an absolute rule, the breaking of which is punishable by death. You can imagine why."

"The guards were present too?" I asked.

"Of course. Also the village carpenter, to repair the casing. He makes most of the cases, by the way, using imported wood." Karnon paused. He looked like he was gasping for air. "When we opened the lid we found . . . lead." He almost sobbed at that word. "I immediately ordered all the boxes opened. There are two others with missing money."

"Did you call for Anaxinos?" Diotima asked.

"Not yet, but he'll know at any moment, of course. There are too many talkative people who know the truth. What I want to avoid, if at all possible, is for Pericles to find out before we know where the money is."

"Yes," I said with feeling. "Believe me, Karnon, I know exactly what it's like to incur Pericles's wrath."

"How much is missing?" Diotima asked.

"As near as I can make out, it's on the order of thirty talents," Karnon said grimly.

That number sounded oddly familiar. Where had I heard that recently?

When I remembered, the pit of my stomach felt like it had fallen through the floor. Thirty talents was the amount that Geros had demanded from Pericles, to hand over the treasure.

I said, "Uh, Karnon, how long has this money been missing?"

"I don't know."

"Bring the torch over here," Diotima said. She was inspecting the cases of gold bars. "Have you noticed everything on Delos is very dusty?" she said, then added quickly, "Except for your home, Karnon, which is immaculate—"

"That is Marika's fine work," Karnon said. "She comments all the time about how hard it is to keep the grit outside, especially with the boys."

"Right," Diotima said. "Apollo's Rest is clean too. Everything else on this island is caked in dust. Even in this apparently enclosed temple."

She wiped her finger across one of the undisturbed boxes. The dust was thick indeed. "I imagine it gets in through the gaps between the roof and the walls. Now look here." She pointed out the tops of the three cases that the slaves had opened.

"This one's dusty." Diotima swiped a finger. There was dust, though not as much as on the tops of the other cases. Diotima took the torch from Karnon and held it close to the second case.

"This one has some dust, but look, you can see where there are the remains of hand prints."

You could indeed.

"This case was disturbed long enough ago that dust has settled over, but not as much," Diotima said. "Now this one . . ." She moved to the third. "This one has large swipes across it that are still clear."

"What does this mean?" Karnon asked.

"It means we're looking at three thefts, not one," Diotima said. "The same person has been here three times, taken treasure, replaced it with lead so you wouldn't notice the difference, and then departed."

"Why take such a risk three times?" Karnon asked.

"How much do these cases weigh?" I asked.

"Lift one," said Karnon.

The cases were much alike, unsurprisingly, since Karnon had said the same carpenter made them. There were rope handles at both ends. I took the handles and lifted. The case was heavy, but not so heavy that I couldn't raise it. I put down the box, with a slight clang of the gold bars within, then lifted two boxes, one on top of the other. That was an effort. I could manage three, but not comfortably.

"You are strong," Karnon commented.

"My father is a sculptor," I explained. "I've been carrying marble blocks for him since I was young."

"Most men could only carry two at a time," he said. "Even then they'd be struggling. It's not the sort of thing you can sneak out underneath your clothing."

On the face of it, this seemed impossible. Nobody could carry away one of these cases in the light of day without being quite obvious about it. At night, the thieves would be risking all sorts of accidents. I said as much to Karnon and Diotima. Neither could suggest an answer.

"Who has access to the temple?" Diotima asked.

"It varies with the treasury," Karnon said. "Only I have a key to the Porinos Naos. All the other temples are open to the public day and night. Anaxinos and Geros have keys to the other treasuries, I think, but I don't know, it's not my business . . ." Karnon shrugged.

"But someone else could have stolen a key," I said. "Everyone on Delos leaves their houses unlocked."

"I like to think the guards would have stopped anyone else who turned up with a key," Karnon said, with a great deal of practicality.

"That's a very good point," I said. "What about the guards?"

"Obviously they're standing here day and night. But they don't have a key."

Diotima said quietly, "They might not have a key, but they're the *only* two men who could have carried off treasure without being noticed."

We all three instinctively looked to the door. It was firmly shut, and Diotima had spoken softly. I didn't think they had heard us. But the guards could hardly have failed to realize that something was wrong. If they were the thieves then we would be in the greatest danger when we exited the temple.

"If they think we know, they could cut us to pieces the moment we exit," Karnon said as softly as Diotima.

"I wonder what the odds are of getting to Philipos?" I whispered.

"Why?" Diotima whispered back.

"Because he could bring soldiers from the fleet."

"The only way out is through that door." Karnon nodded at the double doors through which we'd entered, on the other side of which were two armed and armored soldiers who were almost certainly expecting trouble, and who knew they faced execution if they were captured.

I fingered my knife. It was all I had.

Diotima grabbed my arm. "Nico, be careful," she said.

Be careful? When I was about to face down two trained *hoplites* in full armor?

I pulled my dagger.

"I'm going with you," Karnon said.

"No, you're not."

He could not have been less than forty, he was an accountant who had probably last served in the army twenty years ago, and though he'd kept himself fit he wouldn't last a heartbeat.

Diotima at least had the sense not to say she was going to fight. In times past she would have raced me to the door, but now she had our baby to protect.

"Karnon, I need you to protect Diotima. Once I'm

through, get her clear of here, and get help. The Athenian fleet has plenty of force."

It was so frustrating. Pericles had turned up with enough men to destroy a small army, and we couldn't use a single one of them until we had won the fight for which we needed them. My plan was the only way: to keep the two guards busy while the other two went for help.

Karnon nodded, reluctantly.

"Be careful, Nico," Diotima repeated.

"Of course I will," I reassured her. Then I wondered how I was supposed to be careful while attacking two armed guards.

Diotima and Karnon took a door handle each, ready to fling open the double doors. I stood behind, my weapon at the ready. I decided I would roll out, to duck under any spears that were thrust my way, then come up and with luck, attack them from behind.

I reached down my leg to take my second fighting blade. Diotima's father was chief of the city guard of Athens. On my very first commission, many years ago, he had torn strips off me for not carrying a backup. Now I always had a second blade strapped to my right ankle. It had saved me more than once.

I looked to Diotima and Karnon and nodded. Diotima silently mouthed, "One, two, three—"

They flung open the doors.

I instantly dived through. I landed in a somersault that I executed perfectly, rolled out of it into a jump during which I turned, ready to stab.

"Yaaahhhh!" I screamed to scare them and pushed the dagger in a blind thrust to catch the first attacker.

My feet touched the ground after my jump. My fighting stance ready to kill.

But nothing happened.

There was no one there. The guards had disappeared.

There were plenty of passersby in the sanctuary grounds though. Every one of them had stopped what they were doing and stared at me as if I were some sort of maniac. One woman was so scared she dropped her bundle of laundry and ran away. Several other women screamed and priests moved to protect them. From me.

I lowered my hands.

Diotima and Karnon appeared at the doorway.

"Where did they go?" Karnon asked the air and anyone who might hear.

"Do you mean the temple guards?" one of the nearby priests said. He edged away from me while warily keeping his eyes on my blade.

"They took off a moment ago. I thought you must have sent them on an urgent mission, Karnon."

"Which way did they go?" Karnon asked.

"That way." The priest pointed down the Sacred Way.

We all looked. In the distance, two men were running away. As we watched they both tossed their spears to the right and their shields to the left, the better to run. They tore off their helmets and flung them aside too.

"After them!"

I started running.

The guards had a good head start. If this were open country I wouldn't have even bothered trying, but on tiny Delos they were going to run out of land very quickly, and then I would have them.

I was sadly out of condition. Married life and no recent hard work had seen to that. I was soon puffing hard. But I was gaining on my targets, which meant they'd been living an even softer life than me. I supposed that being a guard on Delos meant having nothing to do but stand around all day.

The soldiers didn't deviate from the path. That was sensible. They were faster on the road, and they didn't risk a fall on the stony ground. It made my job easier. I settled into a steady pace. The worst thing I could do would be to run out of breath when I caught up with two criminals. Though they were two *stadia* ahead, I knew this could only end one way.

By now we were passing the outlying houses of the New Village. These were the ones in which the priests lived—I hoped that someone would walk out a door and blunder into the guards' path, but no one did. Soon we were past those first homes, into the village proper, and about to enter the agora.

I wondered if they would turn left or right when we reached the agora. Either way we would end up following the rough track that circled Delos. I had a ridiculous vision of the three of us running in loops around the island until we were all too exhausted to move. If nothing else it would entertain the onlookers.

We entered the agora. Moira walked out of Apollo's Rest and was bowled over by the man in the lead. She fell backward, he stumbled, the other man took the lead and they kept on going straight ahead into the sea.

No, not the sea. They diverted at the last instant onto the narrow dock where the fishing boats moored. All the boats but two were out at sea, fishing. Damon was on one of the moored boats, doing the same repairs we'd seen him at the other day. At the other boat was a man unloading catch, and another on the pier accepting the baskets of fish.

The guards charged into the man on the dock. He flew backwards, straight into the water, then came up

spluttering and cursing, his arms flopping wildly backwards in total surprise at the dunking. The guards jumped
into the fisher boat. They landed on either side of the
remaining fisherman, picked him up by an arm each, and
tossed him over the side to join his friend in the water.

That fishing boat was still perfectly set for sailing. The
guards ignored the curses of their victims while they set
the sail. One took the tiller. The other rowed to get them
started.

By then I had reached the dock, but they were already
too far from shore for me to stop them.

I jumped onto the other boat; the one that Damon was
in. He had watched the fracas with total surprise. Now he
stared at me.

I pointed at the two escaping guards. "Follow that boat!"

Damon looked to the struggling fishermen in the water.
He saw that they were hauling their soaked bodies back
onto land. He looked at the stolen boat, now beginning
to catch wind, and then he looked at the fishing boat we
were in.

In a trice Damon hauled up the sail from below the
shallow deck and was threading rope through holes in
the sail.

"Quick, Nico, tie two cringles for the spar!" he ordered
me. "I'll manage the clews."

I looked at him blankly.

"Right," he said, perceiving the problem. "You don't
have a *clew*, do you? Do you know how to row?"

"Sure."

"You better start then." He nodded in the destination of
our receding quarry. "Those two are getting away."

I grabbed the oars from where they had been stored on
each side. I pushed them over the side and began to pull.

As I did, Damon got the sail up single-handed. He stepped on me repeatedly as he did, but I couldn't complain.

I had barely made any distance by the time Damon was settled at the steering oar. He nudged it one way, seemed to consider for a moment, then pushed the other way. The wind suddenly filled the sail and we had speed.

"How do you do that?" I asked.

"I feel the wind on the back of my neck," he said. "I've sailed here for so long that I can predict where it'll come next."

That was one advantage we had. Damon knew the winds and the guards didn't.

Damon asked the question I'd been expecting. "Who are they?" He hadn't recognized the guards beneath the armor, not with so many Athenians on the island too.

I told Damon what had happened at the Porinos Naos. He was shocked. He eyed the other boat with a calculating stare. "They're about to turn to port," he said.

That made sense, because if they turned right they would round the point into fifty Athenian triremes. But Damon had obviously seen something I hadn't. I asked, "How can you tell?"

"From the way they're wobbling, and look, they've both moved to port side too soon."

Sure enough the other boat seemed to stall for a moment. Then it went still as the sail turned dead to wind.

"Now we have them!" I exulted.

"Not unless they're fools," Damon said. "Watch."

We were getting closer as they struggled, until I could see the two of them clearly. The one that had been rowing at the start pushed the oars out once more. He turned the boat by paddling. But the boat was pointing head into the wind, and the wildly flapping sail prevented them from turning any more. The other man had stood up, somewhat shakily. He manually pushed the sail to one side and held it there by main strength. The sail filled with wind, pushed the boat backwards in a curve, which completed the turn, and suddenly they were under way.

"He didn't use the ropes. That's cheating," I complained.

"Yeah, but it works," Damon said.

The stolen boat picked up speed again. Damon with his practiced eye turned our steering oar just a nudge, and our boat began a wide sweep that was faster than the other boat.

We continued in this way for some time, making ground. I knew from past experience that sea chases needed patience: things always seemed to move slowly, but the distance fell away before you knew it. I looked behind, to see that we were far from Delos.

I considered how we would capture those two guards when we reached them, which now we were sure to do. Damon would be a good man in a fight, and I had my daggers. In the sort of dirty fighting that was certain to follow, I with my real-world experience of desperate struggles in back alleys would have the advantage over two common soldiers.

"You know, it's a funny thing, Nico," Damon said breaking in on my thoughts.

"What is?" I asked.

"The other day, when you came by with Diotima, and we had the picnic, you didn't ask me what's wrong with this boat," he said.

"All right, I'll ask. What's wrong with this boat?"

"It's got a leak."

I looked down. Now that he mentioned it, the water in the bottom did seem to be filling.

"Looks like the plug didn't quite work," Damon said with his usual irritatingly happy voice. I was beginning to understand why nothing ever seemed to work on Delos; the doors that never quite fit, the hinges that squeaked. If Damon fixed it, it wasn't likely to stay fixed.

"What do we do?" I asked.

"I think we need another boat," he replied.

I understood what he meant. Our only hope of survival was to take that other boat from the criminals. If we didn't, we would drown.

"Can we reach them in time?" I asked.

Damon shook his head.

The plug failed totally. The wooden stopper popped into the air. I grabbed it in midflight. I immediately tried to push the plug back in, but the pressure of the water that now gushed in was far too strong. That meant the boat was about to sink and we would drown. I reflected this had not been one of my better days.

Our boat rapidly filled with seawater. As it did, the hull began to sway alarmingly with the wash of the sea. The hull sunk until it was below water, which was now up to my waist height. The sway caused the canvas sail to become so wet that it was too heavy to remain upright.

The whole craft slowly, majestically turned over. Damon and I dived out. It was that, or stay where we were and be trapped beneath the hull. I was careful not to swim underneath the descending sail.

The sail entered the water and rotated until it was pointing vertically down, which was the direction I would probably soon be going myself.

The only thing above water now was the bottom of the boat, a tiny island far from safety. Damon and I clambered aboard, with some difficulty because it was covered in slime and barnacles. We sat there, on the upturned hull, tired from the effort and with our skin cut by the barnacles.

I watched as the fishing boat we were chasing, inexpertly handled by two criminals whom I desperately wanted to question, slowly vanished into the distance.

I sighed.

"Can you swim?" Damon asked.

I turned my head to tell Damon I could swim, but not all the way back to shore. Delos was a tiny dot in the distance. Then over Damon's shoulder I saw something behind us.

"We're being followed."

Whatever came our way was barely larger than the dot of Delos, but the small vessel that had begun so far away grew rapidly to become a trireme.

"I think it's one of ours," I said, for the trireme had rounded Delos from the direction in which lay our fleet.

All we could do was sit on the upturned hull and wait to be rescued.

The trireme slowed as it approached. I stood up, unsteadily, upon the bottom of the boat, waved wildly and pointed in the direction our quarry had gone.

A head appeared over the side of the trireme. It was Captain Semnos. This boat was *Paralos*.

"Don't stop!" I shouted. "Chase the other fishing boat!"

"Can you catch a line?" Semnos shouted back.

I wasn't sure what he meant, but I shouted, "Yes." I raised my arms to show that I agreed with whatever Semnos proposed.

A sailor appeared over the edge of the fast-approaching trireme. He held a long rope, which he proceeded to pay into the sea beside him. Soon there was a long line trailing behind *Paralos*. *Paralos*'s path shifted slightly toward us.

Semnos had clearly directed his boat so that it would pass by our crippled vessel.

"Do you want help, Nico?" Damon asked.

"Help to do what?" I asked.

"To grab the line as it passes," Damon said.

So that was what Semnos had said, to which I had agreed.

"I'll be fine," I told Damon confidently. "You go first." I wanted to see how Damon caught the rope.

Damon shrugged. "See you on board then."

At that moment *Paralos* passed by. It was like an enormous, rapidly moving wooden wall that missed us by a hand's breadth. I gasped. Any closer and it would have crushed us. Either the steersman on *Paralos* was supremely skilled, or else Damon and I were incredibly lucky. But by luck or skill, we were still alive.

Now the scary wooden wall had passed us by, and the rope was sliding across our hull. Damon dived after it. He grabbed the rope and was swept across the swell into the distance.

It was my turn.

I licked my lips—they tasted of salt—and wondered what would happen if I missed the rope.

Semnos was leaning over the stern. He waved at me. I saw that the rope was about to come to an end. If I dived and missed, I was probably going to drown.

I threw myself in and hoped for the best. I grabbed the rope and it slid through my hands. I let go and grabbed again, at the very end, this time with both hands, and this time I held on. I felt like my arms had been jerked from their sockets. *Paralos* was towing me at an incredible pace. I'd never understood from onboard just how quickly a trireme swam.

I screamed but I was underwater. I took a mouthful.

I automatically swallowed the enormous mouthful of sea. The salt burned my throat. That action made me gasp, and more sea washed in. I gulped mouthful after mouthful, until I managed to close my mouth and keep it shut. My head just didn't seem to rise above the sea. That made me concentrate on surviving. I kept my mouth and my eyes firmly shut, I thought I would drown down there, until some fluke of the sea brought me to the surface. I gasped air, and gasped again, and almost choked on the sea water that now came gushing back up from my abused stomach.

By the time I had finished I felt awful, my stomach muscles ached with the amount I had vomited, but I also felt like I might live, as long as my throat didn't collapse from salt and sea.

It was only now that I realized sailors were hauling on the line. It was a good thing, because without them I could never have clambered along the rope. Someone had dropped a fishing net down the side of *Paralos*. I saw it beside me with red-misted eyes. I grabbed the net with one hand and didn't let go of the rope with the other until I was sure I had a firm grip. I was still traveling a hundred times faster than any man could swim.

I was dimly aware that the sailors were shouting at me. I grabbed the net with my second hand, and instantly the net began to rise, and me with it.

They hauled me over the gunwale and onto *Paralos*. I stood there shaking, and then I felt my intestines spasm.

I had thought my stomach was empty, but I was wrong. I bent double and was copiously sick.

Someone said angrily, "Over the side, you moron! Don't hit the gold!"

But it was too late.

The sailors gave me a black look. They were the ones who would be scrubbing my mess off the deck and wiping the contents of my stomach off the ship's gold fittings.

I looked up, feeling ashamed.

Damon stood there, dripping wet and grinning broadly. "That was fun!" he said.

"Thanks for saving us," I managed to croak to the captain.

Semnos shrugged. "They might not let us fight, but we're still the best damned sailors in the Navy. When your wife turned up in a rush to say you were on a chase and probably in trouble, my men were the first to launch," he said proudly.

"Diotima made it to the Athenian camp?" I said, perplexed. I couldn't imagine how she had gotten there. Had she run? I was worried she might have hurt the baby. "How did she manage it?"

"Carried by four priests, on her orders," Semnos said. "Apparently she was shouting at them to go faster every step of the way. They were sweating like pigs when they arrived. What's our target?" he finished.

"Somewhere ahead of us there's a fishing boat, manned by two soldiers," I told him.

"Soldiers trying to sail?" Semnos smiled. "That sounds like the start of one of our onboard jokes. Don't worry, Nicolaos, we'll catch them easily."

Semnos turned to speak to the steersman, who in turn roared orders that were echoed by the port and starboard officers. At midships were two *aulos* players, musicians who played the double flute. They increased the tempo of their song to match the increased urgency of the mission. Men pulled harder in time to the music, the sail went up, and *Paralos* surged. Having been mercilessly towed along by this mighty beast, I could only imagine with what speed we were cutting through the water now.

"We're close to Mykonos, aren't we?" I asked.

Semnos pointed. "That way, well north of us."

"Oh. Then where are those guards going?"

"Maybe they're as lost as you."

The *proreus*—the officer who commanded at the front of the trireme—was on his usual watch, standing on the very pointy front end. His arm was wrapped around the smooth wooden pole that rose there for that very purpose.

Now the proreus pointed to starboard and yelled, "Captain! Captain, there!"

"Aye!" Semnos bellowed back into the breeze.

"Small vessel, sir!"

I stared where the officer pointed. Sure enough, there was the fishing boat. It couldn't possibly escape *Paralos*, a fast and mighty warship.

The proreus paused, then added, "And a major vessel, Captain."

Out of the sea mist beyond the fisher boat emerged another vessel; a large one, and it didn't look Hellene. The other ship was also heading straight for the fishing boat.

Our Captain examined this new arrival with narrowed eyes.

"Who are they?" I asked Semnos.

"The hull looks Phoenician," he said. "It's a galley, not a trader. Which means they're either pirates, in which case they might run, or they are enemy."

The Phoenicians claimed to be the best sailors in the world, though everyone knew we Hellenes were better. Yet the Phoenicians were the only other sea-going people that Hellene commanders feared. It didn't help that Phoenicea had long been a subject state of the Great King of the Persians. When the Great King had invaded us, twenty-six years ago, the Phoenicians had provided the core of his fleet. If this Phoenician was a fighting ship, then it meant trouble.

Another two boats came into view—they had been hidden behind the first—all three of the same type.

I said, "Three?"

"Usual contingent for pirates, if they have a base near here," Semnos said. "Don't worry, Nicolaos, those three together are no match for us."

I asked, "Are they heading for the fishing boat too?"

"Looks like it."

"Semnos," I said urgently. "We *have* to get there first."

"Pull hard. Maximum speed." Semnos spoke it almost softly, but the effect on his men was instantaneous. The tempo of the *aulos* music increased to a frenetic pace. The rowers were sweating for their drachma-a-day.

It was going to be a tight race. We were fast, but the Phoenician was closer.

I suddenly realized the fishing boat would come alongside the other vessel at the exact moment we got there.

The guards bumped into the other boat, midships. I saw someone aboard throw down a line.

"Disengage," Semnos ordered.

"But Captain," a man objected, "We can take those scum."

"I said disengage!" Semnos shouted.

All around me, I could feel the men's shoulders slump. They were disgusted. And resigned.

But I wasn't. I couldn't believe what I was hearing. An Athenian captain in a powerful ship of the line had just refused to take on a smaller galley.

"What? You cannot be serious, Captain," I said. "Why aren't we fighting them? We're a ship of Athens."

Semnos grabbed me by the front of my chiton. "Don't you remember what my standing orders are?" he said angrily. "*Paralos* is forbidden to engage. If you want to fight, then you're on the wrong boat."

The steersman diverted the steering oar, but only by the tiniest margin necessary to miss the Phoenician. He wanted them to know that we could have sunk them, but chose not to, and he growled as he did it.

I was forced to watch while *Paralos* skimmed so close to the fishing boat I had chased that I could almost have reached out and touched it. Instead, we passed it by at such a high speed that we were gone in an instant. The two criminal guards made rude gestures at our backs.

Semnos stood alone to the starboard side and swore. "By the balls of the dog, by the guts of a constipated goat, by the hairy bum of a—"

"Captain, I apologize," I said, interrupting him.

"What for?" He was puzzled.

"When you said that *Paralos* was not allowed to fight, I took that for a hollow complaint. Now that I've experienced it, I completely understand your frustration. How do you stand it?"

He shook his head. "I ask myself that same question every time this happens."

"THE OTHER BOAT was Phoenician, all right," I said to Diotima and Pericles. The two of them had waited together for our return in Pericles's tent. That must have been interesting, considering their mutual dislike. On the other hand, Diotima was surrounded by empty bowls. I guessed she had spent the time wisely, eating Pericles out of supplies.

Pericles turned to Semnos for confirmation of my statement.

Semnos nodded. "I got a clear view of their deck. That's my evaluation, Pericles."

Pericles visibly relaxed. He had been honest with Anax-inos when we first arrived: his greatest fear was that the Persians would use their newly recovered base in Egypt to launch an attack from the south.

"Three ships isn't anywhere near enough for an inva-sion," Pericles said. "For that you would want two hundred. It might be a raid, of course. Athens runs constant raids against Persian cities on the coast, though usually we'd send more ships than three to hit a city! That's the sort of complement you see from a pirate base. If so, we have nothing to fear from them, with all our ships of the line."

"On the other hand, it could be a scouting party prior to an invasion," Semnos said.

That thought was mildly alarming. Pericles certainly thought so.

"I will order the triremes to patrol Delos," he said. "Those sailors sleeping on the beach every day may as well be doing something for their drachma a day.

Semnos left, to carry Pericles's orders to the other *tri-erarchs*.

Diotima and I stood to go, but Pericles waved at us. "Stay, Nicolaos. You too, Diotima."

Diotima bristled; she didn't like taking orders from Pericles. I hoped an argument wasn't about to break out. Fortunately my wife held her tongue.

Pericles said, "What's this I hear about Philipos becoming your apprentice? He came to me babbling about such a thing. You know he's my closest assistant."

"He wants to learn investigation," I said.

Pericles frowned. "This doesn't sound like you at all, Nicolaos. You prefer to work alone. What are you playing at?"

No one ever accused Pericles of being slow.

I explained to Pericles that his assistant, by his own admission, would have killed the victim if he'd been a little more competent. "Philipos is the only man on the island who not only had a motive but was in the right place to do it," I finished.

"So you gave him a job?" Pericles asked.

"I put him in a position where I can keep an eye on him," I said. "What do you know about him?"

"He comes from a good family," Pericles said at once. This was something I'd noticed before about Pericles: he often judged men by who their fathers were.

"Military man?" I asked.

"Only in the sense that he's served when the state needed brave men," Pericles said. "Philipos is an adequate line officer, but he has no initiative. He's not command material, Nico. He's not like you."

That statement took me aback so completely that I almost staggered. Had Pericles just offered me a compliment? If so, it was the first time in our long association.

"I don't understand," I said, because I could not credit what I had heard. "I've never commanded men in my life."

That wasn't strictly true. I had once commanded the city guard during a crisis, but at every moment I had been acutely aware that I had no idea what I was doing. I had never commanded men like Pericles did every day, or like my father-in-law.

Pericles shook his head. "That's not the point. You act on your own initiative, Nico. Usually you act too much on your own initiative. That's something Philipos will never do." Pericles closed that statement with a hint of contempt.

Pericles was not a man to hide his feelings about an underling. He had probably made clear to Philipos, every day that the lesser man hung around Pericles's house, that he considered Philipos good only for following instructions. Yet Philipos had kept returning, because he wanted to help. It would have been like kicking a faithful dog.

Suddenly I understood why Philipos had acted as he did to try to kill Geros. Philipos had acted on his own initiative, probably for the first time in his life, purely to prove Pericles wrong.

And now this had happened.

I felt sorry for the man. If Philipos proved to be the killer, I was going to blame Pericles.

"Is there any chance those two guards could have been the killers of Geros?" Pericles asked.

"It's possible," Diotima said. "When the protest began that night, the guards made themselves scarce, and who can blame them? Geros might have ordered them to defend the treasury against the entire fleet. "

"So they might have done it?" Pericles pressed. That answer would be very convenient for him.

"They might have gone to the Old Village," Diotima agreed. "In fact, they almost certainly went somewhere out of the way. Nobody saw them all night."

"Then they might be the thieves too," Pericles said.

"Not a chance," I told him. "Accomplices, yes—"

"Almost certainly," Diotima added.

"But to get so much money off this island and then know what to do with it requires skill. Skills a common soldier wouldn't have. Whoever did this knows finance and accounting. In particular they knew how Karnon accounts for the funds. From the evidence this has been going on for some time."

"Then let's move on to the theft of League funds,"

Pericles said. "How are we supposed to explain this to the people of Athens?" He threw his arms up in despair. "Not to mention that an entire Athenian fleet was present when the theft was discovered. That's not going to sit well with the other member states." For a moment I thought he would tear out his hair. Instead he turned on us. "How much is missing?"

Diotima spoke up. "We won't know until Karnon has finished his accounting. His initial estimate is thirty talents." Diotima hesitated, then added, "Pericles, when you keep in mind that there are four thousand talents in that treasury, thirty talents doesn't seem so much."

"It's enough to build three entire war ships!" Pericles exclaimed. "Did the killer take the money?" He asked.

"It does seem logical," I said. "We'll have to look into it."

"What a good idea," Pericles said in his most sarcastic voice. "Don't let me keep you."

"No, but we'll keep you," Diotima said.

Pericles stared at her.

"We need to understand whether there might be some other member state, or some other organization, that might want to target the treasury," Diotima said. "Why is the treasury kept on Delos?"

"Because no one could agree on which city to trust with the money," Pericles said. "That was twenty-five years ago. Now everyone knows that they can trust Athens."

I thought Pericles was more optimistic about that than I felt.

"Also, no one in their right mind would sack Delos. The city that did such a thing would be cursed for all eternity."

"So you don't think a member state would be behind those ships out there?"

"Hardly."

"How many members are there?" Diotima asked.

"A hundred and forty-eight."

"Anaxinos wanted you to convene a meeting of the members, to talk about where the treasure should lie. Yet you refused?"

"Have you ever tried to get a hundred and forty-eight men to agree on anything?" Pericles asked.

"I see your point," Diotima said. She'd seen enough meetings of temple priestesses to know how that would go. "Then let's be sure about this. You still think those ships are Phoenician or Persian?"

"That or pirates. Why are you pressing these questions?" Pericles asked.

"One of the coins we found on Geros came from Kyzikos. Karnon identified the coin for us," Diotima said. "Kyzikos is in the province of Anatolia. Anatolia is on the other side of the Aegean, well inside the Persian Empire. So far inside that we Hellenes don't normally see their coins."

Pericles was visibly disturbed at that news. He stopped pacing. "You think Geros was in some sort of conspiracy with the Persians?"

"Karnon said the coin might have come in trading," I said.

Pericles nodded. "Yes, or the conspiracy theory is correct."

"Or Geros discovered someone who was in a conspiracy," Diotima suggested. To our looks of surprise she shrugged and said, "It's a theory. One of those ideas must be right. No matter which, we have a major thief on the island."

THE SITUATION WAS BECOMING GRAVE

WE WALKED STRAIGHT out of Pericles's tent and straight into Philipos. He was waiting for us.

"You went and chased criminals without me," he complained.

"Sorry about that."

"If I'm to be your apprentice, we need to do things together."

"You're quite right."

"Are we ready to do some detecting now?" he asked.

It was the end of the day, most of which I had spent in a boat chase. I had started off thinking I was going to be outnumbered in a knife fight; instead, I had been sunk, dragged through the sea, almost drowned, and then had to watch while my quarry escaped. I was exhausted. I opened my mouth to tell him so, but Diotima got a word in first.

"As it happens, there is something you can solve for us," she said.

"Yes?" he said eagerly.

"Philipos, you said when you spoke to my husband that you fell into an opened grave?"

"Yes."

"Are you sure?"

"Of course I'm sure," he said. "What other sort of grave can you fall into?"

"What I don't understand," Diotima said patiently, "is

why there was an opened grave in a graveyard that hasn't been used for a century."

That stopped Philipos for a moment. He scratched his head. "I didn't think of that."

"It's too dark to look now," Diotima said. "Meet us there at first light tomorrow."

WE WENT IN search of Karnon. It had been absolutely necessary to report to Pericles first, but now that we were free we knew the accountant would be desperate for news. We also needed to find out about the guards. Who were they?

We went first to the Oikos. The slaves there told us that after the theft had been discovered and I had given chase to the guards, Karnon had repaired to his office at the Oikos, his face a mask of total despair, and had sat there, staring at a sharpened dagger, for longer than anyone had thought healthy.

The slaves had sent for Marika. The relationship between Marika and Karnon seemed to be an open secret. Marika had wrapped a blanket around the accountant and led him to his home, gently, with the help of the slaves.

The slaves worked in administration. I asked them about the guards.

"There are six, sir," the slave said. "They work in shifts."

"Who organizes the shifts?" I asked.

The slave looked surprised at the question. "There's nothing to organize, sir. One pair works from before dawn to midday; another pair from midday to evening; and the third pair the night shift."

"Don't they mix their shifts?" Diotima asked.

"No, madam," the slave said. "Why would they need to do that?"

"Where can we find the other four?" I asked. "I assume they're Athenian soldiers."

"I believe they're all mercenaries, sir."

Diotima and I looked at each other in despair. Those guards were next to useless as protectors of the treasure. Worse than useless, in fact, because they'd given everyone a sense of security that was entirely false.

I went to Karnon's desk, where I found an old piece of papyrus, a brush, and some ink. I scribbled a note to Philipos, asking him to organize a roster of guards from among the Athenian soldiers, to protect the treasury day and night. I gave the note to one of the Oikos slaves and asked him to carry it at once.

"Who organized this fiasco?" I said to the remaining slave.

It had been a rhetorical complaint, but the slave had a ready answer. "Karnon funds the guards, sir."

"But he doesn't manage their shifts."

"No, sir."

The slave gave us directions to the barracks, which were not much larger than a hut, on the outskirts of the New Village. There we confirmed what the slave had already told us: that the guards had their own regular schedule.

"It's an odd job for mercenaries," I commented to them. They looked the usual sort for their line of work: rough, a little unkempt, slightly untrustworthy but competent when it came to looking out for their own skins.

One of the guards said, "The pay's bad, but we get fed, and there's not much chance of dying, you know?" He shrugged.

"There'll be even less chance now," I told them. "I'm replacing you with Athenians for the duration of this crisis."

They took this news as stoically as I expected. But there was also a hint of suspicion.

"Before you ask, none of us knew anything about what those two were doing," one of them said. "We might be mercenaries, but we got honor."

"I'm sure you do," I said, but I was sure of no such thing. It was perfectly possible that one or more of these men was in on the crime, and it wouldn't be the first time a hired man had betrayed a wealthy employer. "Where are you lads from?"

"Me and Axiagos, we're from Macedon," their apparent leader said. "Enalkides and Orotheremes, they're from Crete, right guys?"

The other two nodded.

The guards had arrived in pairs. That was completely normal. Mercenaries often traveled and hired on with a buddy they could trust. Mercenary work was dangerous enough without having to rely on strangers to watch your back.

"What about the two guards that ran?" Diotima asked. She wrinkled her nose. All the time we'd been in the barracks, she had been holding her breath. The smell of sweat and unwashed bodies was strong.

Our friendly guard spat on the ground in disgust.

"Their names are Ippoloxos and Zelmontas. Since you seem so interested, they're from . . ." He paused. "I don't remember. Somewhere on the other side of the sea. Any of you guys know?" he asked the rest of the room.

Every man present shrugged.

"Did any of you know Ippoloxos and Zelmontas before they arrived?" Diotima asked.

"No," they said in unison.

"Hmm," Diotima said.

When Diotima and I arrived at Karnon's house, we discovered that even the two boisterous little boys had gone quiet. We delivered the news that the guards had escaped, and with them, no doubt, any hope of recovering the lost treasure. At this news Karnon had turned a terrible gray, and gravely thanked us for our efforts. Then he wept.

The boys hugged their father and cried with him, though they could not have understood what terrible misfortune had befallen the family. I wasn't sure that Marika understood either, and I did not enlighten her. For it is the law of Athens that any treasurer who loses state funds shall be punished by death. Nor is it one of those laws that everyone knows about but no one ever enforces. That terrible penalty had been carried out in my own lifetime.

I had said as much to Diotima as we walked back to the sanctuary.

"But you'd defend him, wouldn't you Nico?" Diotima had asked anxiously.

"Of course I would, and I'd fail," I told her. "The law applies if a treasurer merely fails to protect state funds, even if he didn't embezzle them himself."

"That's harsh," Diotima said.

"Yes, but it gives city officials a decided interest in making sure state funds stay safe."

Diotima was furious. "This changes things," she said. "Before we were looking for the killer of a man who—I'll admit it—nobody liked much. Now we have to save the life of a good man."

"Assuming the good man isn't also the killer," I said.

"You don't believe that, do you Nico?" Diotima said.

"Try this scenario . . . let's assume Karnon has been stealing from the treasury for years, knowing that so long as he is treasurer he will get away with it. There's so much money flowing in and out that no one will ever know. Then we Athenians turn up to take the funds. Soon someone else will check his numbers. Suddenly he's in trouble."

"All right, I can see that," Diotima said. "He would need to do something to save himself."

I nodded. "He kills Geros, who as you point out nobody likes, and plants on him three coins that appear to come from the treasury. Then during the inevitable murder investigation—which you, my dear wife, are conducting—Karnon can 'discover' the theft of state money."

"Why would he?" Diotima asked.

"Because Karnon knows the missing money will come to light anyway. With Geros dead, and framed by the coins, Karnon can point the blame at the priest. Karnon would be safe."

Diotima looked puzzled. "But wait, you just said that a treasurer must be punished for losing state funds."

"Aha." I smiled. We had come to the clever point in my theory. "So I did. Who is the *second* treasurer on this island?"

Diotima thought about it, then said, "Geros is treasurer to the temples!"

"Yes. In court, Karnon can argue that we should take the word of the law literally. A treasurer must be punished. Geros was a treasurer. Geros is dead. No further action required."

"But Geros wasn't the treasurer for this particular fund," Diotima pointed out. Then she answered her own objection. "But Karnon is a likeable man. Likeable men have been let off for technicalities more unlikely than this."

"That's what I think," I said. "A jury will look for any excuse to save Karnon, especially since Geros looks so guilty of theft, and he a holy a man at that."

"What about the soldiers who ran?" Diotima asked. "Explain them."

I shrugged. "They're in on it with him. He could have had that fast Phoenician boat ready and hidden, which is why we never caught up with the guards. With the guards gone, and with the priest dead, it leaves Karnon looking completely innocent."

"What if the accountant gets caught later?" Diotima asked.

"Caught for what?" I asked. "On the evidence, you'd say Geros was the thief, wouldn't you?"

Diotima nodded.

"Right. Karnon would have successfully thrown all the blame on the dead man. As long as Karnon doesn't steal from this point on, then he's safe from prosecution."

Diotima frowned. "Safe from prosecution for embezzlement, perhaps. But if you're right then Karnon killed Geros. We can still get him for that."

"There is that detail," I admitted. "But we have no evidence."

"Why would Karnon do this?" Diotima asked.

"That's easy. Karnon needs the money to run away with the woman he loves and his two sons. He's completely dependent on his wife's family. The only way he'll ever have enough to leave her is to steal some."

"When you put it that way . . ." Diotima thought about it. She nodded. "Yes, it's possible. Do you believe it?"

"Not for a moment. He's too honorable."

"We have to save him," Diotima repeated. "Think of his family. Nico, they'll starve without him."

We would save Karnon. If we could.

THE GRAVE ROBBERS

T**HE GRAVEYARD WAS** much less intimidating in
bright light. I arrived to meet Philipos without Diotima,
who was taking a slow route upon Plod. This morning, for
the first time, she had complained of pain. My wife wasn't the
type to needlessly complain about her health. I was worried.
But she had refused to rest when I suggested it, and the only
real solution was to solve the case and get ourselves home.

"Where is this grave?" I asked Philipos, because I
couldn't see it. He pointed toward the north side.

We walked that way, but as we approached, Philipos
looked more and more confused.

"I think we've passed it; we've come too far."

We turned back, but couldn't see an open grave, though
there was plenty of rubble and rubbish to trip over.

"Are you sure it was a grave?" I asked again.

"I know a grave when I fall into one, Nicolaos."

I climbed upon a toppled stele for more height to see all
around, but there was no open grave.

We spread left and right in search of the hole.

"Do you see it?" I called to Philipos.

He was out of sight behind a cluster of monuments.
"No. What about you?" he called back.

"No."

We carried on, walking circuitous routes, until we had
reached the end of the graveyard.

"I can't explain it. I promise you it really happened," Philipos said. He was upset that there was no grave. "I wasn't imagining things."

"You didn't drink too much during that barbecue, did you?" I asked.

"Not a drop. I was completely sober."

"I believe you," I said, although I didn't entirely. I was, however, convinced that Philipos believed what he was saying. I surveyed the ruins of the graveyard and decided that unless Philipos was completely mistaken, there was only one possibility.

"Philipos, I need you to go on an errand."

He instantly looked hurt.

"I'm not Pericles, all right?" I assured him.

"What am I fetching?" he asked.

"Go to the village. Find a man named Damon. He knows where to get anything that anyone needs on this island. Tell him that Nicolaos needs shovels, pickaxes, and a few strong men."

"You made the right decision to send for diggers," Diotima said when she arrived. She had passed Philipos on his way for tools and men.

"Thanks."

"I think there's only one possible answer," she said.

Damon and Philipos arrived quickly. With them were four men, four shovels, three pickaxes, and two wheelbarrows. None of the workmen looked happy. I couldn't blame them. This ground was hard.

"It's another hot day, isn't it, Nico?" Damon said, and then he smiled. He always seemed to point out the most unfortunate facts with the most cheery manner. "What are we doing here?" he asked. "Do you want us to dig up this hard ground?"

Diotima nodded to me. "Gentlemen," I announced. "We are looking for a pit that was recently open." I carefully didn't say the word *grave*, but I could see from the men's faces that they knew what I meant. "The pit might still be open," I said. "If so, then that is all to the good. We want to see what's in it. But it's possible this pit has been filled within the last day. In that case we will find some place nearby with loose, recently disturbed gravel. In that case, we'll need to dig down."

The men scowled. They didn't want to dig.

"The good news is, if it's been filled, then the gravel won't be so hard to remove again," I said.

The men nodded at that and scowled a little less.

"Any questions?" I finished.

"What about *psyches*?" one of the men asked.

It was a very good question. I had no idea whether we risked being visited by the spirits of the dead.

Fortunately, my wife came to the rescue.

"Everyone who was buried here in ages past received a perfect funeral," Diotima said smoothly. "We know that must be true because this is Delos, the Sacred Isle. Therefore every psyche has had the proper propitiation and is now safely descended to Hades."

The men nodded at that, slightly reluctantly.

"Besides, all the bodies were transferred from here to the new cemetery at the other end of the island almost a hundred years ago," Diotima pointed out. "Everyone knows a stray psyche follows its former body. If there are any psyches about, they're not here. You may trust me on this, gentlemen, because I am a priestess of Artemis. We are trained to know these things."

The men nodded much more happily at these words.

"Right, get to work," I said. "The first step is, see if you can find that pit, or failing that, look for any recently filled in hole. Surely a recent in-fill would be visible."

The men spread out in a regular pattern under Damon's orders.

As they worked I said, "Philipos, I don't think you've been formally introduced. I'd like you to meet the official detective on this job, my wife, Diotima."

Philipos looked at us oddly. "I thought Nicolaos was the detective?"

"It's extremely unusual," Diotima said. "But I am a priestess of Artemis and my husband is not. Therefore in this place I have a power to judge that you Athenian men do not. A priestess *may* rule men on sanctuary grounds. There are precedents."

There were indeed precedents. The Pythoness at Delphi, the High Priestess at Brauron, the Priestess of the Games at Olympia—all these women ruled their sacred domains. With the authority of the High Priest of Apollo to back her, Diotima could command here on this one specific mission.

"Are you married, Philipos?" Diotima asked.

"I was. My wife died," he said shortly.

"Oh, I'm sorry to hear that," Diotima said.

I took a guess that his wife had died just before Philipos took to hanging around Pericles like a supplicant, but I didn't voice the idea.

"My sons are both grown," Philipos said. "They're in the army now."

Diotima had been right. Philipos was the oldest apprentice in the history of Athens.

"There's not much to learn about agent work," I assured him. "You'll get the hang of it in no time."

Just then the men returned. The search had been quick, but I had expected that.

"We didn't find a thing," Damon reported with a friendly grin. He reached into the first of the barrows. "I brought some wine. Shall we have a drink?"

The men drank while Diotima spoke.

"I expected that result," Diotima announced.

"Then why did you waste our time by making us search?" demanded the man who had asked about psyches.

Diotima's smile became somewhat brittle but she retained her composure. "Because there was a small chance that you would find what my husband and his associate missed," she said. "Now the real work begins. I want you to search again, but this time you are looking for a fallen stele that is weathered on the wrong side."

"What's that mean?" the disgruntled man said. "Weathered on the wrong side? There ain't no right side."

But Damon laughed.

"The priestess is a clever priestess," he said. "She thinks someone covered the pit she looks for with one of the fallen monuments."

"Exactly!" Diotima said.

Damon laughed. "So either they rolled the stele away, in which case the side it's weathered on will be *underneath*, not on top; or else there will be drag marks in the dirt."

"Exactly!" Diotima repeated.

The men began the search again, this time with an air of greater purpose.

"You know, it's still not at all clear why we're doing this," I pointed out. "There's no reason to assume that Philipos's disappearing grave has anything to do with the death of Geros."

"Except that two unusual occurrences at the same place at the same time are too much to accept as coincidence," Diotima said. "We're still searching for a path to the heart of the mystery, Nico."

"I know. But I want to prepare you for disappointment."

"Over here!"

It was Damon who found it. He lay flat on his stomach, his head almost beneath a large stele that had been sculpted in the shape of a cylinder. Damon's left arm was stretched underneath the curve of the stele, dangerously so. I hoped it didn't roll on him.

From this prone position Damon said, "The ground here is soft beneath. I can feel it." He dug his fingers into the gravel. It compressed noticeably more than the surrounding dirt.

Damon ran his fingers along the underside of the stele. "Look, Diotima was right; the inscription on the stone is more weathered underneath than on top."

"Damon, you are a genius," I said. "Well done."

I helped him back up. He wiped his hands on his tunic.

"I suppose we have to move this great big, heavy stone now?" he said in his happy voice.

"If what we suspect is true, it won't be hard to move at all," I said.

I put my hands upon the stele, braced myself, and pushed. It rocked a little, but it was clear that I couldn't roll it on my own. Philipos appeared beside me. Together we were able to make a small amount of progress.

Then suddenly the stele rolled away.

It had been too easy. I looked beside me, startled, to see Damon with a large crowbar. He had levered it under the stone.

"I found this under the bushes behind us," he said. "Also, this wooden chock."

I looked down at his feet, to see that Damon was nudging a large chock under the stone as he heaved. The system worked perfectly. I silently cursed for not having thought to look for these tools myself.

The turning of the stele had exposed the funerary message to easy view. There was a tableau chiseled into the stone, and below it, an inscription. I inspected this with the eye of a sculptor's son, and saw that it was quality work. Likewise the stone itself had quite obviously once been perfectly rounded and polished. It was, of course, cut from local stone, almost certainly from the small mountain that rose in the middle of Delos.

The funerary image showed a baby boy, held in the arms of his father. The baby's arms were outstretched, like a supplicant, toward a woman who sat upon a chair. Her expression was serene, her right hand raised in a gesture of farewell.

The inscription was worn, as Damon had said, but it was still readable. Philipos read aloud.

"I am Akesia, wife of Dorexides, well-deserving of him."

Philipos fell silent. He glanced uneasily toward Diotima, but had the sensitivity to say no more.

Into the sudden silence Damon said in his cheery voice, "She died in childbirth."

That wasn't something I wanted to hear, just at the moment.

Diotima affected not to notice, but I knew Damon's words had upset her. She scuffed the ground on which the stele had lain. "It does look newly filled," she said. "Can we dig it?"

The men sighed, but they knew this was why they had come. They set to work.

Diotima, Philipos, and I sat in the shade and watched the pickaxes rise and fall. The men had removed their clothes. That was normal procedure for workmen who owned only a single tunic. The sheen of sweat upon their backs was soon dripping down their backs in rivulets.

"I'll have to borrow money from Pericles. I didn't bring enough," I commented.

"What for?" Diotima asked.

"To reward the men," I told her. "They're earning their pay today and more."

"They are locals; their duty is to serve the Gods," said my wife the priestess. "That's the only reward they need."

"You have something to learn about encouraging men," I said to my wife.

Philipos dug beneath his own clothing. He pulled out a money bag that looked rather full. "I have sufficient coins," he said. "I'll reward them."

"Thank you, Philipos," I said. I was genuinely pleased to see my apprentice enter into the spirit of investigation.

The workmen traded pickaxes for shovels. They had broken the ground with surprising speed.

"It's hard to believe Geros did this on his own," I said.

"Damon managed to move the stele," my wife pointed out.

"Damon is a strong man. Geros was an old one," I said. "But more to the point, the digging those men are doing is serious."

I called out, "How is the ground, Damon?"

The Delian looked up from the work, wiped the sweat from his brow, and called back, "It's much the easiest hole we've ever had to dig on Delos. The ground here is usually hard as . . . well . . . hard as rock."

At that moment a shovel wielded by one of the workmen yielded a hollow thump.

I got up, so did Diotima and Philipos. We clustered around the grave.

The workmen scraped to quickly reveal a wooden crate of some sort. I was struck by how little earth covered the discovery.

"Could it be an old coffin?" one of the workmen asked. There was slight fear in his voice.

"No," I said firmly. "That looks like a crate to me, don't you think? See how new the wood is. Nothing has rotted."

Indeed the top in view was made of pine so new that the shaved wood was still almost white. The men saw the truth of this. They nodded.

"Whatever that is, it's buried shallow," I said. "How deep was that grave you fell in, Philipos?"

"I don't know. I didn't have a measuring rod," Philipos said. He thought for a moment and then added, "I climbed out easily . . . maybe hip height?"

There was enough dirt removed by now that we could open the box. Damon pulled up the lid and everyone gasped.

Within was a fortune. The entire box was filled with coins. Diotima knelt beside the hole. She held out her hands. Damon scooped treasure with his large plams for her to hold. Coins fell from her cupped hands like water. She peered at the ones remaining.

"They look like the three that we found on Geros," she said. She opened her hands, and the small fortune fell back into the box.

"Fetch soldiers," I said to Philipos. "Fetch honest soldiers. You're an experienced officer; you'll know the men we can trust." Philipos nodded, and left at a run. He knew what I was thinking. We were in imminent danger of a riot when people found out about this. The treasure had to be guarded.

"You men, you stay here," I said to the workmen sternly. As soon as they returned to the village, the whole island would know. "You'll be rewarded for your service," I told them. "That's the security covered," I said to Diotima. "What next?"

Diotima turned to Damon. "Fetch Karnon," she said to the village chief. "Only the Treasurer of Delos can tell us where this money came from."

THE HOUSE OF GEROS

"I'**LL HAVE TO** count it back at the Oikos, but on a rough estimate I'd say there's about ten talents here." Karnon looked up from his position over the grave. "I owe you a great deal," he said. "You have recovered some of the missing money."

Karnon had the villagers and a small troupe of soldiers hoist the boxes. He then proceeded to watch every man with paranoid intensity as they carried more money than most people see in their lifetimes back to its proper home. I sent Philipos with this group, with orders not to let that wealth out of his sight, and more importantly to watch and report on Karnon. I said this to him quietly, out of hearing of the others.

"You suspect him?" Philipos asked, shocked.

"He's clearly not the thief," I said. "He knows better than anyone that the other accountants would catch him. Nor was he at the protest. But pressure can do things to a man."

What I didn't explain to Philipos was the enormous stress Karnon was under because of his home situation. I didn't want the rather intense accountant to do anything rash, such as gather up the rescued money, collect Marika and the boys, and try to catch a ship out. With the bad odor this theft would put him in, on top of everything else, he must surely be tempted. I liked him too much to let him try.

IT WAS CLEAR that we had to learn more about Geros. We'd learned all we could from talking to the Delians.

"How did he get into the Delian Treasury?" Diotima asked.

"The guards let him in. We know that," I said.

"But the guards don't have a key," Diotima pointed out. "Only Karnon has a key."

"Geros must have one too," I said.

"I think he must have," Diotima agreed. "How hard would it be to make one?"

"Trivial for any blacksmith," I said. "They're only metal bars, bent in a certain way. Of course, you have to know where to put the bend for each key."

"But Geros must have seen Karnon's key—many times, I should think," Diotima said. "Geros would know."

"I'm acquiring a distinct dislike of these keys," I said. "Door slaves work so much better."

Diotima nodded glumly. "If Geros had a copy, I know where it is," she said.

We raced as fast as a pregnant woman can race to the home of Anaxinos. There we asked to see the box of keys that Anaxinos had removed from Geros's house. We sat on the floor and compared each of Geros's keys to those that Anaxinos owned.

Geros had three too many.

"No, two too many," Anaxinos said, when we showed him our discovery. He picked up one of the extra keys. "This one goes to the special Treasury of Artemis that houses the Hyperborean Gifts. See the name on the side?"

There was indeed a name on the side. It occurred to me

that naming a key was probably a mistake, but we already had too many problems to go looking for more.

"Meren told us of the Hyperborean Gift. Geros was the keeper?"

"Just so. He had the only key."

"What about this one?" I held up one of the remaining two. The alloy seemed different—it was a different color, and the handle was much more utilitarian, with no ivory.

Anaxinos scratched his head. "There you have me."

"Did anyone open this box after you brought it home, sir?" Diotima asked.

"Certainly not," the High Priest said.

The collection looked the same as the one I had seen when I first found the box in Geros's office. I said as much.

"Then Geros must have had a use for this key," Diotima said. "I'll bet this is the copy we're looking for. Let's try matching them."

But it wasn't. We held pairs of keys side-by-side, to compare the bends. This odd key didn't match any of the others.

Diotima set it aside. "What about the last one?" she said.

We quickly proved that the second odd key also matched none in Anaxinos's possession.

"Send for Karnon," Anaxinos ordered a slave. "Tell him to bring his keys."

Karnon came quickly. One of the two extra keys precisely matched Karnon's key for the Porinos Naos.

"I was afraid of that," Karnon said. He turned an unnatural shade of gray.

"This key looks different, though, from all our usual ones," Anaxinos said. He held it up. "Do you see? Our temple keys have ivory handles and are inscribed with the sun and the bow, the insignia of the divine twins. But this key's handle is a plain, utilitarian style."

"Yes, High Priest," Diotima said. "It's probably a copy. Geros must have acquired the real key and had a copy made."

"Do you have an explanation for this, Karnon?" Anaxinos turned to the accountant.

"No, High Priest," Karnon said weakly. He realized how this looked for him.

Diotima said, "Can you honestly say that your key has been in your sight every moment for the last year?"

"No, of course not," Karnon said. "When it's at home, I keep it in my own bedroom. Nobody else goes in there . . . well, almost nobody." He looked uneasy.

"What about at work?" Diotima persisted.

"Then the key is tied to my belt," Karnon said.

"Even when you're in the Oikos?" Diotima asked.

"Well, the key hangs heavy—you see how unwieldy it is. In my office I lay it on the table before me."

"No harm in that," Anaxinos said.

"None at all," Diotima agreed.

"But nobody on this island bars their door. Has Geros ever come to visit you, Karnon, or waited for you in your office?"

"Yes, many times. He works here too, you know."

"There's the answer then."

"That explains the first of the two odd keys. But what about this last key?" Anaxinos held up the one that matched no known door. "What does it go to?"

"What a very good question," Diotima said. She took the mysterious key from the High Priest's hands, and passed it to me. "I think Nico and I will go find out."

I KNOCKED ON the door of Geros's house. It opened a crack and an eye peered out.

"Nicolaos, son of Sophroniscus," I said brusquely. "We met before. You also met my wife, the priestess Diotima. We are appointed by Anaxinos High Priest of the Delian Apollo to search this house."

It never hurts to overpower a slave with authority.

The slave opened the door, and looked even more worried than he had the first time we'd visited. He rubbed his hands absently and said, "Yes, I remember you. I am relieved to see you."

But he stood in the doorway and did nothing.

"Perhaps we could come in?" I prodded.

"Oh, yes, of course." He stepped back to reveal the atrium and courtyard.

The body of Geros still lay in the traditional position, in the middle, upon a table, with his feet pointing toward the door. The priestesses who had been preparing him when we were last here had done a good job. Geros was dressed in his priestly robes; the staff that he had carried in life was laid beside him.

Geros had lain like this ever since his body had been taken from the murder scene. The days since then had been hot ones.

"Isn't he becoming a little bit . . . er . . . rank?" I suggested.

"Yes, sir. The smell is becoming quite difficult," said the slave.

"You don't perhaps want to bury him?" I asked.

"I have received no orders, sir," the slave said.

"Where are the mourners?" Diotima asked.

The slave blinked at her. "There are none."

"None?" Diotima almost screeched. Such a thing was unheard of.

"Oh, everyone came to pay their respects, as is proper,"

the slave hurried to correct himself. "That was on the first day, and you saw the priests come to prepare him. Since then, there has been no one."

"I shall speak to the High Priest," Diotima said firmly.

"Thank you, mistress." The slave bobbed his head.

"What happens to you now?" I asked him.

"Only the gods know," the slave replied. "I hope they don't turn me out. I wouldn't know what to do."

"Surely someone here could use an extra pair of hands," Diotima said. "I will enquire."

"Thank you, mistress. I don't cost much to feed."

"What is your name?" I asked.

"Ekamandronemus."

That stopped me. His name was a mouthful, even by our standards. Fortunately everyone has a short nickname that their friends use.

"Ah, then what do your friends call you?" I asked.

"Friends?" This was a new concept for the poor man. "Everyone calls me Ekamandronemus, sir."

"Very well then, er . . . Ekam," I said, choosing something swiftly. "May I call you Ekam?" I asked, and spoke on quickly before he could say no. "Ekam, we're going to search your master's office."

"You have already done that, sir."

"We're going to do it again. Very thoroughly. Also every other room of this house until we find what we're looking for."

"And what is that, sir?"

"A keyhole."

Ekam looked doubtful. "I have the master's orders never to let anyone wander about in here."

"That would be the dead master," I pointed out.

We all three looked over at the body.

"I don't think he's likely to object," I added. "Besides which, I and this lady, who incidentally is going to find you a new place to live, are searching for his killer."

Ekam found this logic to be decisive. "I'm sure that'll be fine then, sir. May I bring you refreshments?"

"No thank you," I said. "We'll be here a while, so leave us to it."

"Yes, sir."

Diotima added, "Ekam, why don't you go make yourself a big meal? I am sure that Geros would have wanted you to eat your fill from whatever is in stores."

"As to that, mistress, I have my doubts," Ekam said. He returned to rubbing his hands and looking nervous.

"Nonsense," Diotima said with complete assurance. "Why don't you take my suggestion as a direct order?"

"Thank you, mistress."

There was nothing in the office. I pulled everything away from walls, I moved the desk and the couches. I shifted chests. All we found was an ordinary office.

We moved downstairs to Geros's bedroom, then the storerooms, the kitchen, the public rooms. Nowhere could we find a keyhole to try our mysterious key.

We were ready to give up, and leaving for the front door, when we passed a staircase that we had completely ignored.

We both stopped dead.

Diotima said, "How blind can we get? What about the women's quarters?"

"How did we not think of this before?" I asked.

"Because not even the lowest, most unethical of criminals would store purloined goods in the place where the women live," Diotima said. "It's sacrosanct."

"Except in a house with no women," I said.

There was a door at the top of the stairs. In the door was a keyhole.

I handed the key to Diotima. "You do the honors, my dear."

Diotima pushed in the key. She struggled to turn the handle, so I helped. The bar behind went up, the door opened to reveal Geros's secret office.

Within was an exquisite desk, fine furniture, and rows of empty shelves.

"This makes perfect sense," I said. "Any official visitor to do temple business, like Anaxinos, would be shown to Geros's usual office. Normal men who visit another man's home pass by the staircase up to the women's quarters. It's not the done thing to even notice it."

I found a whole bundle of the dead man's personal papers tied together with string. I handed these to Diotima and kept searching.

Diotima started reading. "There's a letter here saying his funds have been deposited."

"How much?"

"Thousands of drachmae, it seems." Diotima read through the page. She put it down and read the next. "Here's another deposit, for more thousands."

Diotima flipped through the pages before her, her brow furrowed.

"What are you doing—"

"Shhh, I'm concentrating." When she was finished she said, "These letters are all receipts for money received at the bank. I added the amounts and it comes to more than twenty thousand drachmae."

"That's more than three talents!" I said. "Who is his banker?"

Diotima sifted through the papers. "The Antisthenes

and Archestratus Savings And Loan Company," she said in shock.

"Well that explains a lot."

Antisthenes and Archestratus were the two dodgiest bankers in all of Athens. We had had a run in with those two before.

Diotima picked up the next page. "Dear Gods, Nico, Geros owns an estate!"

"What?"

"It's in Kyzikos."

Geros had a coin from Kyzikos on his dead body. Karnon had told us Kyzikos was well inside the Persian Empire. I said, "That is very, very suggestive."

"Isn't it?" Diotima agreed.

But there was still the question of paying for it. I said, "This is ridiculous. No professional priest could possibly have enough money to own an estate."

Diotima waved a piece of paper on which there was much writing. "This is a report from his estate manager." She paused for thought, then said, "Maybe Geros inherited it?"

But I could think of another answer, and so could Diotima.

"We must face the certainty, my dear wife, that this priest of Apollo was as crooked as the keys they use around here."

"I'm afraid you're right. We knew right from the start that Geros was corrupt, but until now we didn't know he was an outright thief." She put down the papers, squared them into a neat pile, and put them in the box, which she handed to me. "These come with us."

We had more than enough to convict Geros for corruption so severe that it would certainly result in his execution. The only problem was, he was already dead.

"This doesn't make sense," I said. "If anyone should be doing the killing around here, it's Geros, to protect his secret life as an embezzler."

"Maybe someone killed him in retribution for his crimes?" Diotima grabbed my arm. "Nico, the word NEMESIS was written above his body!"

"So it was," I said. "But if someone wanted Geros dead for his crimes, then that must mean they knew about the crimes."

"Yes, of course, that's obvious," Diotima said.

"Then all they had to do was tell the world. Geros would have been executed for sure."

"Oh, you're right," Diotima said. "That almost implies that the killer *didn't* know . . ." She sighed. "Why are these murder cases always so confusing?"

"That's why they pay us the commissions."

"They're paying us for this?" Diotima sounded surprised.

My wife had just made a good point. Always in the past we had worked on a commission basis, but this time we had volunteered, in the extreme circumstances. That meant one important thing . . .

"Curse it," I said, "We're doing this for free. I hadn't realized up until this moment. I should have demanded something from Pericles."

"Too late now," my wife said. "Anyway, I'm the detective here, remember? This time, Nico, we're on a mission for the Gods."

"All right then, my detective wife, tell me what we have."

Diotima lay back in Geros's office couch. She shifted about until she felt comfortable. When she was settled, she began.

"We have a dead priest who everyone thinks was an upright man of the highest integrity, but who you proved was corrupt, and now we've proven was a thief and embezzler."

I added, "Plus, everyone still thinks he was a highly moral man, except for the handful of us in the know."

"Handful?" Diotima said. "Two. You and me."

"And maybe the killer," I said.

"Maybe."

"And the soldiers who helped him," I pointed out. "Which they almost certainly did. Geros and the guards . . . that's the right combination for the thieving. I hope the guards were paid well, because if they ever show their faces in Hellas again they'll be executed on the spot."

There was a knock at the door. It was Ekam, the house slave. Now I knew why he looked so nervous.

"You knew this place was here, didn't you?" I said.

"I was ordered never to say anything, sir." Ekam rubbed his hands. It was a wonder the skin hadn't fallen off. "A slave cannot disobey his master, can he?"

That was fair enough. "But once your master was dead you should have said something," I told him.

"And admit to knowledge of crimes that I didn't report, sir?" Ekam said. "How long would a slave like me last then?"

Ekam had a point. He was in an invidious position.

I saw he was shaking. "If you don't mention it, neither will we," I told him.

"Thank you, sir!" He looked most relieved.

"Tell me, what was on these shelves?" I asked. "They're empty now."

"I was never permitted to enquire, sir and lady," Ekam said. "The master was quite secretive—"

"I can imagine."

"But if you want my guess, they were some of the nicer items from the treasuries."

That was my guess, too. "Do you know what happened to them?" I asked.

"I'm afraid not," Ekam said. "Though if it's any help, sir, I was never asked to move any of the items myself."

"Your master didn't trust you?" Diotima asked.

"I think perhaps my master had plans that didn't include me," he replied sadly.

Ekam disappeared, but then returned, bearing a tray of food, two cups, and a flask of wine. From the smell of his breath I had an idea that Ekam himself had been at Geros's good wine, but I was fine with that.

"I know you said not to bring food, sir and lady, but I made something for myself, and I thought you might like a bite."

We had been working long, and the aroma smelled wonderful. Ekam had done himself proud.

I handed a glass to Diotima and placed a bowl of figs beside her.

"He began the thefts years ago," Diotima said. "They were small at first. He kept records. Then the thefts got larger."

"When he discovered he could get away with it," I said. "I bet you'll find it all began after the wife died."

"Why do you think that?" Diotima asked.

"Because you women tend to be the ones who hold the moral compass for us men."

Diotima shrugged.

"What do we have on the financials?" I asked.

"We have thirty talents stolen from the League treasury. Maybe ten of these talents have been recovered from the graveyard. It looks like the remainder is with bankers in Athens."

"And locked up in property in Kyzikos," I added. "We need to talk to someone who knows something about investments."

"Karnon is the only choice," Diotima said at once.

"It would help if he weren't one of the suspects," I said. "How can we trust what he says?"

"Who else here would know about international property?" Diotima asked. "We certainly don't."

I thought about it. "Let's try Pericles first," I said. "Somehow I have a feeling he knows more about dodgy international transactions than he lets on. When he told me how to go about bribing Geros, it was like he was reciting a school lesson."

"There's a letter here of negotiation," Diotima said flatly. "It's recent. For a consignment of small statuaries."

I didn't like the sound of that. I walked over to the empty shelves. Sure enough, there was dust settled everywhere, but clean spaces in the shapes of squares, rectangles and circles. Just the right size to be the stands of small statuettes.

"What treasury would have so many statuettes?" I asked, but I already knew the answer to that.

"He's cleaned out the Hyperborean Gifts," Diotima said, and her voice was deeply depressed.

"We better not tell the Hyperboreans," I said.

"They'll find out soon enough."

As we left, I thanked Ekam for his courtesy. I felt sorry for the poor friendless man with the difficult name. I could well understand why he'd broken into the wine stores. I said, "Also, Ekam, I know from experience that keeping vigil alone on a dead man can be a bit unnerving. I strongly suggest you take some more wine to strengthen your resolve. In fact, I insist on it."

"Sir, are you ordering me to get drunk on my master's best wine?"

"Why, yes, Ekam, I believe I am."

He stood a little bit straighter and said, "I'll do my best, sir."

THE PERICLES CORRECTION

PERICLES WAS ENTERTAINING a visitor, which was fortunate because it was the other man we needed to speak to: Anaxinos. They sat in the command tent, wine by their side in what looked like a spirit of rapprochement. We pushed our way in, which was perfectly acceptable as Anaxinos had a couple of priestly assistants with him, and Pericles had Philipos.

Anaxinos was speaking as we entered. ". . . I have thought long upon this, Pericles, and I believe I can convince you to abandon this course."

"I doubt that," Pericles said. "But say on."

"Then let me recall the terrible days of the last Persian invasion."

"It was long ago. I was a child, then," Pericles said.

"Yes, so was I," Anaxinos agreed. "Your father Xanthippus was one of the great soldiers of that war."

"I am proud to say that this is true." Pericles noticeably puffed out his chest. Say what you like about Pericles's flexible ethics, he was a patriot through and through.

Anaxinos nodded. "It is said that your father was the last man out of Athens when the enemy sacked the city."

"That too is true," Pericles said.

"They say that your father once crucified a Persian officer, for the crime of sacking a temple," Anaxinos said. "Is this story also true?"

"It is," Pericles confirmed. "It happened at Sestos, in Asia Minor, where there is holy ground nearby. The officer had taken for himself the sacred treasures therein."

"Yet you seek to take the sacred treasures of Delos, an act for which your own father had once crucified an offender," Anaxinos said mildly. "So I must ask you, Pericles, what would your father say, could he see you now?"

These words left Pericles speechless.

Anaxinos stood. "Well, I have made my observations. I must be getting back to my duties."

"Before you leave, High Priest, there is something we must discuss . . ." Diotima's voice trailed off.

"Yes?" Anaxinos cocked his head sideways and looked at Diotima in innocent expectation.

"Umm . . ." She obviously wasn't sure how to begin. I knew that Diotima rather respected the High Priest; she didn't want to upset him, but what she had to say was guaranteed to do that. "The thing is, High Priest, that we can prove that Geros, your lieutenant, has been systematically stealing large sums from the treasury."

"Obviously you're wrong," Anaxinos said. "The idea is ludicrous."

At the same time, Pericles said, "He's the one who's been stealing my money?"

Anaxinos said, "No, Pericles, these two young people have already proven that the guards stole the missing money."

"The guards didn't have a key," Pericles said.

The differing reactions between the two leaders was interesting, but the conversation threatened to run at cross-purposes all day. I coughed to get their attention. "I'm sorry to tell you, Anaxinos, that with the evidence we have, any court and any jury in any city in Hellas would convict Geros."

I proceeded to explain. When I demonstrated what we had found in Geros's office, and when Diotima produced the damning papers, Anaxinos fell back heavily into the chair he had recently vacated. He couldn't move until he had drained the wine cup that he had left behind.

"We'll have to inspect every treasury," I amended. "There's no telling what Geros got into."

"What am I to tell the priests?" Anaxinos muttered to himself.

"The truth?" I suggested.

"A truth that could destroy Delos!" Anaxinos exclaimed. "What use is piety when one of the highest can act like this?" He pulled himself up again. "I must think upon this news," he said. "You must excuse me."

The High Priest gestured to his followers, and they departed.

Pericles sat back down, and gestured for us to do so too. "There is something I must say to you," he said.

"We have more for you, too, Pericles," I told him.

"Thank you for bringing this news. It helps our case enormously, though I'm beginning to doubt if that's a good thing," Pericles said. Then he fell silent. He stayed that way for some time before conceding quietly to those of us left in the tent, "Anaxinos might be right when he says my father would not have approved of transferring the treasure. Yet my intelligence tells me that he is wrong. The arguments we brought with us from Athens are as true as ever. The problem is, when those right arguments are said out loud, they sound just a little too . . ."

"Convenient?" I finished for him.

"Just so." Pericles nodded. "A cynical man might misinterpret our actions, not as the result of cool-headed strategy, but rather as a shameful greed for gold."

"I'm sure no one would ever accuse Athens of such a thing," Diotima said.

I winced.

"Your sarcasm is not needed here," Pericles said. "I have enough to contend with, without your pointless humor."

He seemed to be almost shaking. I was taken aback. Diotima stared, but aid nothing.

"Pericles, you should calm down." I found myself advising the foremost man of Athens.

Pericles took a deep breath. "Yes, you are right." He paused again, then said, "The death of the priest now seems somewhat less regretful."

Diotima said, "We actually came here to question you about one of the transactions that Geros made. It would help us."

Diotima produced the deed for the estate in Kyzikos. She explained its significance.

Pericles understood the main point at once. "That estate was bought with League funds."

"Almost certainly," I agreed.

Pericles thought about it. "Kyzikos isn't just some Hellene city on the coast that the Persians happen to have conquered. It's further inland, on the Black Sea."

"Does that mean something?" Diotima asked.

"It means the Persians know for sure that a priest of Delos has bought land inside their Empire."

"How so?"

"In the Persian system every man is a slave of the Great King. Everyone! No matter how free a man seems, he is ultimately a slave. This is the system we have fought for decades."

"I understand."

"Therefore all property ultimately belongs to the Great

King. You cannot buy land without the approval of their officials."

"Therefore they approved Geros, a senior priest of the Hellenes, to buy an estate inside their empire," Diotima finished for him. She chewed on her lip. "You're right, that does look bad."

"Do they know where the money came from?" I asked.

"What do you think?" Pericles replied.

There was shouting outside—*Harpy* had returned from Athens. We exited the tent to see the commotion. The trireme docked where it had been before, at the pier alongside *Paralos*.

The trierarch was first off, with a bag of responses from the letters that had been sent home. I hadn't expected a reply and therefore wasn't disappointed when he indicated there was nothing for me or my wife.

I was, however, very surprised when a lady of rather small stature was helped off the trireme, following the captain. She had a large bag with her, which she dropped gratefully at my feet.

"You can carry that the rest of the way," she said to me.

I couldn't reply. My jaw hung slack in shock. Eventually I managed to gather my wits enough to say, "Mother! What are you doing here?"

"What do you think I'm doing here?" she said. "You send me a letter telling me that your wife, my daughter-in-law, *the mother of my first grandchild*, could be forced to give birth on some remote island with no one to help her? Dear Gods, boy, did I teach you nothing about how to care for your wife?"

"She was quite insistent," the captain of *Harpy* said. He had come to bid farewell to his passenger and, I suspect, to laugh at me. "She turned up at the boat after we sent off the mail at the Athens end. Refused to leave the ship and cursed me when I wouldn't sail at once. I've never before had a respectable matron threaten to whip the crew if they didn't row faster." The captain of *Harpy* shook his head in mock horror and grinned broadly. He took my mother's hand in a gesture of farewell. "Madam . . . Phaenarete, if you ever tire of your family, I would be most pleased to hire you as a deck officer. Well, I wish you luck."

With that he wandered back to his boat, whistling a happy tune. I was fairly sure that before the day was out, every man in the Athenian Navy would know my mother had arrived to help me.

THE MOTHER DIRECTIVE

IT WAS LATE in the day, but that didn't stop my mother from completely transforming our cottage.

Her first considered action was to inspect Diotima. For this I was told to stand outside and make sure no one entered. We had a murder to solve, but I didn't even think about disobeying. Mother emerged some time later to announce that Diotima's pregnancy was in fine condition, and very close to the end. My wife looked mildly embarrassed but, she had to admit, relieved to know that an expert on childbirth was with us.

The next thing Mother did was place statues of Eileithyia, the goddess of childbirth, around the room. Most men know nothing about her, but because I was the son of a midwife I was more knowledgeable than most. Mother then made offerings at each of these statues and recited prayers beseeching Eileithyia to assist both mother and child.

Mother put her hands on her hips and inspected her handiwork with approval.

"This is where the birth will take place, if Diotima doesn't make it back to Athens in time. We've done everything we can to gain divine assistance. At least here on Delos Diotima has the most chance of intervention from Eileithyia."

"Why is that?" I asked.

"Because Eileithyia came to us from Hyperborea," my mother said.

My jaw dropped for the second time that day. "Say that again?"

"Hera, the mother of the gods, sent Eileithyia all the way from faraway Hyperborea to Delos, to assist with the birth of the gods Apollo and Artemis. Everyone knows that, my son."

"Everyone who is a midwife knows that," I said. I wondered what my mother would say if I told her I could introduce her to some real live Hyperboreans. But this wasn't the time to mention it.

I had to admit the arrival of my mother relieved the fears of both Diotima and myself. We left her to continue turning the cottage into the perfect birthing chamber while we went out to solve a murder.

THE HYPERBOREAN SURPRISE

IT WAS TIME to inspect the Treasury of Artemis, the one place for which Geros had the only key. Diotima and I were quite certain what we would find. The papers in Geros's secret room had clearly said that Geros had found a buyer for the Gifts. The empty shelves in that same room suggested strongly that they were already gone. I could only hope that Anaxinos would not be too upset when he saw the truth.

Philipos joined us, in his official capacity as my apprentice. "I found the boat," he announced when he arrived.

"What boat?" I asked.

He looked hurt. "Nicolaos, you asked me to find which boat went to the Old Village the night Geros died."

So I had, and it was so long ago that I'd completely forgotten.

"You're never going to guess which one it was," he said.

"You're right, I won't guess because you're going to tell me."

"It was the dinghy, the one that's chained to a rock and has the oars inside."

Diotima and I shared a look of total surprise.

"But that's the emergency eject system," she said. "People aren't allowed to use it for anything else."

I asked my assistant, "Was there another death that night . . . a natural one, I mean?"

"No."

"Are you sure of this?" I asked.

Philipos managed to look smug. "I measured the keel, just like you said. I measured the keel of every boat in the New Village. All the others are fishing boats; their keels are much wider and deeper."

"What about the triremes? Do they carry tenders?"

"I checked. Some do, but they're all much longer, for ten men or more."

"Whoever took it must have been desperate," I said. "I wonder who it was? Philipos, you have done well."

"Thanks!"

It was then that Anaxinos joined us with his usual cloud of priests.

"Which treasury holds the Hyperborean Gifts?" I asked Anaxinos.

"The one closest to the Temple of Artemis," Anaxinos said, reasonably enough.

We stopped there, and Anaxinos produced the key that had once belonged to Geros. The steps to this building were barely set off the ground.

Anaxinos pointed the key toward the slot in the door, missed the hole on the first try, then carefully got it right on the second. He pushed. The key resisted several times, but finally made it all the way in with some extra effort and a few unpriestly swear words.

Anaxinos began to turn. This key had an extra handle of ivory to make the turning easier. The door made its now familiar clunk as the key released the bar, then squealed to set our teeth on edge as it opened a fraction.

Anaxinos sighed. "I hate it when that happens." He put his hand on the door but stopped for a moment and faced Diotima and me. "I suppose you realize this is a waste of time. Everything will be in order."

The High Priest pushed the door. It swung slowly inwards.

"I reveal to you the Gifts of the Hyperboreans."

Light from over our shoulders filled the small space within.

Inside there was shelf upon shelf of votive statues. Some large, some small, all of them works of art.

Diotima and I stared at this open-mouthed.

"I can't believe it," my wife said.

"See, I told you the Gifts would all be here," Anaxinos said. The tone of his voice was almost gleeful. "Geros could never have so forgotten himself as to steal these devout gifts."

Diotima and I could only look at the perfectly placed, very beautiful statuettes.

"You are astonished at the exquisite beauty of the gifts?" Anaxinos said, misinterpreting our dumbfounded expressions. "So am I. I wish we knew who these Hyperboreans were, so that we can thank them properly."

Diotima and I could have helped him out there, but this wasn't the time to tell him. I suddenly realized that behind us, completely unnoticed, Damon had sidled up, ostensibly to see the excitement. I caught his eye and shook my head ever so slightly, to tell him we would not give away his secret.

Damon smiled.

"This is a complete and utter surprise," Diotima said.

"Why?" Anaxinos asked, puzzled.

"Because I thought it would be ransacked!"

ANAXINOS AND HIS priests made their way off, after locking up behind them. No doubt they would spend the rest of the day talking amongst themselves about what idiots the detectives were. Damon likewise sauntered off, secure in the knowledge that we hadn't betrayed his secret.

This left Diotima, Philipos, and me to contemplate total failure.

"It doesn't make sense," I said. "How could the Gifts— the statuettes—all still be in the treasury? Is our entire theory wrong?"

"None of the facts seem to match any other facts," Philipos complained. "Is it always like this?"

"Usually," I said, "Right up to the moment when things click together. Then it all makes sense. You just have to move the facts back and forth, and work out why they connect, even when they don't seem to."

"Don't worry, Philipos," Diotima said. "I feel we have enough facts. We'll get it, but it might take a few more days."

"Well, we have to solve it soon, or you'll be stopped by childbirth." I counted on my fingers. "According to my calculations, you have ten days to go."

At that moment, Diotima gave a startled groan. Suddenly there was a pool of water by her feet.

"Honey, are you all right?" I said. "Are you hurt?" I put an arm around her. She seemed to stand there in shock.

"Oh, I've seen that before," Philipos said. "It means you're about to be a father, Nicolaos."

"What?" I said stupidly.

"My waters have broken, Nico," Diotima said. "My labor just started."

"It's too soon!" I said in alarm.

"You better tell the baby that, then, because it disagrees."

I told myself there was no need to panic. Nor was there, but that didn't stop my heart from racing.

"Dear Gods. Philipos, we really need you now. Help me get Diotima to the cottage, would you?"

My mother recognized what had happened at once. Philipos waited outside while my mother laid Diotima on our bed and announced that she was beginning contractions, whatever that meant.

"Is that good?" I asked.

"It's perfectly normal," my mother assured me. "Go do something else for the next half day or so. We don't need you here."

"But what about the baby?

"Calm down, Nico," she said. "I've done this hundreds of times."

"But Diotima hasn't!"

"I can't give birth on Delos," Diotima said. "I can't break the Goddess's sacred rule."

"Is there time to get her to Mykonos?" I asked Mother.

"No," was her short reply.

"We'll get you onto one of the triremes," I said, relieved that I had an answer. "Pericles will give us one. It can stand off the coast."

"But then the murder won't be solved, Nico. We'll fail our mission." Diotima seemed genuinely upset. She never accepted failure.

"Do you think I care? You're more important." I took her hand in mine. "Does it hurt?"

"Only when I breathe," she said.

"Don't stop doing that!" I said, alarmed.

"Good idea. Nico, listen to me." Diotima sat up. She seemed quite certain about something. "I have time."

"Time for what?"

"To denounce the murderer."

"You must be joking. You're having a baby—"

"Yes, I'd noticed," Diotima replied coolly. "Nico, I was joking when I said it only hurts when I breathe. I'll declare who is the killer, then you make the arrest while I go have the baby. There's plenty of time for everything."

"You're not going to risk my grandchild!" my mother said.

"No, Phaenarete," Diotima said. "I'm certainly not. But there are women who work right up to the moment they give birth, aren't there?"

"Yes," said Phaenarete dubiously. "But they mostly work on farms."

"Then think how easy my work will be!" Diotima said persuasively. "All I have to do is talk for a while."

I said, "I don't think this is a good idea . . ."

"Trust me. What could possibly go wrong?" my wife said.

My wife had gone delirious in her labor. "Don't you think it would help if we knew who the killer was?" I pointed out.

Diotima said urgently, "I want to try. Nico, I have time, honestly. It's like we said to Philipos: I'm sure we have all the facts, we just haven't worked out yet how they fit together."

"That would seem to put a stop to the plan."

"Nico, we're facing failure either way. Let's get up to the sanctuary grounds. It's the only place where everyone can meet. We'll start explaining the facts to everyone—the whole island—so that every witness is there. We'll take it slowly and try to work it out as we go. All right?"

"Aren't you supposed to be having contractions?"

"I *am* having contractions, they're just not very painful yet."

I looked to my mother. "Is Diotima right? Do we have time to denounce a murderer and then get her back here safely?"

Phaenarete shrugged. "Sometimes they come quickly; sometimes they take a long time. How much time do you need to denounce a murderer?"

"Usually it's a long meeting with lots of shouting. Never more than, say, half a morning, usually much less."

Phaenarete lifted Diotima's tunic and checked certain arrangements on my wife that are normally for my eyes only. She dropped the tunic and said, "You have time. But then you get straight back here after. I suggest you have a stretcher ready and waiting."

"Nico, we have to do it," Diotima said.

This was insanity. I looked out the window. Night was falling.

"If we're going to do this, we'll have to be fast," I said.

I went out to issue orders to Philipos. He was waiting beyond the door, looking solicitous. I was touched by his care. He looked up expectantly as I approached.

"Philipos, my apprentice," I said. "We're still on the job. Go to Pericles and Anaxinos, and ask them to assemble the people of Delos."

HARD LABOR

THE MEETING WAS held at the same place where the protest had occurred, not so many days before. How things had changed.

Assembled were the villagers of Delos, the priests and priestesses of the sanctuary, and Karnon and his assistants. Of the Athenians there were Pericles and all the captains of the triremes. The common men were back on the beach. Pericles had insisted the men stay with their boats. They had patrolled during the day because of the threat of the three ships that Semnos and I had seen. Pericles was unwilling to leave the fleet unguarded at night, and he wanted them ready to launch at a moment's notice. The exception was *Paralos*. Semnos and his crew had come to watch us.

It was dark by the time everyone was present, milling about, and with much murmuring from the crowd. Torches were lit. I heard several voices in the crowd loudly comment that dinner was being missed and ask if this couldn't wait until the morning. The answer, though they didn't know it, was that it certainly couldn't. Every now and then I heard a slight moan from Diotima, who sat upon a comfortable stool that I had carried. My mother stood anxiously by Diotima, but we had not told anyone that our detective was in labor. I silently prayed to Mother's goddess Eileithyia for deliverance for my wife.

Anaxinos wanted to begin with a lengthy speech, which

we cut short. I needed to keep us moving at a brisk pace. I swallowed heavily, and hoped nobody saw me do it. The highest probability was that by the time we were finished, my wife and I would look like the greatest idiots Athens had ever produced. The only way we could avoid that would be to solve the murder even as we explained the facts. We had talked it through while we waited for everyone, and had agreed that the way to proceed was to logically unfold the facts as they had occurred, dissecting each one, and hope that inspiration would strike.

Diotima stood to speak. She did not have a loud voice, and had to shout to be heard. "I shall begin with something that happened long before the Athenians arrived. Something that is known only to a few, but which you all must learn if there is to be justice."

Anaxinos flinched. He knew what was coming.

Diotima said, "For some time, a number of years, Geros had been stealing from the treasure of the Delian League. He used the money to buy an estate and fine things for himself."

This instantly caused angry shouts from the priests. One said, "How could he do these things without us noticing?"

"Because Geros had a key made up," Diotima said. "Geros borrowed a key, probably from Karnon, and had the local blacksmith copy it. Your blacksmith here is an old man, flooded with work. He probably didn't even notice what he was doing."

I held up Geros's copy of the key for all to see. "Do you see this one is different from the official keys in its color and its form?" I said. "The handle is bare metal, with no ivory handle, the material is a darker iron, and if you looked up close, you would see no inscription. This is a mere piece of metal bent to the right shape."

People nodded.

I jumped across to the Porinos Naos and, in full view of the crowd, used that copied key to open the door, as Anaxinos had done before. There were exclamations from the many who had not heard the news of Geros's extra key. Then I pulled the door shut and returned to Diotima.

"How could he hide the money?" another man asked.

"Geros was using a bank in Athens to handle all his transactions." Diotima produced the sheaf of papyrus that we had removed from the dead man's office. "I'm sorry to have to tell you that we can easily prove Geros did these things. I must also mention that his bankers are possibly the most dishonest of their dubious kind. They would not hesitate to misappropriate temple funds."

That caused Anaxinos to purse his lips in distaste. "Then should they not be prosecuted?"

I answered that one. "Unfortunately the bankers will claim that they did not know the source of their client's funds. Nobody could prove otherwise." I sighed.

Anaxinos looked askance at the large wad of papyrus in Diotima's hand. He put up his hand to the angry priests. "I have seen these proofs that the priestess Diotima claims, and unfortunately I find them persuasive. We must accept for the moment that what she says is true. Geros had stolen from the treasures. This does not answer the question of who killed him, nor solve the pollution upon the sacred isle."

Diotima nodded. "You are right, High Priest. The killer must still be found." She took a deep breath. "Now knowing this, I want you to imagine what Geros must have felt when the Athenians arrived."

She paused to let them think about that.

"Geros's problem was really quite simple," she went on.

"When the Athenians turned up, demanding the Delian League's money, he must have been terrified. He knew the money would be accounted before it left Delos—Karnon would see to that—and then the theft would be discovered."

"But no one would know it was Geros who had stolen the missing money," Anaxinos objected.

"People would find out very quickly, High Priest," Diotima said. "Imagine if Geros had not died, and the theft was discovered. We would have instantly interrogated the guards who stand before the treasury. They would have told us of Geros's trips into a temple to which he supposedly had no key, and no reason to visit. As it happens, Geros had enlisted two of the guards—he had to, so that they would let him pass—which would have made catching them all so much the simpler."

"I can see the logic of this," Anaxinos conceded.

"Thus imagine the situation in Geros's mind. He had committed a larceny so enormous that it was probably the biggest theft ever made in the history of Delos. When Pericles announced that he was taking the treasure, Geros foresaw his own arrest, trial, and certain execution."

There were noises from the crowd, ones not quite so hostile as before, that suggested the people saw the logic of this. They could feel themselves in Geros's position. It probably helped that he had not been well liked.

Diotima went on, "High Priest, remember when Pericles announced his plan. He almost won you over with his rational argument. I don't like the idea of moving the treasure any more than you do, but we could both see that Pericles's idea had some merit."

Anaxinos nodded. "That is true."

"But Geros was present too," Diotima said. "He realized

straight away that he did not dare let the Athenians take the treasure. He not only objected, but he promoted an argument between you and Pericles."

"The anger I felt was real," Anaxinos said.

"Yes, sir, but your rational head would have ruled you had not Geros interrupted," Diotima said.

"Perhaps." Anaxinos clearly wasn't convinced. "Go on with your tale."

"Geros immediately agitated the whole island against Athens. That wasn't difficult, with the way many of the people felt. You yourself the next day made your own feelings about Athens known to us, High Priest."

Anaxinos blushed. "That was in drink," he said.

"Yes, of course, and there's nothing wrong with hating the greedy, is there?" Diotima assured him. "You have nothing for which you need apologize, High Priest. In fact, from your point of view, *anyone* who removes treasure from the sacred precinct has committed the most terrible crime."

There was general shocked silence at these words, until a priest with a full black beard interjected, "Here now! Are you accusing the High Priest of murder?"

I wondered if she was too, but Diotima ignored the interruption. "Thus, by evening, Geros was leading a revolt against Athenian arrogance."

"We all admired him for taking the moral stand," the priest with the black beard said.

"The Athenians admired him too," I told him. "For the same reason. But he was fooling all of us."

They all looked doubtful.

"The barbeque that ended the protest suited both Pericles and Anaxinos," Diotima said. "The social mixing restored peace. That is true, is it not, Pericles?" Diotima prodded. "You were happy for good relations to be restored."

"Yes, of course," Pericles said the only thing he could, though I knew quite well Pericles couldn't have cared less as long as he got his money.

"It suited you, too, Anaxinos?" Diotima asked.

Anaxinos nodded. "Conflict is never welcome here. Anything that restored peace had to be good."

"It didn't suit Geros though," Diotima told them. "He needed conflict. I don't think at that stage Geros knew what he was going to do next. He only knew that he had to keep the Athenians at bay until he could cover his tracks. Or make a run for it. But I suspect he wanted to make good with the treasury."

"How could you possibly know that?"

"Geros's motives at that point are hidden from us, but what he did is known. He needed to consult with someone. He sent a message back to someone in the village."

That was a pure guess on Diotima's part, and I knew it. But we both knew it was the only way to explain the result that followed.

"They arranged a clandestine meeting. That immediately suggests the two did not dare be seen talking together."

"How do you know this?" someone asked.

I took over. "After the barbeque, Geros departed northwest to the old village. The gate on the path there is the only one on this island that doesn't squeak, by the way. Someone, presumably Geros, had oiled it. It was the path to where he stored his stolen goods, but that comes later. What he did that night, after the barbeque was over, was to go on his own to the old village. There he met someone. We know this because he was observed all the way there, and at the old village there was someone waving a torch. Obviously, they met."

"Who followed him?" a young, scowling priest demanded.

"I did," I said. I stared down the questioner, who scowled even harder but said nothing, then I cast my glance across the crowd, daring anyone to ask the next question. To my relief, no one did.

"Who was this someone whom Geros met?" Diotima asked the rhetorical question. "At this stage we couldn't tell. But we knew for sure that whoever it was, they had used the emergency eject system to row themselves around the island to the old village."

"How do you know that?" Anaxinos asked.

"Because the keel of the emergency eject rowboat exactly matches the marks on the sand by the old village," Diotima said.

"Proves nothing. It could be any fisher boat," one of the villagers said.

"No, it couldn't," Diotima said. "Philipos, our assistant, measured. The keels of the larger boats used for fishing are all wider and deeper, as anyone would expect."

"The other rowboats, then," the villager said.

"Are all tied at the docks, in easy view of the agora, where people were walking back and forth all night, because of the barbeque. No, it was the emergency eject, which no one ever looks for except in an emergency. Not that it matters for our investigation, anyway. What is important is that a rowboat, taken from the New Village, was used to row to the Old Village."

"How do you know the small boat didn't come from a larger one offshore?" someone asked.

"In the middle of the night?" I asked. "There are fifty trireme captains present. Gentlemen," I called out.

"Which of you would willingly sail your boats at night, in shallow water, close to an island?"

No one stirred. I wasn't surprised.

"So you see," Diotima said, "the rowboat that landed at the Old Village *had* to have come from somewhere else on the island."

Heads nodded. Diotima had logic on her side.

All this time I had been feverishly watching the faces of the audience, to see if anyone reacted strongly to these revelations. But too many people did. If there was a guilty party, he wasn't obvious.

Diotima now came to the first of the questions that could cause us to fall flat on our faces. She took a deep breath, preparing to speak, but then gasped and her left hand went to her stomach. I don't think anyone else noticed, but she doubled over just a fraction.

After a moment Diotima said, "Then the next question is, who was in the boat?"

No one volunteered, which was hardly surprising. Diotima looked at me. I looked at her. There was no choice but to go with our guess.

"There could only be one answer," Diotima said with a confidence I knew she didn't feel. "It had to be someone from the village. Only a villager would think to use that rowboat; of the Athenians the only one who might even know about it is Semnos, and he was at the Athenian camp."

The faces in the crowd watched Diotima expectantly. No one objected to her reasoning.

Diotima spoke on. "But if it was a villager, why didn't Geros simply speak to him—or her—during the protest? No one would have noticed during the confusion. No reasonable person would leave the sanctuary, where Geros was present, walk to the village, take the rowboat no one is supposed to take, and then row all the way back to where they'd come from." Diotima shook her head, slowly. "It doesn't make sense, does it? Therefore the person who rowed from the New Village to the Old Village had to be a local who was *not* at the protest, and who didn't want to be seen there. There was only one such person of any importance."

Diotima looked straight at Karnon.

There was a long, long pause, during which Karnon was silent. But the accountant knew a correct calculation when he heard it. He said in a defiant tone, "All right, I admit it. I was the one who met Geros."

I breathed a sigh of relief.

"Would you like to tell us why?" Diotima asked in such a way that she made it seem as if she already knew the answer. Diotima and I had a good guess, but only Karnon could confirm it.

Then Karnon did something that surprised me. He beat his right hand against his bald head, the way a man might when he admits to doing something stupid.

"Very well, I will tell you everything. Geros was black-mailing me."

The crowd exclaimed at this.

"And the reason?" Diotima asked coolly. She had her hands placed over her stomach. It was a natural posture, but I knew she was pressing in, and that she was in some pain.

"I don't know how, but Geros had discovered that I was dipping into the Delian funds," Karnon said.

The way he phrased it, it took a moment for everyone to realize what he meant. When they did, there was uproar.

I said loudly, over the hubbub, so that it was clear to

everyone present, "Thus you see, there were *two* thieves, acting independently, both stealing from the treasure of the Delian League; and one was blackmailing the other."

Anaxinos said, in a choked voice, "But . . . Geros, my second in command, and Karnon, the most trusted accountant in all of Hellas? They were *both* thieves?"

"I'm afraid so, High Priest," I said.

The respected leader of Delos was in deep distress. Someone brought a stool, and Anaxinos sat down heavily.

Karnon knew he was in trouble. He shouted, "Hear me out!"

He had to wait, but when the crowd quieted, he went on.

"I wasn't actually doing any harm. You have to understand that. The money I was taking was money I had made on top of the funds."

Karnon turned to Diotima and me. "Remember I told you that I used investments to increase the League funds?"

Diotima said, "You did. You said you invested much of the League funds, and returned the profits to the Treasury."

"Well, I channeled away some of that extra profit before it ever reached the coffers," Karnon said. Then he held out his hands in supplication to Pericles, the most senior League member present. "I would never have stolen the real funds."

That was a fine line, and I had a feeling the combined leaders of the Delian League were not going to appreciate it. Karnon looked from one to the other of us wildly and pleaded for understanding. "Geros found me out. I don't know how. He threatened to tell everyone what I had done. He also threatened to tell my wife back in Athens about Marika and the boys, or at least, he tried. My wife would divorce me and then I'd be left with nothing, no way to support Marika. When I realized what he was getting at, I confess I was a willing accomplice, to help him hide his own thefts."

"You *knew* that Geros was stealing funds?" Pericles said to Karnon. "But it was you who announced that the treasury had been robbed. With your own thefts to hide, why didn't you keep quiet?"

"I can answer that." Diotima smiled. She enjoyed any opportunity to outsmart Pericles. "It's simple. From Karnon's point of view, Geros's death was a gift from the Gods. With Geros dead, Karnon could announce the entire theft, and then let us decide that the whole crime was the work of the priest. Do you see? Karnon would still have the money he had misappropriated, and yet be completely in the clear."

Karnon looked like he was about to cry, but he nodded. "The Athenian priestess speaks correctly. When I ordered my slaves to start the accounting, I knew what they would find. I expected all the missing money would be put down to Geros. Then when the money moved to Athens I would cease my own thefts and be completely safe."

Anaxinos said, "But why, Karnon? Why did you destroy your integrity?"

Karnon turned to the High Priest. "For my family, of course! I needed that money so I could free myself from my wife's family and leave with the woman I truly love, Marika, and my sons." Karnon sobbed.

"Then this means Karnon killed Geros," Pericles said.

"I admit I stole profits," Karnon said as he wept. "But I did not kill the priest."

The other priests shook their fists. One of them shouted, "Bring a rope!" Another shouted, "A likely story!"

"A likely story, indeed," Diotima said, holding up her hand for attention. "Karnon could not have killed Geros."

"What!" all the priests exclaimed as one. Most of them looked upset.

I had to admire what Diotima was doing. From this point on I knew she was making the deductions as she went.

Diotima said, "It's true. The rowboat was gone from the Old Village by the time of the murder. The evidence of Philipos proves it. He reported that he saw the light. Then he saw Nico and Geros talk. But after they parted, Philipos returned to the camp down the waterline, and he *never mentioned seeing the boat*. It must have already gone. Which, by the way, is consistent with Nico's catching Geros as he was returning from the conference with Karnon."

"How do you know Karnon didn't return later to kill Geros?" someone asked.

"Because there is only one keel track at the beach," I said at once.

"There are ways around that," Pericles said.

"Complex ways, that require the man in the rowboat to know that two random Athenian operatives are going to creep through the graveyard and see his light," Diotima said. "Because it's certain that he didn't see us. If he had, Karnon would have fled the island."

"Hmm, I see your point."

"I have not explained the next part of the mystery," Diotima said. "Here I hand over to my husband."

I knew what had to come next. We had discussed this beforehand, and saw no choice if we were to solve the killing.

I said, "I must admit my own complicity in a crime. You see, ladies and gentlemen of Delos, I was sent to find Geros on a mission."

"You are treading into dangerous territory, Nicolaos," Pericles said icily. "This is not open to discussion."

"I fear it must be, Pericles, if you ever want this treasure to live in Athens."

I turned quickly to the crowd, before Pericles could argue.

"Pericles sent me to offer Geros whatever it would take to convince him to cease his resistance."

There were outraged murmurs and a few shouts amongst the priests at this news.

"You admit this?" Anaxinos said in shock.

"I do, High Priest, and I am sorry to say I accepted that commission. I can only console myself that from what we know now, Geros would probably have died anyway."

"I suppose, after all that you have said, that you will tell us that Geros accepted this bribe," Anaxinos said sadly.

"He did."

"I ask out of curiosity, to find out how much the integrity of a priest of Delos is worth. How much did you offer?"

"Geros demanded thirty talents," I said.

There was a collective gasp from everyone present.

Someone muttered loudly, "Dear Gods!"

I said, "The ironic thing is that, if Geros had simply admitted to me that he had already ransacked the treasury to the tune of thirty talents, Pericles would not have cared one little bit. Geros made the mistake of thinking that Pericles has any ethics worth speaking of."

"NICOLAOS!" Pericles shouted.

"Which of course he does," I finished smoothly, and grinned broadly. I was enjoying every moment of this. "But not when it comes to the good of Athens. Pericles would have let Geros keep the money he'd stolen—after all, it was the same as the bribe we'd offered—and then Athens would have made off with the treasury and everyone would have been happy, more or less." I cast an uneasy eye at the

High Priest, who could not have been happy hearing about such underhanded dealings within his sacred sanctuary.

"Geros must have thought that the Gods had smiled upon him when Nico made his offer," Diotima said. "He saw a chance to save himself. He had ten talents hidden on Delos, but he also had ten talents stored with a banker in Athens, and ten talents already spent on assets. Thus he couldn't return the stolen money, but he *could* return the bribe money."

"Geros mentioned none of this to me," Karnon said. His brow furrowed. "Why would he not tell me?"

"Because Geros didn't know of this offer until after you had left," Diotima said.

"I see."

"After Geros parted from Nico, he was seen walking toward the New Village. We wondered why he did this. Geros wasn't seen anywhere else until his death. Where did he go?"

Diotima paused to let everyone think about that. Then she said, "The most obvious answer is that he went to see Karnon. They had only just parted, but now he had important news. He went to tell the accountant about the bribe."

"I deny this!" Karnon shouted.

"Yet consider, Karnon, if you knew, and if the sums came out even, would you have raised a fuss? Especially since you have your own . . . ah . . . family issues to consider."

"Perhaps not," Karnon conceded.

"There you see it, then," Diotima said. "The Athenian bribe offered Geros the lifeline he desperately needed."

She paused, to let that sink in. I could see heads among the crowd nodding slightly. But most weren't. The priests were not entirely convinced. As for the villagers, their expressions were stony.

"There is every chance Geros went somewhere else, or spoke to someone else," Diotima said. "Now we must leave that thread and turn to the Hyperborean Gifts. The evidence from his house suggests Geros had taken the Hyperborean Gifts. Yet when we checked the treasury house, they were still there. How could this be?"

"Geros put them back, perhaps an outburst of honesty?" Anaxinos said.

"It does seem the obvious conclusion, doesn't it?" Diotima said. "There are only two keys to the treasury house of the Delian Artemis, where the Hyperborean Gifts are kept. Geros held one, High Priest. The other was held by you."

Diotima paused, and then she gasped a little. She clutched at her stomach and I knew the pain of childbirth was becoming too much for my wife. I moved to support her, but she waved me back. There was a murmur among the crowd. I think some—at least some of the women—had begun to guess she was in labor.

When the pain had passed, Diotima said, "Of course, by the time the gifts returned, Geros was dead himself. That suggests there is another thief, or another criminal of some sort."

That caused another eruption from the priests. They stepped toward Diotima—it seemed to them that she had just accused Anaxinos of murder. I stepped in front of Diotima, and I was gratified to see that the combined captains of the Athenian Fleet also moved to defend an Athenian.

The meeting was on the verge of riot.

"Stop!" Pericles ordered. Then he looked to Anaxinos, who nodded.

"Pericles is correct," said Anaxinos. "There must be calm here." He turned to Diotima. "Proceed as you must, priestess," he said. "I assume you realize that a war on this small island is not to your advantage?"

"I do, sir," Diotima said. "There is almost nothing that can be said about these killings that doesn't antagonize *someone*."

"So I see," said Anaxinos dryly. "I feel somewhat antagonized myself. Explain your words."

"Yes, sir," said Diotima politely. She continued loudly, over the hubbub. "The fact is, Delos relies on keys to protect its treasures. It's not like how it's done in many other places. On Delos, except for the Porinos Naos, there are no guards or slaves to watch who goes where. On Delos, it all comes down to who can hold a key."

Diotima held up one of these keys, for everyone to see. "This is the key to the treasury of the Hyperborean Gifts. The only one. Geros kept it. We found it in his house. On the face of it, then, it was not the key used to open the door to return the gifts. But now we must note that most people on Delos leave their doors unguarded, and the slave of Geros is rather fond of wine, and maintenance men from the village tend to wander in and out of everyone's homes."

Diotima let them think about that. She finished with, "Almost any villager could have grabbed that key for a day."

"But who would want to return the gifts in such secrecy?" one of the priests asked.

"The Hyperboreans, of course," Diotima said. "The Hyperboreans have gone to enormous lengths to send these fine gifts to Delos. They would be absolutely furious if they knew the Gifts were stolen."

There was general laughter at this. "The Hyperboreans are far, far away," the priest said.

"Are they?"

Diotima walked over to Damon, standing to the side.

She said quietly, "Damon, I promise on my honor and my life that your people will not suffer for this. Anaxinos has too many other problems than to worry about some friendly immigrants."

Damon thought for a moment, looked to Moira for silent advice, she nodded, and then Damon nodded, slowly.

Diotima put her hand upon his high, broad shoulders and said, "Let me introduce you to Damon, Chief of the Hyperboreans."

There was great clamor at this announcement.

"Is this true?" Anaxinos said in amazement.

"It is true," Damon said. He explained the history of the Hyperboreans, as he had to Diotima and me in the dead of night.

"All this time you thought you were running Delos, High Priest," Diotima said to Anaxinos. "When in fact, all this time you have been running the Sacred Isle in partnership with the Chief of the Hyperboreans."

"This is hard to believe," Anaxinos said. I knew what he was thinking, and likewise everyone else. Damon seemed like the most simple of simpletons . . . most of the time.

I said, "Have you ever noticed, sir, how Damon always seems to be there with the right answer when there's a problem to solve?"

Anaxinos thought for a moment, his hand on his chin, before he nodded.

Diotima shot me a happy smile, and I returned it. I knew what she was thinking. The way that had turned out, we both now knew exactly who had killed Geros.

Diotima made the announcement. "Ladies and gentlemen, priests and priestesses of Holy Delos, the murderer of Geros was—"

"Pirates! Pirates!" People on the eastern side of the

crowd were screaming in fear. I looked and saw there were indeed armed strangers streaming in from that direction.

But no pirate would ever be so stupid as to attack Delos when there were fifty triremes guarding the island. This was something entirely more dangerous. Pericles and I, and every other man with combat experience knew instantly what we saw. There were men emerging from the dark, to the east and south east. They didn't run, but walked steadily. At first they were mere figures, but as they approached the detail became apparent. Some wore the unmistakable leather and bronze scale armor of the Persians, with the unmistakable shafts of spears in hand. Others wore no armor, but looked like sailors in tunics with typical Phoenician caps.

Not an armed invasion, as Pericles had feared, not pirates as might be expected. This was a targeted raid, by the Persians, on Phoenician ships, and I had no doubt what the raiders were targeting.

"Not pirates," Pericles shouted. "Persians . . . Phoenicians . . . Raiders."

There was no doubting who led us now. Though he spent all his time on politics, Pericles was a *strategos* of Athens. There was no one to match him on Delos.

Villagers and priests were stumbling backwards, away from the advancing attackers.

Semnos drew his short sword. It was the sort that sea captains liked to wield, of no use on a battlefield, but handy for close quarters fighting. Like everything else about Semnos, his sword was the last word in elegance: decked out in silver filigree, with a handle of finest leather, brightly colored ribbons at the pommels, and a leaf-shaped blade of perfectly polished iron. It also looked very sharp.

Semnos jumped to the top of a high plinth upon which

stood a statue of Apollo. He hooked his left arm around Apollo, and hung there at an angle, his right arm high and his sword pointed to the stars.

Semnos yelled in a sea captain's voice, which is to say his words echoed across even the rapidly developing battle. "*Paralos! Paralos* to me!"

This was a slashing raid, with swords and spears and a battering ram to take the treasure of the Delian League before anyone could react. The men of *Paralos* were the only common fighting sailors present; all the other Athenians were commanders of trierarch rank. The other sailors were all on the western beach, tending to their ships. They might as well have been in another country for all the good they could do here. This fight would be over one way or another before any body of men could arrive.

The men of *Paralos* pushed through to their commander.

Semnos shouted, "*Paralos* follow me!" He jumped from the statue.

Here on land, Semnos didn't have to protect his ship. He was free to engage the enemy. Semnos led his men forward like a fighting sailor, with his weapon at the ready and a steady charge. The men followed their captain. It was only then that I realized none of them were armed, except for their personal knives. All their weaponry was back on their ship.

Pericles saw the problem too. He shouted in his command voice. "Trierarchs, form a battle line, single file."

The trierarchs were the only men here with weapons, all short swords, all designed for use at sea, none of them even remotely long enough to suffice for a phalanx in the manner that Hellene soldiers liked to fight. But they would have to do something, because right now, the only thing standing between the Phoenician raiders and the entire fighting fund for our war against the Persians was the crew of *Paralos*.

Karnon ran over to me. "Nicolaos, those men will get into the treasure at any moment."

"Don't worry, Karnon," I told him. "I know it looks bad, but they'd need a battering ram to get through that door. I'm sure they've got one, but by the time they can bring it up the other men from the ships will be here."

Karnon said, "Uh, Nicolaos, do you remember when you opened the treasury, just a moment ago?"

"Yes, of course I do."

"Do you remember how you slammed the door shut and then hurried back to your wife?"

"Of course I do."

"Are you holding the key of the treasury door right now?"

"Of course I . . . uh oh . . ."

I stopped speaking, realized the key wasn't in my hands, and desperately looked about the ground around me. There was no key.

Dear Gods, I had left the key in the door.

All the raiders had to do was push that door open.

Karnon turned to Pericles, who was shouting orders to the trierarchs with sword drawn. Karnon snatched Pericles's sword from him.

Pericles jumped backwards, thinking that Karnon intended to attack him. I had thought so too, until Karnon shook his head.

"Give back that sword," Pericles commanded.

"You don't need it," Karnon said. "You're the General."

"So? What in Hades do you think you're doing?" Pericles barked.

"I haven't spent my whole life tending the treasure of the League to see it go like this."

Karnon didn't wait for more small talk. He turned and ran into the mêlée, waving the sword. The struggling sailors closed in around him and that was the last I saw of Karnon.

Pericles didn't stop to swear. Instead he commanded.

I had to get back that key.

But first, there was something else that was even more urgent.

I went over to where Diotima and Damon stood. I said, "Damon, I need you to take Diotima and my mother, and all the women and children and the old people away from here. Can you do that?"

Damon nodded. "Yes, of course."

"Before you go, there's something we need to settle . . ."

"Yes?" he asked.

"Diotima didn't finish her explanation. I'll finish it for her. It was you who killed Geros, wasn't it Damon?"

He paused for a moment, and then he nodded.

"Yes, we did it," he admitted. "It was Meren, actually. She stabbed him while I held him still."

"Because of the Gifts, of course," I said.

Damon nodded. "Meren kept an eye on the treasury and the Gifts—in her role as our priestess of the Hyperboreans, you understand. Geros never knew. Then, one day, the Gifts were gone. It didn't take long to work out that Geros had taken them. He was the only one with an official key. A few days later we watched while he visited the Hyperborean Treasury, ostensibly on business, and didn't raise an alarm though the place was ransacked. Then we *knew*." Damon scowled and spoke angrily. "Our people had worked for decades to fill that treasury with the gifts of our devotion to the Goddess, and this evil man was about to sell them."

"You didn't raise the alarm yourselves," I said.

"That would have given us away," Damon said. "While we were thinking about what to do, you Athenians turned up. It gave us the perfect opportunity to punish Geros and make it look like you Athenians did it."

"Thanks very much for that."

"You're welcome," Damon said with a straight face. "We got the location of where Geros had hidden the Gifts before we let him die. Turned out we were only just in time to stop a sale."

"Then Meren wrote NEMESIS above his body," I said. I had thought at the time Diotima had explained it that whoever had written that word must have been a priestess.

"That's right," Damon said. "After that we crept into Geros's secret office, grabbed the Gifts, and put them back in the treasury. It was a good morning's work. Then all was right with the world!"

"Can we trust you?" I asked, because I was planning to put Diotima into the care of two murderers.

"Are you planning on robbing the Goddess?" he asked.

"No, of course not."

"Then you can trust me."

But did I trust him? It was in Damon's interest to eliminate Diotima and me before we told the world that he and Meren were guilty. It would be so easy for Damon to eliminate Diotima, and then hope the Persians killed me in the battle, and then he and the Hyperboreans would be safe.

I weighed the option of trying to kill Damon, right now, on the spot, as the course of least risk. But it wouldn't work. There was a battle right in front of us, and if Diotima wasn't moved at once, then my wife in labor would be caught in the middle of it.

"You're not worried about the loss of the Delian League funds?" I asked him, still searching for some reassurance that I could believe.

"The League money was never part of Delos," he said.

Why was the most reasonable man on this island the murderer? I wondered if Damon had sounded this reasonable when he approached Geros, prepared to kill him.

Damon must have understood my indecision because he said, "Nico, we killed Geros because he stole the Hyperborean Gifts. He stole *our* gifts to the Gods."

I would have to believe that this murderer was an honest man.

"Go then. Take Diotima . . ." I thought about it. "Go north."

It was the only safe path. The Sacred Way to the New Village would take the women and the older priests too close to where the raiders had landed. The path to the east was blocked by buildings. They could get around, but it would be slow. West was the direction the enemy had come from. But to the north, all they had to do was climb over the low stone wall.

Anaxinos was somewhere in this disaster, but I didn't know where, and if he was calling any orders then no one could hear him. I followed the example of Semnos. I jumped up to join Apollo on his plinth and I bellowed, "People of Delos! Women and old men to go north with Damon. Follow Damon. Go north. Now!"

I reasoned that the more people who were with Damon, the safer my wife would be. Besides, it was the right thing to do.

To my surprise, it worked. The villagers and the older of the priests immediately began to stream north. I could see their heads swivel as they looked for the village chief.

Many couldn't see him in the crush. But they knew the way to go and they followed it.

"You can trust me, Nico."

My mother had Diotima by one arm. Meren the murderess had her by the other arm.

Diotima clutched my hand. "Nico, be careful."

"You're about to give birth, and you're telling me that?"

"My baby's going to have a father."

"A mother, too."

I kissed her. She kissed me. That was all we had time for before we had to go our separate ways.

I had no choice but to leave my detective wife in the midst of childbirth, in the hands of the two murderers she was about to denounce, while I went to retrieve a key that might very well get me killed.

All in all, I had had better days. I would have to hope that I lived long enough to see my child. I would have to hope Diotima lived long enough to give birth. I would have to hope my wife survived the birth. I would have to pray that our child lived.

I had all these depressing thoughts as I worked my way around the fight, running where I could behind the backs of the combatants, dodging swinging swords, thrusting spears, and the occasional sling bullet. From where I stood, all I could see were the backs of struggling men. The sailors of *Paralos* were so far into the action that I could barely see them at all. I could hear shouts though, and screams as men were wounded or died.

I guessed that there were three shiploads of attackers, matching the Phoenicians we had seen at sea. That suggested three hundred attackers on the ground here, give or take, assuming their commander had had the sense to leave a strong force behind to secure his ships.

Pericles had the trierarchs lined up and ready to attack. It would be fifty men against three hundred, and those fifty with no armor and only short swords. Luckily Pericles knew the ground, having been to Delos many times before.

I ran up to our Pericles, who was in the midst of calling orders.

"I have to secure the treasury door," I told him. I avoided telling him why.

"That's your problem," Pericles said. "I'm taking these men to flank them on the left."

"You don't want to ring the treasury?" I said, surprised.

"No. That would be static defense with no cover. Outnumbered as we are, we'd die quickly. We must remain alive with maneuver to give the men from the ships time to arrive. If you need to secure that door, go quickly. The enemy will soon have the temple enveloped. They'll start taking boxes."

I nodded and ran. Pericles shouted to the trierarchs to march left.

Behind the trierarchs, the younger priests, and the middle-aged ones, and those of the village men in good shape stood in an awkward line, with grim expressions. They knew they wouldn't last more than a moment against the professional soldiers of the Persian Empire. If the raiders broke past the navy men then it would mean their deaths, but they would not give up the Sacred Isle without a fight.

A hand clapped me on the back. I turned in surprise. It was Philipos.

"I'm the military man here," he said.

I wasn't going to argue with that.

"What's our objective?" he asked.

"The Porinos Naos. I blundered, Philipos, I left the key in there."

Suddenly I felt like the apprentice.

"Don't worry, Nico, I'll get you there."

I chose the two priests of the nearby group that seemed least afraid. "You, and you," I pointed at them. "Come with me."

"Why should we?" the younger of the two demanded aggressively. Apparently I had chosen a stupid priest.

"Because you can stand there doing nothing useful, or you can help save your sanctuary," Philipos told him. The older man gave the younger a nudge. The young priest nodded.

The priests and I followed Philipos, who strode purposefully across the battlefield. "Do you see the steps to the Porinos Naos?" he asked them.

"No," they said in unison.

"Neither can I," he said. "But they're through that cluster of men there."

"Yes. Of course," the older priest said.

"We're going straight there. Running."

"Through the fighting?" the older man asked in dismay.

Philipos said confidently, "If you don't look at the enemy, and you don't threaten them, they won't touch you. I promise. I've been in lots of battles, and a man in combat only cares about the men who can hurt him. Those Phoenicians and their Persian overlords have Athenian sailors with knives to worry about. They'll think you're frightened priests running away in a panic, you see?"

They looked dubious.

"Feel free to scream a little as you run through, if you like," I added helpfully.

What I didn't tell them was that I thought we'd be lucky if any of us made it.

"Oh, and another thing," I said. "If you make it through and I don't, could you please pull the key from the temple door and run away with it? Thanks."

The priests nodded.

Philipos squared his shoulders and seemed to stand taller. "Are we ready? One, two, three, go!"

We ran.

Acting the part of a terrified man was quite easy. I reached the back of our line and actually elbowed one of our men out of the way. At a party it would have been rude, in a mêlée it was suicidal. I came face to face with a Phoenician with a deep black beard, dark olive skin, ringleted hair, and a big sword edged with blood that he held aloft in his right hand.

I stared at the Phoenician and held up my hands in surrender. He stared at me in surprise. I kicked him in the nuts.

His nuts were armored. There was some sort of bronze plate beneath his tunic. Pain shot up my leg. I'd kicked him with the same foot that I'd hurt when I walked into the wall, on the night Geros died.

All that saved me was that the man's armor had dug into his groin, doing sufficient damage that he took a step back. I swore, favoring my good foot. He raised his sword to drive it into me, but the man I'd elbowed had recovered his balance and drove *his* dagger into the back of the man who was about to stab me.

I didn't wait to see him fall. I took two steps forward and tripped over a body sprawled upon the dirt. I skidded in his large pool of blood. The dead man must have been killed by one of the sailors from *Paralos*, because I came eye to eye with a throat that had been opened by something sharp. I could actually see the tubes inside.

I rolled over, only to see a soldier stand above me with a spear.

He drove it down at my neck.

I grabbed it with both hands—how I'll never know—and struggled to keep it from entering my throat. The sharp leaf-shaped point was so close that I went cross-eyed staring at it. I had the spear by two hands and tried to push up and sideways. But my killer was a big man and all he had to do was lean down hard. I was doomed.

Philipos flew from nowhere, straight into my attacker. They rolled sideways into the legs of two Persian troopers, both fully armored. Those two saw what was happening and drove downwards with their weapons. Other Persians saw Philipos stricken on the ground. There wasn't a thing I could do. A dozen blades went into an honest man of Athens. The last word I heard him scream was, "Nico!"

Philipos was gone. I would have cried, but there was no time. Somehow I had to get myself out of here, surrounded as I was by the men who had killed him. Still lying flat on the ground, I pulled a leather helmet from the dead body of a Phoenician. I struggled with the straps, and it seemed to take forever. Then I knelt to lift the body of the helmet's former owner over my shoulder. I stood with a heave and staggered toward the Persian rear.

"Wounded man!" I croaked in Persian, and the enemy soldiers in their back row looked at me, saw that I held one of their comrades, and to my relief they moved to let me past. The swathes of fresh blood covering the front of my tunic must have helped.

I made it to the steps of the Porinos Naos. There was the key, still sticking out of the key hole, and there was the enemy. Two of them—Persian by their appearance—were in the act of opening the door. They turned to see me as I laid down my load.

"Wounded man," I said in Persian. These two Persians would probably take me for a Phoenician speaking their language. "Need help?"

"No."

They turned back to their task of turning the key to raise the bar. I heard the now familiar clunk and the door swung open.

I knifed the first man from behind, in the right kidney, slit the throat of the second man before he could react, then returned to finish the first.

At that moment the two priests arrived—from the dirt on their hands and knees I guessed they had crawled all the way. They saw me, a figure in a Phoenician helmet and covered in blood, with fresh corpses at my feet, shrieked, and turned to run.

"It's me!" I said in Greek. I had to take the chance. I removed the helmet so they could see my face. They looked nervously at the death around them, but they stayed.

"Right, men," I said confidently. "I want you to go inside, throw down the bar, and then load as many of those treasure boxes as you can against the door on the inside."

"Lock ourselves inside a small temple with a fortune in gold that's being attacked by hundreds of men? Are you insane?" The younger priest's intelligence hadn't improved since he'd last spoken.

I said, "If you go in there and block the door, you might be the only ones still alive by tomorrow morning, and you will have saved for Hellas the treasury that will save our country. Does that seem like a good idea to you?"

They both nodded.

"Right. In you go."

They jumped in, swung shut the door, and I heard the bar fall. I waited until I could hear boxes being pushed into position against the door. Those boxes were so heavy with metal that even a battering ram would have a sorry time trying to break in. For the first time I felt confident. Confident at least that even if every Athenian in the sanctuary grounds was killed, the men from the ships would still have time to get here and overpower the raiders.

I could have saved myself by going in with the priests, but I had something more important to do. I was on the wrong side of the battleground from my wife. I looked across the sea of struggling men.

The sailors from *Paralos* had taken fearful casualties. They had thrown themselves into the fight to buy time, armed only with their daggers, and they had paid the price.

Men were beginning to arrive up the path from where the Athenian fleet was beached. I felt a surge of relief. Each new arrival was armed with the boarding axe so beloved of navy men. Those axes wreaked terrible damage upon an unarmored man. I knew, having once fought with one myself. They would not do much against a fully armored hoplite, but these raiders from Phoenicea were all in light armor. The tide was turning our way.

I rolled over the dead man I had carried to the temple, and quickly unlaced the leather he wore. I put this on myself, and tied it loosely. Then I pulled the all-important key from the treasury door and shoved it beneath the armor. Now with a spear in my hand I took a last look at the treasury door, then strode north.

I went unmolested. I ran slightly east of north, trying to act like a soldier carrying a message, going deeper into their rear but thinking to round their flank to the outside and make my way north to find Diotima.

The route I needed took me further to the east than I guessed. It occurred to me that the raiders must have landed very close to Karnon's house, where Marika and her two sons were. I hoped they were all right. Persians are not above slaughtering the innocent. I especially hoped that Karnon's sons hadn't taken it into their heads to charge at boatloads of landing enemy. If they were as brave as their father, they might have done that very thing. But Marika was a sensible woman; if she had a chance she would have bundled herself and her boys into a hiding place. At least, I had to hope so.

Pericles had made progress. The ad hoc unit of combined navy captains had descended upon the enemy from the direction I was running towards. I stopped for a moment to catch my breath, then began a strong run.

I soon reached the edge of the battle. I came across an Athenian and a Persian locked together in a death struggle, rolling over and over on the hard ground. I left my spear in the back of the Persian and kept running, bursting through the line before anyone saw me coming.

This almost got me killed. A Hellene sword thrust at me, and only the leather I was wearing prevented me from taking a sword to the chest.

"Athenai! Athenai!" I screamed, and I tore off the helmet and threw it aside so my own people wouldn't destroy me.

"Let him through!"

The command came from Pericles. I hadn't noticed him until that moment.

I didn't stop. I kept running. I passed by all the other treasury houses and the temples. I hurdled the low wall without pausing. I ran the path to the Lion Terrace.

By the time I got there I could barely breathe. I bent over, hands on knees, gasping for air.

The villagers who waited there, the women and the few children and the old people, watched me as if I might hurt them. But Moira came up to me.

"They're by the lake," she said. "I'll show you."

We hurried to the lake's edge. There was no one there but Damon, looking very distressed.

"Nico," he said.

"Where's Diotima?" I cut in.

Damon pointed out over the water.

"She's in *the lake?*"

"On the barge, Nico," Damon said. "We had to get her off the island."

"Why?"

"The proscription against giving birth," he reminded me.

I could hardly believe what I was hearing. I said, incredulously, "There are a hundred dead bodies back there in the sanctuary, and you're worried about one tiny baby?"

"Not me," he said. "Diotima. She insisted."

That sounded like my wife. "She would," I said morosely.

"I couldn't let her go to the emergency eject system," Damon said.

"No, of course not," I agreed. The dinghy was on the other side of the island. Even to reach it would require getting past the raiders.

"There was no point carrying her to the Athenian triremes. All the sailors are in the battle."

"They are now," I agreed.

"That meant the only place not on the island that we could possibly reach was the lake, and there was the barge. It's a nice, big platform."

"But isn't the lake part of the island?" I asked.

"A lake's like a small sea, right?" Damon said, reasonably.

"I suppose . . ." I said dubiously.

"So if she's on the barge, then she's not on the island. That's logic, right?" he said. "I rowed them there myself, Nico." He put a consoling hand on my shoulder. "If the raiders reach us, it's the safest possible place on Delos right now."

That was a very good point. Damon had not known how the battle was going. If the raiders had come to the Terrace of the Lions, then those on the ground would have been in great danger, but a woman in the middle of the lake would have been left alone. Damon had done the right thing.

"Thank you, Damon."

Then I heard it, a heartrending scream of pain.

I flinched. We all three stared at each other, Moira, Damon, and me. We were all thinking the same thing, but none willing to voice it.

"How long has she been screaming like that?" I asked.

Damon shrugged.

There was silence, for a long time, then another scream, longer and much worse than the first. I thought that nothing ever screamed like that except in the face of imminent death.

That was my wife who had screamed, and now she was silent. The silence was more unnerving than the screams. I willed her to scream again, so that I would know she was still alive. But there was nothing.

I walked out into the water. "Nico! What are you doing?" Damon said.

"I have to see what's happening," I told him.

"But she's giving birth, man. That's woman stuff."

"I don't care."

I still wore the Phoenician armor. I unlaced it as I waded and dropped the leather in the water.

I began to swim when the water reached chest height.

A suspicious voice upon the barge called out, "Who is it?"

It was my mother who called. It was dark, and all they could see in the water was an approaching man.

I said, "It's me, Mother."

I hauled myself up onto the barge. Phaenarete simply stood there, shoulders drooped. She looked exhausted.

Meren was crouched at the other end, busy doing something I couldn't see.

In the middle of the barge was a pallet made of old blankets, and clothing. The Hyperboreans had taken whatever they could find and then donated the clothes they were wearing to give Diotima a bed.

Diotima lay there. Her eyes were closed. She looked peaceful. She opened one weary eye, then the other.

"I hope that's not your blood," she said.

"Mine?" I looked down. I still wore the exomis I'd been wearing when I skidded through enemy blood. The lake water had spread the color everywhere until I looked like an axe murder victim. "No, I'm fine," I said.

My mother took a bundle from Meren. She turned around to me and said, "Nicolaos, my son, I present to you your daughter."

I had a daughter.

My mother handed me the bundle, and made sure my arms were in the right place to hold a baby.

My mother said the ritual words, "Do you accept this child?"

I looked down. The little girl in my arms looked up at me with big eyes, and I could have sworn she recognized her father. She was the spitting image of Diotima's mother. That made the next bit easy. Diotima and I had already discussed what to name the baby if it was a girl.

I completed the ritual. I said, "I accept this child. I name her Euterpe, daughter of Nicolaos, daughter of Diotima, granddaughter of Euterpe and of Phaenarete."

Then I leaned over, so that Diotima could see her baby. She struggled to sit up. Meren placed an old, dirty blanket behind Diotima's back.

My mother had turned away from this scene. Then she turned back and repeated the ritual words, "I also present to you your son. Do you accept this child?"

Twins? Suddenly I felt faint.

"No wonder you were so tired," I said to Diotima.

I tried to take hold of my son, discovered I didn't know how to hold two babies at once, and passed little Euterpe to her mother.

I took my son in my arms.

"I accept this child," I said. "I name him Sophroniscus, son of Nicolaos, grandson of Sophroniscus and of Pythax."

TAKING LEAVE

THE NEXT MORNING I went to see Karnon. Diotima didn't come with me. She was busy, back in the cottage, exhausted, feeding our children and trying to get some sleep. Instead I was accompanied by my friend Damon.

Karnon was waiting in his home, with Marika and the boys. He no doubt expected the executioners to come some time during the day. After all, he had confessed in front of hundreds of people to the theft of state funds. Marika looked frankly terrified.

"I'm sorry about your friend Philipos," were Karnon's first words.

"So am I."

The body had been discovered earlier in the morning, with more than a dozen wounds and numerous dead around him. Pericles had promised a state memorial. Philipos would be leaving us as a someone.

I said to Karnon. "I've come to let you know about your travel arrangements."

"To Athens, for my trial?" he asked bitterly. "Why bother?"

"No, you'll be going a different direction."

I pulled out a scroll that I'd had hidden beneath my tunic. "I figure that a man who knows as much as you do about finance and owning mines must know something about estate management."

"Perhaps," Karnon said. "I've never tried."

"Here is the deed of ownership for the estate in Kyzikos that Geros bought." I held it out.

Karnon took it, with a bewildered look on his face.

"Kyzikos is behind the Persian border, *beyond the reach of Athens*," I added helpfully.

Karnon's face lit up with hope.

I said, "Damon has the island's largest fishing boat waiting for you. On board you will find a chest with the ten talents that Geros had hidden in the graveyard. That should be more than enough to get you going as a major estate holder."

"Are you sure you want to do this?" Karnon asked me.

I shrugged. "It's less than Pericles was willing to pay in bribes to get the treasury."

"Thank you."

"You'll want to avoid Mykonos on the way. It's the first place Pericles will think to look. Damon says his men know some sneaky routes. There's a risk here, Karnon. You'll be carrying a lot of money."

"We'll manage," he said it confidently, like his old self. Good.

"The boat will beach outside your house," Damon said. "There might be problems if you're seen in the village. It will be here any moment."

I turned to speak directly to Marika. "How quickly can you be packed? You'll need clothes for all weathers, good sandals if you have them, and a little food to get you started. You can buy the rest on the way. Oh, and whatever toys the boys own, I suppose. No more than a single chest."

"I can be ready before you drink that wine," she said.

"Go."

Marika flew.

Karnon laughed. "I owe you my life, and the happiness of my family. How can I thank you for this?"

He probably thought it was a rhetorical question, but I had an answer. "By taking the blame for Geros's killing."

He looked at me quizzically, then at Damon, and then back to me. "That is more than a fair deal. Would you like a signed confession?"

That was an interesting idea, but, "It might look contrived," I said. "A simple absconding felon should be sufficient." I clasped his hands. "Good luck."

I FOUND PERICLES in the home of Anaxinos, where a great deal of diplomacy was patching up certain embarrassing problems on both sides.

Pericles had something to say. "Anaxinos, I have thought much about the words you had for me, when you asked what my father would think of this situation. You are right. The treasury of the Delian League should remain on Delos."

"On the contrary," Anaxinos said. "I must insist that you take the treasury of the Delian League with you."

"What?" Pericles was shocked.

"I find that the presence of the money here on Delos has had a . . ." Anaxinos seemed to struggle to find the right words. He finished with, "A lamentable influence on even the most holy. If even the finest priest can be corrupted, then what must this wealth be doing to my other people?"

"Great wealth can have that effect," Pericles commiserated.

"I advise you to watch the people of Athens most closely, Pericles, lest they too allow themselves to love gold more than the gods."

"I will keep it always in mind," Pericles promised.

"Then I bid you leave, with the treasure, and a safe journey to you."

"A very safe journey," Pericles said. "Considering what we'll be carrying."

Pericles left, to take command of the greatest treasure in Hellas, wealth which would protect our land and our people.

"I congratulate you on your fatherhood, young man," Anaxinos said to me.

"Thank you, sir," I said, and I grinned like an idiot.

The High Priest of the Delian Apollo bade me sit and eat with him. I was more than happy to do so.

"I notice that Diotima managed to avoid giving birth on Delos," Anaxinos said. "That was well done, though perhaps not quite so urgent considering the carnage in the sanctuary grounds."

"Yes, I imagine you will have some purifications to perform," I said.

Anaxinos sighed. "That is putting it mildly. We'll be doing catharsis rituals for the rest of the year. Have you seen how much blood there is out there?"

"Yes sir."

"Still, I admire a priestess who can stick to her duty in even the most dire circumstances. If you two are ever interested in moving to an island, let me know."

"We'll give it every consideration, sir."

Anaxinos sipped his wine. "There is one theological issue that you and I need to address," he said.

That surprised me. "Me, sir? I'm not very good with theology."

"But you're the man to speak to about this problem. You see, in her haste to avoid giving birth on holy Delos, your wife has managed to give birth on the precise spot where the divine twins Apollo and Artemis entered the world."

"Oh." I think my face must have fallen at that.

"I believe Diotima is the first woman to give birth in that lake since Leto herself. Then there's the minor detail that she birthed twins. How shall I put this? The theological implications are tricky."

I started to sweat. I had no idea how I was going to fix this.

Anaxinos ate a fig while he thought about it. "Why don't we try to forget it happened?" he suggested. "If anyone asks, your wife made it to one of the triremes and produced your children there."

"An excellent idea, High Priest."

I TRIED TO go back to the cottage, only to be told firmly by my mother that my wife was sleeping. I tiptoed away to the only place I could think of: Apollo's Rest. There I found Captain Semnos eating, drinking, and talking with Moira.

"Captain, your face!" I exclaimed.

"It's nothing," Semnos said proudly.

Running down the left side of Semnos's face was a jagged scar, from the top of his jaw to his mouth.

"Got into a scuffle with a Persian officer with a decent blade," Semnos explained. "But the man died for his pains."

"Tough fight," I said.

"My men gave as good as they got. One thing is for sure," Captain Semnos said. "They won't be calling the men of *Paralos* pretty boys any more."

Semnos grinned, and suddenly his face was transformed. That scar should have disfigured any man. But on Semnos it made him look like the most daring and raffish of handsome pirate captains.

Every woman in Athens was going to feel faint when they saw that roguish face.

———

A few days later it was time for my new family to leave sacred Delos. I went to thank Damon. He could have killed Diotima and me. Instead, he had done the honorable thing.

"Come back and see us some time," Damon had said.

I laughed. "Not for a while. We'll be busy. I can't imagine traveling with babies."

Damon grinned.

"I admire the work you Hyperboreans do," I said, and shook his hand. "I hope the next Priest of the Gifts doesn't steal them!"

"Haven't you heard?" Damon said. "Anaxinos has assigned a new Priest of the Gift. Or Priestess, rather."

"Oh?"

"It's Meren," Damon said.

I tried hard not to laugh. "That's convenient," I said.

"Very," Damon agreed with a straight face.

THE END

AUTHOR'S NOTE

WELCOME, DEAR READER, to the end of the book, and the start of the author's note.

Here I'm going to talk about what's real and what's not in the story that you've just read. If you haven't finished the book, turn to the front now, because everything from this point on is spoilers.

THE HOLY ISLE of Delos, its sacred laws, the sanctuary, the temples, the priestly community, and the village are all real. Delos really was the birthplace of Apollo and Artemis in the belief of ancient peoples.

The Delian League was real, and so was its vast war fund. The infamous incident when Athens took the Delian Treasury is very real. It was a major turning point in history.

The mysterious people of Hyperborea, and the Hyperborean Gift are probably real (more on that later).

The fictional parts of this story are that there was a murder when Athens took the treasury, that there was a Phoenician raid, and that the Hyperboreans are hiding out on Delos.

YOU HAVE JUST witnessed the birth of the short-lived but very important Athenian Empire. When Athens lifted the Delian Treasury, it became crystal clear that the Delian League—a collection of independent city-states joined

together for mutual defense—had turned into a set of client states that had no choice but to go along with whatever
Athens wanted.

The alliance of the Delian League was remarkably
similar to the modern NATO. Both were designed to deal
with a threat to Europe from the East. Both had the very
latest in military technology. Both were (and are) unwieldy
in their organization. Even their funding squabbles are the
same.

The Delian League was founded twenty-five years
before the time of this story. The member states contributed a kickstarter of 460 talents. We know that because it
comes from a book called *The Athenian Constitution*, written
by none other than the famous philosopher Aristotle. Aristotle says the member states appointed a well-respected
man to decide the size of each city's levy, based on how
wealthy each was. They would have continued that funding
level year after year. After twenty-five years, and taking
into account some expenditure to run the combined navy,
it makes a pool of four thousand talents look about right.

It's known that some years after it was relocated to
Athens the fund held between 4,000 to 6,000 talents. I have
taken the low estimate to be the position when the money
was held at Delos, and the high to be the peak position in
Athens.

It's a bit tricky to convert currency across two and a
half thousand years, but if we assume the average wage in
ancient Athens, and the modern working wage are equiva-
lent, then four thousand talents comes to about three
billion modern dollars. So at the end of the book, Nico and
his friends are fighting to save a three-billion-dollar fund
for the defense of their country.

Out of curiosity I looked up the annual budget of

NATO, and was amazed to discover it's a bit more than two billion euros. The similarity between the Delian and NATO budgets is remarkable. It goes to show what a significant organization the Delian League was.

THE REASON ATHENS offered for the removal of the treasury was precisely the one Pericles gives in the book: fear of a raid that could steal that enormous amount of money.

This excuse was greeted by the people then and by people today with complete cynicism; and yet, Pericles and Athens had a reasonable argument.

Raiders were a very real threat. The Athenians themselves had been raiding Persian-controlled cities along the coast of Asia Minor for decades. A typical Athenian raid comprised ten or twenty ships that could hit a city without warning, do damage, steal stuff, and get out before anyone could react. The Greeks deeply respected the ability of the sea-going Phoenicians, who they knew could return the favor at any moment. I put the Phoenician raid in the story to demonstrate how straightforward it would be. At a much later date, in 69 BC, Delos was almost wiped out by a pirate raid.

It's worth noting that for the five years following this story, Athens used the "liberated" funds pretty much only for defense spending. To that extent their motives were honest.

Then, after forty-one years of conflict, Athens and Persia signed a non-aggression pact. The Athenians found a new use for the Delian Treasury. They misappropriated large amounts of it for public building in their own city, including the Parthenon.

Thus, the money that Nico and Diotima saved in this

story is the same money that will be used ten years later to build the Parthenon. They have done the world a greater service than they could possibly know.

PERICLES IN THIS book has a very poor opinion of the decision-making abilities of the League. The real Pericles almost certainly thought the same. His actions alone tell us that, but he also once made a very revealing speech over a different matter.

At one point Sparta, Corinth, and a large number of other city-states formed an alliance against Athens. The Athenians went into a mild panic, but Pericles told them they had nothing to fear. His explanation tells us everything we need to know about how Pericles viewed management-by-committee. This is what he said about that alliance (from Thucydides, book 1, section 141, paraphrased for clarity):

> *They have no central authority to produce quick, decisive action. They have equal votes, they come from different nationalities, and every one of these is mostly concerned with its own interests—the usual result of which is that nothing gets done at all, some being particularly anxious to avenge themselves on an enemy, and others no less anxious to avoid coming to any harm themselves. Only after long intervals do they meet together, and then they only devote a fraction of their time to their general interests, spending most of it on their own separate affairs. It never occurs to any of them that the apathy of one will damage the interests of all. Instead, each state thinks that the responsibility for its future belongs to someone else, and so, while everyone has the same*

*idea privately, no one notices that from a general
point of view things are going downhill.*

Pericles was speaking of an enemy alliance, but I for one
can hear with what heartfelt emotion he is really thinking
about his own problems with the Delian League.

Thus Pericles is horrified when Anaxinos says he will
call a meeting of the League to decide the fate of the treasury. Pericles can all too well imagine a meeting of 148
member states trying to decide anything.

DELOS REMAINED A sacred isle for many centuries,
well into Roman times. This is very lovely for modern
visitors, because the ruins are extensive and show all sorts
of interesting architectural developments as the centuries
passed. It's a nightmare for me, because I have to subtract
from site maps everything that wasn't there in the time of
Nico and Diotima.

Delos has no natural fresh water supply. Later settlers
built a cistern system (which modern visitors can see). In
Nico's day, the availability of water put a limit on the size
of the population. Nothing much grows on Delos. The
island's miserable soil is even mentioned in a poem by
Homer.

The Porinos Naos is the oldest of the temples to Apollo.
It was decommissioned and turned into the treasury for the
Delian League.

I want to mention a few ruins, visible and famous today,
that were *not* there for Nico and Diotima.

The theater that you can see today was built 150 years
after Nico's time.

I desperately wanted to include the two most famous
statues on Delos, but alas they are dated to 300 BC, 150

years after this story. They are statues of two enormous phalluses, each on a pedestal. The phalluses were erected, so to speak, by a winner at the Great Dionysia, which was an arts festival held in Athens. My previous novel *Death Ex Machina* was set at a Great Dionysia. The erect parts have been snapped off both statues, which must have been painful, but the testicles are in good order. A surprising number of women like to be photographed standing beside them.

THE TERRACE OF the Lions was built by the people of Naxos, in about 600 BC. The lion count is usually given as nine to twelve, or maybe sixteen. Nobody knows. I've gone with ten, because ancient Greeks loved to use multiples of ten, in much the same way we tend to work with twelves. The surviving lions are heavily eroded and were moved into the museum at Naxos, except for one, which was taken by the Venetians hundreds of years ago.

HYPERBOREA WILL BE known to you if you're a Conan the Barbarian fan. What is less well known is that this fantasy land might have existed.

Hyperborea in Greek means "beyond Boreas." Boreas was the name of the cold north wind that blew across central Europe. So Hyperborea is a land far to the north, beyond the cold. Which is how it ended up being stolen for Conan.

At first glance Hyperborea has about as much reality as Atlantis. There isn't a shred of archaeological evidence for any such place.

The difficulty is that, unlike Atlantis, a lot of very credible writers talk about Hyperborea as if it exists. Herodotus says that Hesiod wrote about the Hyperboreans. Unfortunately that piece of Hesiod has been lost, but Hesiod was

Europe's first non-fiction author. If Hesiod wrote about them, then he *thought* they existed, rightly or wrongly. There's also an archaic poem that talks about Hyperboreans that probably wasn't written by Homer but which is from the same sort of time period.

Herodotus himself provides the best evidence. He says the Hyperboreans decided to send gifts to the sacred isle of Delos, the birthplace of Apollo and Artemis. You might be noticing a plot element here. Yes, I ripped it off Herodotus.

The story is much as Meren gives it in the book. The gifts were carried by two young women, who were sent on the long journey with five male warriors to protect them. The young women died while on Delos. It's not clear what killed them, but disease rather than violence is kind of assumed since the women were greatly honored. Herodotus states point blank that their tomb is on the left as you enter the temple of Artemis at Delos, and that teenage boys and girls sacrifice to them.

Now this is a very precise detail! There might not be two Hyperborean women in that tomb, but the Greeks *think* there are. If you ever visit Delos, by the way, you'll be able to go to exactly where the tomb was, because the ruins of the Artemis temple are well known. Just walk to the entrance and look left. Sadly there's nothing there now, but you'll also be standing on a spot where Herodotus himself certainly stood.

Herodotus states that when the Hyperboreans realized that their emissaries might not return, they decided to continue to send gifts every year, but to pass them on from one people to the next. To protect their gifts, the Hyperboreans wrapped them in sheaves of wheat. Then they gave the gifts to their neighbors, with a request to hand them on to the next people to the south.

The Hyperborean Gift thus turned into an international game of pass-the-parcel. The gift was handed along until it reached Delos. Multiple authors speculated about the paths the gift took, in an attempt to work out where exactly was this Hyperborea. The ancient people themselves were none too sure.

Herodotus states that the Hyperborean Gift was still turning up on Delos right up to his present day. This is a detail impossible to ignore. Herodotus first "published" his work at the Olympics of 440 BC. There were obviously people from Delos present. If the gift was not turning up as described, they surely would have put up their hands and pointed out that he was wrong. It doesn't absolutely prove that Hyperborea existed. But if not, then someone was playing a strange game (which might be the case).

The two things you are certain to find on any Greek beach are sand and Swedish backpackers. The idea that some Scandinavians in classical times might have quietly migrated south is very unlikely, but not completely outrageous.

PERICLES'S SCHEME TO bribe Geros is cynical, yet consistent with the real Pericles, who never let idealism get in the way of pragmatic politics. The modern image of Pericles as an idealistic statesman is a slight whitewash.

There was an incident one year in which a Spartan army invaded Attica. The Spartans made it all the way to the walls of Athens.

Things looked bad for the Athenians, but Pericles said he would fix it, all on his own. He went to meet the enemy commander, carrying with him a number of bags that clinked heavily. After they had finished talking, the Spartans turned around and went home.

At the end of the year, the public accounts showed

that there were ten talents missing from the Athenian state treasury. Sixty thousand drachmae! Men had been executed for smaller discrepancies than this. Pericles's only explanation for the missing money was that the ten talents had been spent "for necessary purposes."

The city accountants looked at this enormous gap in the state funds, and then with straight faces signed it off. They knew perfectly well that Pericles had bribed the commanders of the Spartan army.

The Spartans knew it too. When they heard what the Athenian account books said, they fined their own leaders a lot of money. More than ten talents, in fact.

Everyone thought this was hilarious. For decades afterwards, any Athenian who spent money on illicit activities would explain to his friends that he had spent the money "for necessary purposes," and then everyone would fall on the floor laughing. This joke even made it into one of the great comedies written by Aristophanes.

This not only proves that Pericles was willing to bribe people using state funds when the good of Athens called for it, but it also set the going rate for a Spartan General at ten talents. Thus Nico is stunned when Geros demands three times that, thirty talents, and Pericles instantly agrees. Pericles can afford to be complacent because in return he will "liberate" four thousand talents.

ANAXINOS SPILLS THE beans on what he really thinks of Athens after he becomes drunk. Later Diotima mentions there's a poem that says wine is a window into a man's soul. She's not thinking of *in vino veritas*. That's a Latin phrase and won't be written for probably a couple hundred years. She's thinking of a poem by a great poet of the archaic age, a man named Alcaeus.

Alcaeus was the second of the two great poets of his time. The first of course was the infinitely more famous Sappho, who was called the Tenth Muse by Plato. Incredibly, Alcaeus and Sappho not only lived at the same time, but it's certain that they knew each other. Alcaeus writes of Sappho in a poem, describing her as if she were a goddess. For this reason many assume the two were lovers.

CHILDBIRTH WAS INCREDIBLY dangerous in ancient Greece. It was incredibly dangerous everywhere in the world, until modern medicine gave doctors the tools to save a mother in trouble.

The mortality rate of mothers was probably the same as what you'd find in Europe in the 1700s and early 1800s. This is known to vary between about 1 in 30 and 1 in 50, depending on locale. That being the case, Nico is right to be terrified for Diotima.

Phaenarete, the mother of Socrates (and Nico), was a real person and is known to have been a midwife. Plato mentions this fact in one of his books about Socrates.

A midwife in ancient Greece had practical knowledge, of course, but very little understanding of what was going on, and no knowledge of anatomy. The midwife was as likely to spend time praying to the goddess of childbirth as she was to assist the birth. Human dissection was absolute anathema to the Greeks. Nor was there any such thing as surgery. The C-section, named for the much later Julius Caesar, is not known to have been practiced in Greece.

CLASSICAL ATHENS DID have people whose job was to keep the accounts. Athenians took their accounting very seriously.

There was a group of ten city officials, elected yearly,

called the Hellenotamiae. They were the official city treasurers, their job was to manage the money vault buried beneath the Parthenon. The sums they handled were vast.

The Athenians, being the untrusting souls they were, checked the accounts on a regular basis. On one occasion, the numbers didn't add up. The ten treasurers were instantly charged with embezzlement.

We know about this because what happened next was mentioned in a subsequent court case for which the documents have survived:

> *Then again, your Hellenotamiae were once accused of embezzlement . . . Anger swept reason aside, and they were all put to death save one. Later the true facts became known.*
>
> *This one, whose name is said to have been Sosias, though under sentence of death, had not yet been executed. Meanwhile it was shown how the money had disappeared. The Athenian people rescued him from the very hands of the Eleven, while the rest had died entirely innocent.*

The Eleven was the official Athenian body responsible for carrying out state executions. In other words, Sosias had been in the hands of his executioners when they retrieved him. The implication of the "it was shown how the money had disappeared" is that it was a mistake in the books.

So the other nine treasurers died for an accounting error.

Modern accountants might feel that the classical system for dealing with an error in the books is slightly harsh—making it to partner status would be something of a triumph—it was however a very effective way to make sure that the people counting the coins paid close attention.

Thus Karnon takes it for granted that he'll be executed for his skimming of the profits from the investment fund. Nico certainly saves his life when he gives him a ticket off the island.

Historical sources tell us that there were two accountants assigned to the Delian League to manage the treasury. Both of them were from Athens, which was an acknowledgment that Athens was by far the biggest contributor to the League. I have converted this to one to keep the character list manageable.

The electrum coin from Kyzikos is perfectly real. There are surviving examples. Electrum really is a mixture of gold and silver and there are a very small number of mines where it is naturally occurring.

KARNON'S MARKET MANIPULATIONS would be hideously illegal in the modern world, but were perfectly legal in the ancient. There was no such thing as a market regulator back then. There were however very extensive import and export rules and duty payments. Since Karnon is in modern terms a one-man NGO, he can avoid even those costs.

It is easy for him to set aside part of the profits made in these ventures into his own personal account, as long as the money he skims is profit made away from Delos, and taken before it reaches Delos. Karnon is correct that Athenians were masters of watching the entire value of a treasury and everything that goes in or out. But the idea of accounting the entire value chain of an enterprise is a concept for accountants in the far distant future (and remains an accounting challenge to this day).

CATHARSIS TO US means a cleansing of the spirit, but

the original meaning in ancient Greek was a ritual cleansing, like consecrating a church. The first person to use catharsis in our modern sense was Aristotle, when he wrote about the great tragedies.

The catharsis of Delos really did happen as Anaxinos describes. The story is told in *The Histories* by Herodotus. The graveyard really does seem to have contained graves—at least based on the description from Herodotus—which was unusual for the period because cremation was the norm.

THE RULE ABOUT neither dying nor giving birth on Delos is absolutely for real.

You're probably wondering what the penalty was for dying, and so am I. Presumably things couldn't get much worse for you anyway. Alas, we'll never know.

Despite the rule against death on Delos, there is a fair amount of death in this book. Geros's killers know the rule as well as anyone, but they don't hesitate to kill him because from their point of view it's the lesser of the evils. Nico is ready to fight and even kill the guards, because it is simply necessary. Likewise Karnon at the end waits to be executed. If that had been carried out, the Athenians would have taken him offshore on a trireme to carry out the sentence. Of course there is also a serious battle that leaves hundreds dead.

So the rule against dying on the island is broken, and in every case there's a practical reason. The Greeks would not necessarily think this a disaster, as long as the necessary purification (catharsis!) is carried out afterwards.

They're not being irreligious when they do this, not even the murderers, in their own way. Instead they are practicing a certain amount of doublethink. It's exactly the same doublethink that we use in the modern world. Take for example the governor of a US state who goes to church and ascribes to the ten commandments, including thou shalt not kill, and then goes to work the next day and signs a death warrant for a condemned prisoner. There are many such modern examples of daily life not quite matching religious ideals.

Ancient people were as inconsistent as us. We know which rules we'll break, and which we won't. After reading a large number of ancient books, I think I have a pretty firm grip on where they'd break with doctrine, and where they'd strictly adhere. The defense of the island at the end of the book is very clearly a moment where the Greeks will ignore the rule against death in favor of self-defense.

DOOR KEYS WERE in use in classical Greece. They worked exactly as Nico describes in the book. Most keys at the time were for temple doors. It is said that the Greeks also invented the keyhole, though I doubt it could ever be proven that they got it first. Classical Greek keys looked a lot like the crank to start a vintage car.

You can forget about carrying keys in your pocket, though. There is at least one surviving key that is actually inscribed as such, and it is more than forty centimeters long. That's about sixteen inches. If you're interested, you can find that key in the Museum of Fine Arts in Boston. It was a key to a temple door and is dated to the 5th century BC, the same time as Nico and Diotima. Thus it's not only reasonable but virtually certain that the treasury doors on Delos were opened with keys.

Keys, however, were an unusual technology for most people. It was possible for a normal adult, who was neither a priest nor an accountant, to get through their lives without ever seeing a key. The paradigm that we are used to—that possessing a key gives you access to what it protects—would have been a bit dubious to your average classical Greek. It seems obvious that a guard can intelligently recognize who is valid and who is not, and thus outperforms these new-fangled keys. Indeed to this day, when we really want to protect something, we assign armed guards. Thus Nico and Diotima have trouble getting their heads around the idea that they have to think in terms of who owns or can steal a key.

I COULDN'T RESIST playing a joke on you, Dear Reader, when I named the slave Ekamandronemus. I'm well aware that some modern readers find the ancient names a bit of a challenge. I try to avoid the difficult ones, but I made an exception for poor old Ekam. Of course I *must* have classical names. I can hardly call all these nice ancient people Fred and Jane.

I always use genuine names from the period, and I try to pick ones that are fairly intuitive to an English speaker. Fortunately there are classical names such as Moira and Damon to fall back on. There's only a limited stock of those, so I use them sparingly.

Historical characters of course get their true names, but with modern spelling. Hence for example Pericles. Philipos is of course the modern Philip.

Nico is quite right that classical Greeks used a lot of nicknames. Thus even Nico is taken aback by a slave named Ekamandronemus.

GEROS'S BANKERS ARE the Antisthenes and Archestratus Savings & Loan Company. It looks like a completely made-up, random detail, but this was a real bank of the fifth century BC based in Athens. Banking was a very new invention at this time—no more than a few decades old—I use A&A in my stories whenever dodgy financiers are required. They first appear in *The Pericles Commission*.

I may well be traducing completely honest men, but since Antisthenes and Archestratus died 2,400 years ago I'm probably safe from a slander claim.

PARALOS WAS A real ship of the time, and her duties were as the good Captain Semnos describes. *Paralos* and *Salaminia* were sister ships. Nico and Diotima normally travel on *Salaminia* when they are being wafted to their various missions. *Paralos* was so respected that Pericles named his second son Paralos in honor of the ship.

Though they were theoretically interchangeable, my vague impression from reading the sources is that *Salaminia* tended to get the diplomatic missions, and *Paralos* tended to take the religious jobs. I've formalized that in the stories.

The real *Paralos* will go on to play a much darker part in Nico's family history. Fifty-five years after the time of this story, Nico's younger brother Socrates was sentenced to die in an infamous trial. But straight after the sentence was declared, it was realized that *Paralos* had left for Delos, on exactly the same mission as occurs in this book. It was a rule of classical Athens that no prisoner could be executed while *Paralos* was attending religious duties. Thus Socrates was put in chains and had to wait. The return of *Paralos* to Athens was the signal for Socrates to be executed.

WHEN DAMON AND Nico chase the guards by boat, I included a moment where the guards tack into the wind.

That was quite deliberate, but it will raise the eyebrows of historians of sailing. Tacking requires a fore-and-aft rig.

All major ships of the classical world had a square rigged sail. There were no exceptions, and you can't tack with a square rig. Or at least, not very well.

Yet it is possible that small sailing dinghies and fishing boats in the fifth century BC *might* have had a type of fore-and-aft rig known as a spritsail.

The earliest known use of a spritsail comes from ancient Greece, in the second century BC. Boats clearly rigged as spritsail appear on vase illustrations. I take it as likely that if spritsails are common enough in the second century BC to be iconic, then early versions could be around with Nico and Diotima in the fifth century BC. I also would not be surprised if the Phoenicians invented the spritsail before the Greeks got to it, but that's the merest speculation.

The spritsail and its close relative, the lateen rig, were in definite and common use across the Mediterranean by the end of the classical world, and they are both natural evolutions of the square rig. Simply lower the spar of a square rigged ship, twist it round to point fore-and-aft, do a lot of annoying work to reshape the sail, and suddenly you have a primitive but workable rig for tacking. It's because it's such a natural evolution that I think it must have come earlier than we think.

YOU MIGHT BE wondering how Diotima managed to still be pregnant at ten months. It's because Athenian months are lunar. Every month is twenty-nine days. Therefore every classical Greek woman gives birth at ten months.

First sons were *always* named for the paternal grandfather. That rule was so universal that historians have used it to trace ancient families across centuries. Girl names were slightly more flexible, though you'd still expect a family name to be repeated over generations.

Thus we leave our heroes as happy new parents.

Nico and Diotima have come a long way since their early days as crime fighters, investigators, and secret agents for Athens. I thought for fun I might repeat the jacket copy of their very first adventure, *The Pericles Commission*. Here it is:

> *Nicolaos, the ambitious son of a minor sculptor, walks the mean streets of classical Athens as an agent for the promising young politician Pericles. Murder and mayhem don't faze Nico; what's really on his mind is how to get closer (much closer) to Diotima, the intelligent and annoyingly virgin priestess of Artemis, and how to shake off his irritating twelve-year-old brother Socrates.*

How things have changed.

Pericles is no longer a struggling young politician. He is the leader of the world's newest empire, and overwhelmingly the most influential man alive. There's a good reason why they call this the Age of Pericles. Little does anyone know that Pericles will one day hand over that mantle to a rather annoying young fellow named Socrates. Nico has finally achieved his lifelong ambition to shake off his little brother. Socrates is serving his time in the army. He won't be out for another two years, but then he'll be back to annoy Nico.

Nico's doing well, too. He not only got the girl, but he's got a family.

Now Nico and Diotima must face their greatest challenge yet. They're going home to raise some babies.

GLOSSARY

Apollo

God of the sun and of healing. A major god of the Greek pantheon.

Artemis

A major goddess of the Greek pantheon. She is the Huntress. Her weapon is the bow. When Zeus wants to send a message he often assigns the job to Artemis, in which role she is something like a divine hit girl.

Delian League

An early version of NATO, and that's no exaggeration. The Delian League was a mutual defense alliance of most of the city-states of Greece, and by implication, the major European states. Corinth and Sparta had been members during the Persian Wars, but dropped out later. That left Athens as the most powerful member. The Delian League morphed into the Athenian Empire.

Delos

A small island not far from Mykonos. It was the birthplace of two gods: the twins Apollo and Artemis. For the Greeks, Delos was a place for worship and the greatest reverence. In some sense Delos was like the Switzerland of the ancient city-states. It was neutral turf where nation states could meet to do deals. Hence the Greek alliance was founded during a huge meeting at Delos, and thus became known as the Delian League.

Drachma, Tetradrachma, Obol

A drachma is the standard unit of currency, but too large an amount for everyday use. A tetradrachma is four drachmae, and way too large for anyone but merchants. Shoppers in the agora use obols. Six obols make a drachma.

Eileithyia

Goddess of childbirth and midwifery. Sorry about the weird spelling, but that's the way it is. The ancients had a whole slew of extra deities, most of them specialists, who we don't much hear about these days. But if you were a woman back in classical

Greece, you would know all
about Eileithyia, because she's
the one who's going to keep
you alive when you give birth.
Nico's mother is a midwife
and therefore an expert on
entreating Eileithyia. Legend
has it, incidentally, that this
goddess came to Greece from
Hyperborea.

Hyperborea   A lond described not only by
Herodotus, but also by other
respected and credible men,
including Hesiod, Europe's first
non-fiction author. Hyperborea
is located beyond the cold north
wind, often taken to mean
Scandinavia. Every year the
people of Hyperborea sent to
Delos what became known as the
Hyperborean Gift. The gift was
encased in a sheaf of wheat. No
modern person knows what the
gift actually was. Many people
assume both Hyperborea and the
Gift were myths, but Herodotus
states very clearly that the Gift
was delivered right up to his own
day.

Leto　　　A Titan goddess, one of Zeus's many girlfriends. Why Hera didn't divorce Zeus remains a mystery. Instead Hera hunted Leto, who hid out on Delos, where she subsequently gave birth to Apollo and Artemis.

Month / Pregnancy　　　Diotima is ten months into her pregnancy. There's a good reason for that: the Greeks used lunar months! In the classical world every month is twenty-nine days. That played havoc with the yearly calendar, because 29 into 365 doesn't go, but more to the point for this story a ten-month term was the norm.

Nemesis　　　A mere word in modern English, in classical Greece she is a deity. Nemesis gives to mortals whatever they deserve. In the original version that could be good or bad. In later versions it became all bad (presumably due to a lack of well-deserving people).

Oikos of the Naxians　　　An administration building. The foundations of the Oikos can be seen today. Oikos is a strange word in classical Greek. Technically it means household— the family home is an oikos—but it could also be used in parallel meanings. Like many ancient Greek words, it has found its way into modern English. The variant spelling eco has given itself to the modern word economics. Some people have used the word oikophobia to mean an irrational fear of household appliances (I'm not making this up, but I wish I were).

Phoenicia   A famous ancient land now Lebanon. They invented the alphabet that the Greeks adopted and which became our own. They were unbelievably good sailors. At the time of this story, Phoenicia is a client state of the Persian Empire.

Porinos Naos   The oldest temple to Apollo on Delos. It is built of a type of limestone called poros, hence the temple name. By the time of this story the Porinos Naos has become the treasury house of the Delian League.

Stoa of the Naxians   A stoa is a covered portico. It's
a nice, shady place to hang out.
The Sanctuary at Delos has the
Stoa of the Naxians. In Nico's day
Athens was the main protector
and supplier to Delos, but a
hundred years before, the main
benefactor had been Naxos. The
Naxians did an outstanding job
of donating fine buildings to the
temple area. They also donated
the lion statues that face the lake.

Temple of Artemis   It's incredibly old. The ruins you
see today are of the third (maybe)
Temple of Artemis on this site.
It was built long after Nico's
time. The temple in Nico's day
really does have a tomb to the
Hyperborean women on the left
as you enter.

Treasury Houses   Most temples had a treasury,
not unlike the treasuries that
accumulated in medieval
cathedrals. Delos had so much
wealth that there were five
separate treasuries. There are
surviving inventory lists for some
of the temples, so we have a
fair idea of the sort of offerings
they kept. It mostly amounted

to finely wrought items of precious metals. The treasuries were accounted for individually. It's wrong to think of the entire temple complex on Delos as being one big financial account. In addition Delos stored the treasury of the Delian League, which was a fighting fund with no theological implications.

Trireme

The warships of the classical world. Long, low, sleek, incredibly fast, with a battering ram built into the prow. In modern terminology they would be classed as Destroyers.

ACKNOWLEDGMENTS

THANKS AS ALWAYS to my wife, Helen. Every time I say there wouldn't be a book without her, and every time it's true.

Catriona's friends like to photograph my dedications to her and post them for maximum embarrassment factor. I'm afraid I've added fuel to that fire with this book.

Megan likewise has put up very well with a father who writes, as she approaches her senior school years. She was six when I started *The Pericles Commission*. If I am lucky I will talk her into drawing the map for this book.

Janet Reid is a literary agent who took a chance on a classical Greek crime novel back in 2008, and here we are with book number seven. That success is largely due to her. As super agents go, it's a tough choice between Janet and Nico.

My superb editor at Soho Press announced her impending nuptials to Soho's Director of Marketing while I was writing this book. By the time you read this they will be thoroughly married.

Congratulations to Juliet and Paul!

7/17